CHEF DENNIS'S ALB

In mixing bowl, mix 2 lbs. lean gr[...]
1/2 t. ground cumin, pinch of oregano anu [...]
ingredients into 1-oz. meatballs. In a large pot, sauté in 3 oz. of
butter: 1 c. diced tomatoes, 1/2 c. di[...]d green chilies, 4 cloves
chopped garlic, 2 medium chopped onions, 1 lb. chopped green cabbage, 1 finely diced medium zucchini, and 1/2 bunch cilantro. Add 3
qts. beef broth. Just before broth comes to a boil, add the meatballs, one at a time. Add salt and black pepper to taste. Simmer
for 30 minutes. Top with chopped cilantro just before serving.
Serves 12 to 15.

NOTE: This is even better the next day.

SALSA MEXICANA

Mix 5 canned green chilies, diced, with 5 large tomatoes, peeled and
finely chopped. Add 1 or 2 cloves minced garlic, 1 minced onion, 1
T. chopped fresh cilantro, 1 T. vinegar, and 1 T. oil. Mix. Season
with salt and black pepper to taste. Serve with blue corn chips.

JUANITA ORTEGA'S CHILI RELLENOS

In a 9- by 12-inch casserole, continuously layer 3 small cans
chilies, split and laid flat, 3/4 lb. grated Monterey Jack cheese, and
3/4 lb. grated longhorn cheese until all ingredients are used, ending
with cheese on top. In separate bowl, mix in blender 3 whole
eggs, 3 T. flour, and 1 6-oz. can condensed milk. Pour mixture
over chili-and-cheese casserole. Bake in 350° oven for 30 minutes. Top with 6-oz. can taco sauce and bake 30 minutes more.

NOTE: Can be reheated.

CHE THOMAS'S GUACAMOLE

With a fork, mash 2 large ripe avocados into coarse pulp while
blending in 2 or 3 T. lemon or lime juice. Add 1/2 t. salt and 2 to 4
canned chilies, chopped. Makes about 1 1/2 c. guacamole. Serve
with chips.

The
27*INGREDIENT CHILI CON CARNE MURDERS

The 27*INGREDIENT CHILI CON CARNE MURDERS

BASED ON CHARACTERS AND A STORY CREATED BY *VIRGINIA RICH*

NANCY PICKARD

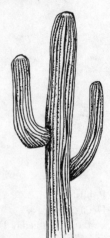

Delacorte Press

Published by
Delacorte Press
Bantam Doubleday Dell Publishing Group, Inc.
666 Fifth Avenue
New York, New York 10103

The trademark Delacorte Press® is registered in the U.S. Patent and
Trademark Office.

ISBN 0-385-30227-4

Manufactured in the United States of America
Published simultaneously in Canada

CHAPTER 1

3:30 P.M., Saturday, May 3
Northcutt's Harbor, Maine

For the first time in her life, Mrs. Potter welcomed bad news.

When it arrived, she was alone in the kitchen of her cottage in Northcutt's Harbor, Maine, preparing albondigas soup for company for dinner the next night. "Albondigas" sounded so much more elegant than "Mexican meatballs," which is what it was. Mrs. Potter knew from experience that her guests were bound to ask, What's that wonderful smell coming from your kitchen, Genia? They'd look impressed and befuddled when she replied, Chef Dennis's Albondigas Soup. Albondigas? they'd say. And what's *that* when it's at home? She had learned to hold off her translation until after they'd tasted and murmured their compliments. Only then would she confide, serenely, that yes, Chef Dennis always did make the best Mexican meatball soup I ever tasted. By then, of course, it would be too late for her guests to look doubtful and say, "Mexican? Oh, well, I don't know about spicy foods . . . I hate to be difficult, and I know you've gone to a lot of trouble, but maybe I'll just skip the soup, if you don't mind, Genia." Albondigas was spicy, all right, but subtly so, and gentle enough for most tummies. Sometimes Mrs. Potter mischievously liked to inform skeptical guests that the essential oils of at least one of the seasonings—cilantro—was used in the preparation of pharmaceutical digestive aids. So there!

The soup *was* an odd selection for a dinner party in May, she conceded, and more like a rib-sticking lunch that one might serve on brisk autumn days. But Maine was enduring a dreary, chilly spell that made folks want to burrow deep into their blankets of a morning, and which seemed to Mrs. Potter to practically cry out for food that would warm body and (one hoped) soul.

That's why her menu for tomorrow night included the soup. It would be preceded by Salsa Mexicana with blue corn chips as an appetizer, and followed by hot apple cider and ginger cookies for dessert. The salsa, with its tomatoes, onion, green chilis, garlic, cilantro, vinegar, and drop of oil, was as refreshing as a salad and low-cal to boot, if one didn't overindulge on the chips (150 calories for 10 enormous ones, surely more than any one guest could, with any degree of virtue, consume). And if it wasn't quite as nutritious as a real salad, the soup would make up for it.

Unfortunately, the rainy cold spell set Mrs. Potter's right shoulder to aching, where an old wound she'd once received had healed. The emotional hurt of it had not, quite. Her right arm, burned around the same time, felt stiff and awkward as she maneuvered her paring knife.

Perhaps that's why I feel so restless and discontented today, Mrs. Potter thought as she diced onions. *And clumsy,* she added when her knife slipped, gouging her cutting board. *It's just a physical thing, that's all,* she thought, *like the depression some people suffer in weather like this.*

Ordinarily, Mrs. Potter would have been happy to spend a stormy afternoon cooking for friends. But on this particular afternoon, she'd poured a glass of good burgundy wine to sip while she worked, and hadn't even tasted it yet. She'd put on her favorite apron—purchased at a church bazaar in Northcutt's Harbor—and promptly stained it when she poured the wine. She'd tuned her kitchen radio to a station playing some of her favorite music—Benny Goodman, Guy Lombardo, the Mills Brothers—but it didn't make her tap her foot or inspire her to waltz now and then around the room with an imaginary partner.

She couldn't even seem to keep her mind on the ingredients, and narrowly escaped several mishaps—like noticing just in time that she was about to measure chili powder instead of cinnamon into the ginger cookies! Mrs. Potter could usually cook without even thinking much about it, "with one eye on the recipe and the other on the children," as a nanny of her acquaintance used to say. But on this particular rainy Saturday in Maine, none of the usual ingredients to a happy day in the kitchen were blending to a create a happy cook.

As she worked at her sink, she occasionally glanced out the rain-streaked window above it, hoping to catch a glimpse of the ocean down at the gentle, curving cove where the Atlantic spanked the rocky shore. But even when she squinted, she couldn't see a thing except the trees right outside her window. Rain dripped like tears off the branches of the ever-green trees, making even *them* look despondent, poor things—as who wouldn't be after standing out in this weather for so long? It looked like the whole world ended at the edge of her trees. Where normally that might have imparted a warm and cozy aura to her cottage, on this day it left her feeling secluded in a cabin at the center of a very small universe, and a sadly colorless one at that. All of the world's brightness and color was inside today, in the yellow of the zucchini and the green of the chili peppers. She hadn't yet planted geraniums in the red clay pots that perched outside on her window ledge, so there wasn't even that bit of crimson to brighten the day. Mrs. Potter, ordinarily not a great sigher, sighed. She imagined her guests arriving in cars on which the windshield wipers had been put to constant use, shedding their oil slickers and umbrellas in her hallway, making quickly for the welcoming blaze in her fireplace in the living room. She felt sure they would be comforted by her choice of companions and her menu.

So why don't I feel comforted? she wondered.

Instead, she felt uncomfortably distracted, as if something were tugging at her mind, trying to get her attention like a child at her elbow. She stayed her hand just as it was about to chop twice as much cilantro as she needed. Whatever was on her mind, it certainly wasn't dinner tomorrow night!

"I hope I'm not coming down with something," she said aloud.

Mrs. Potter cleared her throat. No, not scratchy.

She sniffed. Not stuffy.

Finally, she pressed the back of her right hand against her forehead, but her skin felt cool.

So it wasn't physical, whatever ailed her.

"Well, *some*thing's the matter with me today."

Actually, she would realize later that there was something about her menu that was even odder than its inappropriateness to the season. But Mrs. Potter would not fully appreciate that fact until after she received the telephone call that seemed at first like good news.

And that was still a few minutes away.

She lifted a pretty sprig of cilantro, held it to her nose, and sniffed again. What a lovely, distinctive fragrance it had! There was a hint of peppery onion to it that revived memories of fresh-cut grass at her childhood home in Iowa. Sometimes that seemed like only yesterday. Today it felt long ago—all of her six decades and even more, if that were possible. Mrs. Potter tore a small leaf off the cluster—cilantro was like parsley in appearance, although the leaves were more feathery and less flat—and chewed thoughtfully on it. Yes, there's a heat to cilantro, she decided, which produces quite a dramatic contrast to the cool freshness of its aroma.

"Such an *interesting* herb," she pronounced, as if to an invisible companion. "And all the rage, which astonishes me."

Mrs. Potter saw no reason to feel embarrassed about talking to oneself; most of her friends did it, they admitted. If you didn't discuss things with yourself, how did you ever decide anything? In recent years, she thought she detected increasing notes of patience and tolerance in her arguments with herself and she hoped that meant a melding of the many sides of Eugenia Andrews Potter. Of course, since Lew's death, and without him to bounce her ideas back to her with all of the funny, intriguing little spins and twists he put to them, talking to herself came easily.

She plucked the peppery leaf off the tip of her tongue and washed the remains down the drain. Until recently, who, outside of professional chefs and devotees of Southwestern food, had even heard of cilantro? "Now it's everywhere," she observed, as she began chopping it with her paring knife, "including places like scrambled eggs and omelettes, where it has no business poking its pungent self."

Why, only a few years ago, pesto was the fashionable herb that turned the whole world green, she recalled. (The "herb du trend," as her friend Gussie Van Vleeck had jokingly put it.) Before that, we grilled ourselves to a crisp over Texas mesquite. And what a number of small fortunes *that* must have earned for some enterprising cowpokes. Mrs. Potter smiled. Her fellow ranchers down in Arizona got such a *kick* out of the mesquite fad; they figuratively doffed their ten-gallon hats to those smart Texans who devised such a brilliant (and profitable) method of open range weed control! The only thing to compare to that kind of money-making in Arizona was the "harvest" of rare cactuses, which retailed for upward of ten thousand dollars each, but that was illegal, an ecological tragedy, and certainly no cause for amusement anywhere.

Using the flat of her knife, Mrs. Potter slid chopped cilantro into the frying pan in which diced tomatoes, green chilis, zucchini, chopped garlic, onions, and green cabbage were already sautéing in three ounces of butter. In a large, separate pot, three quarts of meat broth was bubbling its way to a full boil. While those ingredients cooked, Mrs. Potter turned her attention to the albondigas themselves. After putting two pounds of lean ground beef (lean was important so that the soup wouldn't be fatty) into a big mixing bowl, she added to that a half teaspoon each of garlic powder and ground cumin, along with pinches of oregano and ground cilantro.

"I'm worried about oregano," she confided to her invisible companion as she measured the dependable old herb into the meat mixture. "I think it went 'out' when cilantro came 'in.' Is poor old oregano the dodo bird of herbs?"

Her companion kept silent, perhaps reserving judgment.

Mrs. Potter, however, felt herself cheered a bit.

How Peter, the restaurant owner she had known in Nantucket, would have adored this ridiculous conversation she was having with herself. "Potter," he always said, "you're one of my guys." But her smile quickly faded at the actual memory of that friend, who had turned out to be so much less than one. It was to him that she owed the ache in her right arm and shoulder.

Well. Mrs. Potter straightened her shoulders. Gingerly. She'd lost some awfully good friends in the last few years, but who of her age hadn't? The death of friends was to be expected in one's sixth decade, although perhaps not in the untimely manner in which some of them went. She rubbed a knuckle under one eye, but was careful to keep the tips of her fingers away from her eyes. Even though she had washed her hands after chopping the onions and green chilis, she didn't want to take a chance with the pain their juice could inflict on innocent eyes. What a good defensive weapon they would make! A woman could pour their juice into a spray bottle and have herself a nice domestic variety of Mace to carry in her purse. Mrs. Potter briefly entertained the notion of a *Cookbook of Kitchen Weapons*. Besides chili peppers, there was yucca root, which fit your palm like a club and was certainly big and hard enough to knock somebody out cold. And there was that funny-looking vegetable—what was the name of it?—with its hard bulbs and tough root, which you could swing like a club. You could probably beat somebody nearly to death with sweet fennel in its whole root form. Now, there was a rather nice ironic twist—done to death by sweet fennel! And then, if you were worried the courts wouldn't let you off on the grounds of self-defense, you could always eat the evidence, as in that classic Roald Dahl short story that most people remembered only as an Alfred Hitchcock TV show. "Lamb to the Slaughter," that was it. And of course, there was the onion juice.

(Mrs. Potter recalled a friend from years ago, when she, Lew, and the children were still living in Pennsylvania, who had claimed that a woman could wear mascara or chop onions, but not both at the same time. As Mrs. Potter never wore any more eye makeup than a dab of gray shadow, she didn't have to worry about the agony of onion tears blending with mascara. Her own favorite method for preventing onion tears was to chew bread while she chopped.)

She sniffed away incipient tears that had nothing to do with onions.

"Nothing like a rainy day and pretty music to make a person sentimental," she told her invisible companion. "Not to mention maudlin and macabre!"

The next time she sniffed it was to inhale the soft fragrance of simmering vegetables. At least there was one thing she wasn't losing with advancing age: her sense of smell.

"The things you take comfort in, Genia!"

What *was* all this morbid dwelling on dying and old age today? She felt as if she needed a magic elixir, perhaps a jolt of instant youth to cheer her.

Like a visit from her grandchildren. "Did I mention how perfect they are?" she inquired of her silent companion.

Mrs. Potter glanced outside again.

Still raining, and harder now.

She dipped a spoon into the vegetable mixture cooking in butter and lifted a fragrant sample of it to her mouth to test for taste and doneness. Yes, the onions and cabbage were soft enough and delicious.

As Mrs. Potter licked warm butter off her lips, she thought wryly, *I'm not losing my sense of taste, either*, and glanced at her waistline. It missed her late afternoon swims at the ranch, not to mention her two-mile daily walks from the ranch house to the rural post box. Here, all she got was an easy hike into town to pick up her mail, and she'd even avoided *that* the last few days, although she religiously stuck to her usual thirty minutes of daily calisthenics. But she felt cooped up—especially at her waistband!—and sluggish, the effect of too many generous meals with too many generous Northcutt's Harbor friends. Some of them were coming to dinner tomorrow night so that she might return their favors. Hence, the Albondigas Soup. It always tasted better the second day, when the cumin had calmed down a bit.

Since the vegetables were ready to add to the meat broth, Mrs. Potter abandoned the meatballs for the moment in order to slide the sautéed vegetables into the big pot. By the time she had the meatballs rolled, the broth was nearing a boil, which meant it was time for her to drop in the albondigas, one by one. She liked this part of the process; sometimes it was all she could do to resist the impulse to toss in the meatballs like tiny basketballs into a hoop. It was only the prospect of splashing boiling broth that dissuaded her. Each little orb disappeared beneath the surface of the dark, fragrant brew; when they were cooked clear through—and thus lightened of their fat content—they would float nearer the top, like cheery little ground-beef corks.

She set the burner to a simmering heat and the timer to thirty minutes.

"There. I do believe I've earned a cup of tea."

The glass of wine still sat on the kitchen counter, untouched. At least it looked pretty.

Mrs. Potter boiled water and poured it over a bag of blackberry herbal tea. She lightly toasted half a piece of whole wheat bread, dabbed a bit of chilled apple butter on it, and cut off a little chunk of mild cheddar cheese (for the protein and calcium, she told herself). Taking cup and plate to her kitchen table, she eased herself down onto a chair. When she uncrooked her fingers from the cup, she felt a twinge of pain in her forefinger; rainy weather made her touch of arthritis act up. Carefully, she touched the back of that finger to the outside of the cup, and let the heat soothe it.

She picked up her toast, took a bite, and sighed again. It wasn't like her to feel melancholy. But she still greatly missed Sindhu, her noble weimaraner, so cruelly murdered some time ago, following the annual baked bean supper. She missed Harvard Northcutt and Cole and Regina Cogswell, too, on days like this. Once upon a time, she would have been able to walk down to Harvard's cabin to share coffee and wonderful conversation with him, or meander in the rain down to the Cogswells', where she'd be warmed by sunny smiles from both Coley and his beloved Regina. Small comfort that all three of those human friends had been older than she when they died—like Sindhu, they died too young, and too soon, and it was small comfort to recall the part she'd played in revealing the identity of their killer. She missed them, and others, and still resented very much that she never had the chance to say good-bye to any of them.

"If only we knew ahead of time," she mused. "But if we knew, would we feel worse because we couldn't keep it from happening?"

Mrs. Potter caught herself woolgathering—"and in the worst, maudlin way again!"—and jerked her attention back to the stove, to check that the soup was simmering nicely without boiling over.

It was then, ten minutes before the soup was cooked, that the telephone rang, changing first her day and then her life, and bringing into her cottage the bad news that seemed at first like very good news to Mrs. Potter.

CHAPTER 2

Mrs. Potter grabbed the telephone as eagerly as if it were a door she might fling open to admit a welcome visitor.

"*Patrona?*"

"Ricardo! *Buenos días. Cómo estás tú?*"

She recognized instantly and with great affection the deep, melodious voice of Ricardo Ortega, her ranch manager of nearly twenty years. *Patrona* or *la patrona* were the Spanish honorifics by which she was known at Las Palomas. They were the graceful, respectful Latin equivalent of "boss," or, as the feminizing *a* at the end of the word declared, "boss lady." Mrs. Potter couldn't even imagine that brash phrase leaving Ricardo's mouth. Lew Potter, her late husband, had been *el patron*.

In response to her question, Ricardo declared himself well, and he inquired politely as to her health. Those amenities covered, he commenced to apologize for "bothering her." It wasn't their appointed time for his semiweekly ranch reports.

"You're not bothering me at all, Ricardo, quite the opposite. I'm delighted to hear from you. I'm just sitting here with a cup of tea, waiting for some soup to boil, and feeling useless. Now that you've called, I'll be able to convince myself that we've conducted ranch business and that I've actually accomplished something worthwhile with my day. Fire away. What's happening, Ricardo? How are Juanita and Linda, and Bandy and Ken?" And, she wanted to ask but managed to restrain herself from adding, everybody else in the valley?

The "valley" was Wind Valley, a magnificent expanse of rolling prairie in the middle of several mountain ranges in the high Sonoron Desert north of Mexico. Her ranch, Las Palomas—which meant "the doves"—consisted of fifteen thousand beautiful (at least to her) acres hard against the mountains at the eastern border of the valley. Juanita was Ricardo's wife of nearly forty years, mother of their five children, grandmother to their nine grandchildren. She was also Mrs. Potter's dear old friend and helpmate with the cooking and cleaning at the ranch. Linda was Linda Scarritt, their eldest grandchild who was living with them and working at the ranch in the year between high school graduation and college. Ken was Ken Ryerson, who cowboyed part-time for Mrs. Potter and Ricardo. And Bandy Esposito was the old man of the valley, the one-time illegal alien who'd worked at Las Palomas since long before the Potters bought the ranch.

"We have a situation down here that needs your attention." Ricardo spoke with his customary ease and confidence. "I'll explain later." What that meant, she knew from long, frustrating experience, was that he couldn't discuss it over the *phone.* The ranch was still on a party line, which seemed to Mrs. Potter's city friends akin to saying she raised dinosaurs down there in Arizona. "I know this is an imposition on you, *patrona,* but could you come back sooner than you planned?"

"I imagine so. When do you need me?"

"*Mañana.*"

"*Tomorrow?*" While her voice expressed disbelief, her mind raced over what it would take for her to accomplish the impossible. Good gracious, she'd have to call her guests, cancel tomorrow's dinner, get her local couple over here to the cottage to clean and close it up for her, change her tickets, pack her bags, ask somebody to drive her to the airport in Bangor. . . .

"Ricardo, do you *know* what you're asking? Do you realize you could probably buy a new bull for what the airlines will charge me for this?"

"*Lo siento mucho, patrona.*"

"Well, you don't *sound* very sorry."

He laughingly suggested, "You may dock my pay for it."

"As our grandchildren would say, *right.*"

"No, I believe they'd say, *yeah, right.*"

They snickered together over that, two doting grandparents, enamored of their grandkids. There was nothing, Mrs. Potter thought later, *nothing* in Ricardo's words or manner to indicate real trouble or serious concern. There was only this highly remarkable request of his: for her to come home now. But he asked it so calmly that there was no hint, no hint at all . . . Later, she would remind herself that one of the secrets of Ricardo's magic was that he always appeared to be equal to any occasion. If he ever felt insecure, it never showed; always he displayed a patriarchal self-confidence that was balanced by his modesty and good nature. There was no way, she would try to comfort herself later, no possible way that she could have suspected . . .

Of course, in the end she acquiesed and promised him she'd come, although she did attempt to worm information out of him first.

"Juanita is all right, isn't she?"

"Of course, *patrona*. You know vinegar never spoils."

"I'll tell your wife you said that, Ricardo. And Linda?"

"*Muy buena*. Working hard."

"Ken? Bandy?"

"They're well. Not working as hard as Linda."

"They're not your granddaughter, either."

He teased her a bit too. "The cattle are fine. The fences are well. The barns are in good health. Your house sends its regards. The valley misses you. And one more thing," he said, tossing it off casually, "I have taken the liberty of calling a meeting, at your house, for tomorrow night, *patrona*. There will be the McHenrys and the Amorys, Charlie Watt, Che Thomas, the Steinbachs. Eleven or twelve of us in all."

Mrs. Potter could hardly believe what she was hearing. "Ricardo, I'm speechless, although obviously not entirely so. You got the Amorys and the Steinbachs to agree to meet at the same place at the same time? How ever did you manage that?"

"I had a talk with Gallway Steinbach. Played Dutch uncle, you might say. Or Mexican uncle, I guess." He chuckled. "Told him the whole valley knows he's fooling around with Kathy Amory, and that she's not only too young for him, she's also too married, and that it's a rotten way to behave toward Lorraine and Walt, and that he is making an old fool of himself, and he'd better put a stop to it. Shook him up so badly, he agreed to come to any meeting I asked him to."

"Well, don't mince words, Ricardo."

Mrs. Potter shook her head in wonder over her ranch manager's ability to tell difficult people—like Gallway Steinbach—difficult things. She knew perfectly well that he'd phrased it much more tactfully and sensitively than he'd just implied to her. Lew Potter had used to joke that if FDR had only had Ricardo Ortega in his cabinet, the world might have avoided the war. (When Mrs. Potter and her contemporaries spoke of "the war," they meant World War II.) But there were times when Mrs. Potter wondered if Ricardo took his role as valley patriarch a bit too seriously. "Sticking his nose in where it doesn't belong," was how his wife, Juanita, often put it. "It's going to get that man in trouble one day!"

The people he had asked to the meeting were her neighbors and, for the most part, her friends. Most them were part-time ranchers like herself, having purchased their land for investment or "hobby" reasons. Their land abutted hers at various angles.

At the northeast corner of Las Palomas and closest to Tucson were Kathy and Walt Amory, the attractive young couple who owned Saguaro Ranch, which was named for its rare fan-shaped saguaro cacti, known as "crested" saguaro. Walt and Kathy owned a computer software company in southern California. It was Kathy who was, for reasons nobody in the valley could fathom, flirting with scandal by flirting with another neighbor of Mrs. Potter's, Gallway Steinbach. And that wasn't the only problem Walt Amory had, as Mrs. Potter happened to know from a very good source: Ricardo. Ricardo was chairman of the board of a small bank in Nogales where Walt Amory had recently applied for a refinancing loan for his ranch. "He won't get it," was how Ricardo had put it, "at least, not if my opinion counts for anything. I feel real sorry for Walt and Kathy, but they got in over their young heads when they bought that ranch and they can't expect our little bank to bail them out. We're probably their last resort. They should have stuck to computers." Ricardo and Mrs. Potter had shared a rueful smile when he said that, for although Ricardo ran Las Palomas in the black, they both knew what a struggle it was in some years, even for the best of ranchers, which he was. It was nearly impossible, they knew, for naive youngsters like the Amorys to make a go of it. "Still," Ricardo had said sympathetically, "it's sure a hard way for them to learn one of life's little lessons."

Over the fence to the north of Las Palomas, and just east of the Amorys, were Marjorie and Reynolds McHenry. They were a reclusive elderly British couple who owned Highlands Ranch, the biggest spread in the valley. Marj and Rey were rumored to be descended from minor British royalty, and it was said that they'd moved to the U.S. to avoid regressive taxes in England. They were known for bankrolling right-wing politicians, and not only in the United States, it was suspected by people in the valley. Nobody really knew what went on behind the electrified fences and the guarded gates at Highlands Ranch. For Ricardo to get them to agree to come out from behind their elaborate security system was something of a coup in itself—especially as he often said publicly that he would oppose any politician the McHenrys backed for any elected office, anywhere in "his" valley, county, or state. And in that part of Arizona, Ricardo Ortega's word carried substantial weight. If he said to vote *yes* or *no*, there were people who'd pull the lever without even looking at the issue or the candidate, but merely on Ricardo's say-so.

There was Bureau of Land Management acreage directly to the east of Las Palomas, beyond the Rimstone Mountains. And then, moving on to the southeast, was Charlie Watt's place. Its name, Section Ranch, was as plain and practical as the man who owned it, and a total contrast to the fancy dude ranch that adjoined it to the south, toward Mexico. That was the C Lazy U, which was owned and operated by Mrs. Potter's good friend, seventy-year-old Che Thomas. Che was such a savvy businesswoman, at least according to Ricardo, that she had no trouble getting loans whenever she wanted them. "What I'd like to know, though," he often said, "is where Che gets the money to go gallivanting around the globe like she does." Che, who'd grown up in the valley a few years ahead of Charlie Watt and Ricardo, was quite the glamorous world traveler now.

On around to the west were the Steinbachs, sweet, self-effacing little Lorraine, and Gallway (whom Lew Potter used to refer to as "Gall-stones," because Lew always said he "had a lot of gall"—like chasing another man's wife, as rumor had it), who owned the Lost Dutchman Ranch, named for a legendary gold mine. Gallway was the retired comp-troller of a major petroleum company; Lorraine had raised their five chil-dren, none of whom ever seemed to make it out to Arizona to visit their parents very often.

That made eight people, with Ricardo and Mrs. Potter making it ten. She wondered, briefly, who the eleventh person was? Or did he say twelve? But she was more immediately concerned with the amazing and unprecedented fact that her ranch manager, whom she trusted possibly above all other people on the face of the earth, had set up a meeting of her neighbors, in her home, without even her by-your-leave. Mrs. Potter thought: if anybody else had done it, Ricardo himself would call it wildly presumptuous!

"What in the world's gotten into you, Ricardo?"

"You read Agatha Christie, don't you, *patrona*?"

"What? I read what?"

"Mysteries. Aren't you a great mystery reader?"

"Yes, but what does that have to do with—"

"Usual flight time?"

"Probably." She answered his question since he didn't seem at all in-clined to answer any of hers. He seemed, in spite of what he had hinted was some sort of serious situation, almost amused, even a little tickled by his own cleverness, if that's what it was, and by her surprise. "I'll call if it changes."

"*Hasta mañana.*"

Until tomorrow.

"I guess so," she replied with a touch of asperity. "But I'll tell you this, Ricardo—there is not *enough* time until tomorrow." Constrained by his secrecy and by the blasted party line, she couldn't think of anything else to say except adios, but she made sure she slipped that in. She never let anybody leave her without a farewell, not anymore, not after all the peo-ple to whom she hadn't had a chance to say good-bye. "*Con cuidado,*" she added impulsively. *Take care.*

"*Y tú,*" Ricardo replied.

And you.

Mrs. Potter hung up the telephone, and then stood for a moment staring out her kitchen window. Finally, she shrugged and smiled. She trusted Ricardo Ortega's word implicitly. He was such a fine man, so highly regarded in the valley. She considered it a point in her favor that he clearly felt an affection for his employer that was equal to hers for him and Juanita. If all else failed, she sometimes joked to her children, when the Potter family faced St. Peter at the Pearly Gates, they could all claim, "Yes, but Ricardo liked me!"

If he asked her to return home, she would do it.

If he felt the need to call a meeting in her home, she would willingly open her door to her neighbors.

And the truth was, he didn't even need a good excuse.

She smiled again, this time at the rain outside.

Bad news might be awaiting her at the Nogales airport tomorrow, but for now she felt as if she had been given wonderfully good news, which was that she had an excuse to go . . . home.

It was then that she looked over at the soup, and thought of the salsa and corn chips she had planned to serve tomorrow night. She finally realized what was especially odd about her menu: it belonged in Arizona, just as she did. Cilantro and cumin were definitely not the seasonings for a proper pot of Boston baked beans or clam chowder!

"*Gracias*, Ricardo." Mrs. Potter moved briskly into action to clean up her kitchen. Her shoulder felt much better now, and miraculously, the ache seemed to have left her finger. "*Muchas, muchas gracias, mi amigo.*"

When Mrs. Potter migrated every year from her childhood home in Iowa, then down to the ranch, and then up to Northcutt's Harbor, she liked to cook and serve the local fare. That might mean corn on the cob, fried chicken (dipped in milk and battered either in biscuit mix or in flour with a pretty heavy sprinkling of paprika), and tall icy glasses of lemonade (with sprigs of fresh mint plucked from her herb garden) in Iowa. It called for blueberry pancakes, oyster stew, and boiled lobsters in Maine (not all at the same meal, of course). And it certainly dictated guacamole and chips and salty margaritas and chili con carne in Arizona. Yet here she was, one month into her wanderings from daughter to daughter to son, from one old friend to another, and she had been fixing the best soup in Arizona . . . but in Maine.

"Go home, old dear," she advised herself as she swept the vegetable leavings from her cutting board into the sink and washed them down the disposal. "And just as Ricardo suggested, the sooner, the better."

Whatever had possessed her, she wondered now, to break her own habits and to turn herself into a nomad at this time of the year? This was a time when she was usually happily ensconced at the ranch, watching the winter slip away from the high desert while spring, in all its lovely, delicate hues and fragrances, tiptoed slowly, quietly into the landscape, gliding ever farther north from Mexico as the days lengthened into summer.

Mrs. Potter suspected that she knew what had driven her out of her beloved ranch house: an unaccustomed restlessness, and a strange desire to snap—as if it were a thin twig—the long-established routines of the seasons of her life. Clearly, that twig was proving tough to break; it refused to snap clear through, as presently proved by her overwhelming desire to go *home*.

"That's what's been wrong with me," she diagnosed.

No wonder she'd been moping about the rain. It was Arizona sunshine she craved. And was it any surprise she felt sluggish and slow? She missed her crisp mountain air. Now she understood her own melancholy. She was *homesick*, just like a kid.

Mrs. Potter gazed lovingly around her cottage.

Yes. But Sindhu was gone. And this wasn't home.

Without spilling a drop, she poured the soup into a tureen to cool. She'd refrigerate it tonight, then give it away before she left in the morning.

"Perhaps I'll make another batch when I get home."

She broke into song, substituting a word for "California": *"Arizona, here I come!"*

CHAPTER 3

4:30 A.M., Sunday, May 4
Las Palomas Ranch, Arizona

Linda loosened her grip on Taco's reins, allowing her beloved horse to pick his own way over the sharp pebbles, between the boulders and dark mounds of thorny ocotillo shrubs. She winced at the noise of their passage through the bottom of the canyon at the base of the steep mountains that rose on either side. It seemed to her that Taco's hoofs beat like drumsticks against the skin of the earth.

They were following her grandfather.

"He'll kill us if he finds out," Linda whispered.

The horse's ears flicked back in response.

It wasn't true, of course. She couldn't imagine her grandfather hurting anyone, much less killing them. And certainly not his most adored grandchild. A grin flashed on Linda's face, and then was gone. She knew perfectly well that Ricardo Ortega treated every one of his nine grandkids as if each was the most special to his big, generous heart. In Wind Valley she was known as Linda Ortega, after her grandparents, although that had never been her name. Her mother, Francesca Ortega, had married Les Scarritt, who was a fellow graduate student in anthropology at the University of Arizona, and she was their only child. To the rest of the world she was Linda Scarritt, but she was Linda Ortega to the valley. "Juanita's Linda." "Ricardo's Linda."

In this, her eighteenth spring, Linda was living with her grandparents and working for Mrs. Potter during the year she had convinced her parents to let her take off before the college she didn't particularly want to attend. It had helped a lot when her parents won a fellowship to travel to the jungles of Brazil for an anthropological field trip for the bulk of this same year. That made them much happier to leave her in her grandparents' charge rather than turn her loose in some dormitory on campus. She hadn't talked to her mother or father in nearly six months, but she enjoyed their letters—especially since they hinted that Francesca and Les were so fascinated by their work they might want to stay in Brazil another few months, which would give Linda a longer reprieve.

"Grandpa needs us," she whispered to Taco.

Half a mile ahead of them, her grandfather was also on horseback. Patches, his big paint gelding, kept a steady pace across the canyon floor. Her grandfather was the finest horseperson she'd ever known. But thank God he was a little hard of hearing at the age of sixty-seven. That was probably the only thing standing between her and discovery at this moment; when he was younger, her grandfather had seemed to possess the ears and eyes of an Indian scout. Or, maybe more appropriately, an Aztec scout. Now he wore glasses, even to work cattle—with a band to hold the bifocals on his head—and a hearing aid, which he hated. She was counting on the probability that he hadn't put it on for this strange, mysterious, early-morning ride of his.

He rode without ever pausing, like a man with a destination.

"*A dónde vas, Abuelo?*" she whispered.

Where are you going, Grandpa?

"*Y porqué?*" she added.

And why, for heaven's sake? Why did he leave the house at three o'clock in the morning, two hours before his normal rising time, while even the horses were still asleep in their corrals? Why did he saddle up Patches and ride out before the morning shadows began to fill the mountains? And why did he set off all alone—he thought—into the high plains that led into these canyons east of Mrs. Potter's house?

Linda was alert to her grandfather's odd behavior lately because her grandmother had put her on the track of it. And so she had jolted awake when she heard him moving almost soundlessly in the corridor outside his and Juanita's bedroom. While he had slipped on his cowboy boots in the kitchen, Linda had hurried out of her bed and into her own thermal underwear, jeans, boots, turtleneck, and sweatshirt. Grabbing her fleece-lined jacket off the coat tree by the back door, she'd quietly followed him into the backyard and then to the horse barn that lay between the Ortegas' house and Mrs. Potter's. She didn't want Bandy, who lived in the apartment over the garage, to hear her either, or he might limp over to the window and stick out his head—or possibly a rifle—and shout, "*Quién va?*" (*Who goes there?*) If he didn't hear her, as old and hard of hearing as *he* was, then one of his "nephews"—the illegal aliens he often sheltered— might. So she had to be careful. Her grandfather was still moving quietly too.

She'd hidden herself behind a shoulder-high manzanita bush and spied in puzzlement as he threw a saddle on Patches and then led the horse at a walk out of hearing distance of the house. She had then scurried into the barn to saddle her own horse and follow the horse and rider that her grandmother had dubbed the "Old Centaur."

"Keep an eye on the Old Centaur," Juanita had instructed her.

And that's what she was doing, watching with growing concern as the Old Centaur moved off the canyon trail and started up a frighteningly steep, narrow, hairpin path that led to the top of a sandstone formation known locally as El Bizcocho. The Biscuit. Not that the climb would frighten *him*. As far as she knew, nothing scared Grandpa. She reined Taco to a halt, unsure of how to proceed. Darn! How were she and Taco supposed to follow him up there without being noticed?

"Grandpa!" she protested, under her breath. "What are you doing?"

From the top of El Bizcocho, you could see the whole valley in every direction. Linda knew that because she'd climbed it many times on foot and once, holding her breath most of the way, by horse. It was a spectacular 360-degree panoramic view all the way into Mexico, and clear up into Tucson. It took your breath—the little you had left—away. That was your reward for getting to the top.

But who'd want to at this hour?

It was just one more unlikely thing for him to do.

This man, who she loved possibly even more than her own father, this man who other people idolized and the whole of Wind Valley respected, seemed tired and distracted lately. And that was in itself so unusual that it had prompted her grandmother to say, "You keep an eye on that man, *hijita*. If he's sick and he has a heart attack and falls off that horse out there someplace in the wilderness, I want you to be the first to know it." She'd frowned sternly at her granddaughter. "So I'll be the second to hear of it."

And so she'd been following him, feeling furtive and guilty about it, and afraid that he'd find out.

She wasn't scared of her grandfather—far from it—but she couldn't have borne the disappointment that might appear in his eyes if he knew she and Juanita were conspiring against him, as if he were a feeble old man who couldn't take care of himself. What a thought!

"It's for his own good," her grandmother had insisted.

Linda had tracked her grandfather's movements for the past couple of weeks, and reported back daily to Juanita. So far, there'd been nothing of any consequence to say, as far as she could tell, except for the worrisome fact that he'd developed a habit of getting into his pickup and driving aimlessly around the valley. At least, it had seemed aimless to Linda, as she had observed him staring over other people's fences, or following a slow-moving tractor down the road as if he had all the time in the world.

And then there was his odd behavior last night, after supper.

After dessert, and without telling Juanita where he was going, he left the house and walked up the hill to *la patrona's* compound. There, he'd let himself in with the key that Mrs. Potter kept under a potted cactus, then turned on the light in the front hall. From outside, hidden in the shadows by the patio gate, Linda had watched a second light come on, this one in *la patrona's* study. Linda had crept nearer and watched through a window as her grandfather sat down in Mrs. Potter's chair, behind Mrs. Potter's desk, and used the telephone there. One, two, three, four, five, six times, he dialed numbers. Each time he talked into the phone, although Linda suspected that a couple of times he spoke to an answering machine.

"What does he want to say to people that he doesn't want me to hear?" was what Juanita demanded when Linda reported back to her.

"Maybe it's a surprise party for you, Grandma."

"My birthday's in July. We were married in December."

Linda flushed even before the punch line hit.

"This, as you may not have noticed, is May."

Each report that Linda made to her grandmother only seemed to set Juanita more stubbornly on her husband's track, and that made Linda feel as if she were caught like a calf in a squeeze chute. The dilemma was that she trusted her grandmother's judgment, too, especially when it came to the subject that Juanita Ortega knew best . . . which was, as everybody knew, Ricardo Ortega. "That man," as Juanita habitually referred to him, was her mission. Taking care of him was the job at the center of her life.

Linda, a modern girl in spite of her very traditional heritage, both envied and pitied her grandmother for that attitude. As much as Linda adored her grandfather, she didn't think she'd like to sacrifice her life to a husband, not even one as grand and elegant as he. Neither did Linda want to turn as bossy and fretful and sour as Juanita could be sometimes. Linda just wanted to finish growing up and get a job on a ranch here in the valley—maybe even eventually become the first woman foreman in the valley—and get happily married to a special, handsome man, and have their own ranch someday, and raise a wonderful family as her grandparents had done. Or she wouldn't mind being like Che Thomas over at the C Lazy U dude ranch. Now there was a woman, strong as Grandma but happier because she was focused on her own life instead of on a man. Maybe it could all come true. Someday. Maybe even sooner than someday, if her parents didn't absolutely insist on college for her.

And then there'd been the change in her grandfather that both she and her grandmother had noticed in the last twenty-four hours: he'd lost that weary, worried expression, he'd straightened his shoulders and seemed full of confidence again. Something had happened to cheer him, Linda felt, but she didn't know what it was, any more than she knew what it was that had seemed to weigh him down to begin with!

The mystery was driving her grandmother crazy.

"*Now* what's going on?" she'd demanded. "You find out!"

I'm trying, Grandma!

On El Bizcocho, her grandfather disappeared from her sight behind a stand of sweet cedar trees.

Linda rolled her shoulders, trying to unbunch the vise of muscles that locked her upper body. Her thighs gripped Taco's sides as if she and the horse were molded from the same quivering muscular flesh. Linda forced her legs to relax. But then Taco moved forward, so she had to rein him up short again.

Linda wished *la patrona* wouldn't go away so often or for so long, and she suspected that Juanita held the same opinion, although she would never speak ill of her old friend and employer. Juanita might have a tongue sharpened on everybody else's hide, but she never honed it on Mrs. Potter. Except in the most indirect ways. Like the other day, when she'd muttered within hearing range of both Ricardo and Linda, "Too much responsibility for one old man." To which Ricardo had responded, in his usual calm and good-humored way, "Such a young woman to be married to such an old man." Linda had been happy to see the spark of laughter in her grandmother's eyes at that perfect, most gallant riposte. It was just like him. And just like Juanita. It had tempted Linda to think: everything's okay. But everything wasn't, it couldn't be, or why would he be out here like this, doing whatever weird thing he was doing? *Why* was he climbing to the top of El Bizcocho?

Actually, she wouldn't have put it past the smart old man to be doing this to her on purpose, to have detected her presence behind him and to be taking this gentle and rather humorous—if dangerous—way of shaking her off his trail. And afterward, there'd be a small lesson for her, something about how he'd intuited her presence from a telltale toss of his horse's mane, or somesuch impossible thing that only he could sense.

She thought of what her grandmother would say to that: "The man doesn't know everything." It was Juanita's stock answer to anybody who praised her husband excessively.

But Linda wasn't at all sure that was true. Ever since she was a little girl, starting with the first time she ever looked up into those kind and knowing brown eyes of his, she'd suspected that her grandpa was as close to omniscient as a mortal man could be.

The wind through the canyon blew the fragrance of juniper to her.

She tugged the sleeves of her jacket down over her wrists and turned the sheepskin side of her collar up against her neck. She nudged Taco forward a few paces, then paused again beside a couple of great sycamores that grew from the dry, sandy creek bed. Linda glanced up, checking the sky. It was clear, with no sign of one of those murderous spring squalls that could transform a dry wash like this into a roaring river that could sweep unwary people or animals to their deaths by drowning, or by bashing them against the boulders. In the cloudless sky she could see the moon clearly, but there wasn't much of it, only a sliver to light their course.

Ricardo Ortega, on Patches, climbed slowly higher.

El Bizcocho, The Biscuit. Its twisting upper trail belied its cozy, domestic-sounding name. Linda knew it to be a difficult ride in daylight, more suited to mountain goats than horses; she fervently wished her grandfather wouldn't attempt it at all, ever, much less at night, and especially on one as moonless as this.

Linda wanted to yell: Grandpa! Come down!

She whispered, instead, "What are you up to?"

Taco's ears flicked back again. He lifted his right foreleg and set it down noisily. Her beloved horse was all too attuned to his mistress and all too ready to "converse" with her by whinnying or shaking his bridle or stamping his feet in response to the language of her body and her words. It was her grandfather, of course, who had taught her how to establish such a bond between herself and an animal. He, himself, was uncanny in the way he handled animals; whether it was dogs, cows, or horses, they responded to him as to nobody else in the valley.

No more whispering! she commanded herself, feeling a flutter of panic at the thought that her grandfather might hear them. *Grandpa!* she pleaded silently. *Come down from there! Let's go home and go back to bed and then get up at a normal time and have breakfast with Grandma!*

A sudden soft clatter of pebbles made her shift nervously in her saddle. Squirrels. Desert rats. Linda felt as if one of them had crawled up her spine. She didn't like being out in the mountains at night like this, with only a dark new moon to light their paths. She thought of coyotes. Wild dogs in packs. Raccoons. Rattlesnakes. She shivered again.

Grandpa, *por favor*!

Suddenly there was a sound in the distance she couldn't mistake—the noise of an engine, probably a truck.

Damn hunters! They must be over on state land to the east.

If they crossed onto Las Palomas, Grandpa would fix their wagon for sure. Maybe that was why he was out tonight, looking for trespassing hunters. *Oh, but Grandpa, that is dangerous, trying to patrol alone, at night, on horseback. You'd never let Ken or Bandy or any of us do it. What can you be thinking of?*

The noise of the truck grew louder, coming closer.

It drew her attention to the ridge opposite the one on El Bizcocho where her grandfather had come into view again and pulled Patches to a halt at the top. She could just barely see him now, horse and rider outlined against the night sky with its first hint of dawn rising. She looked back toward the opposite ridge. She could just barely see the truck, too, although she could tell that it looked about the size of a quarter-ton pickup, a common type of vehicle in these parts, but she couldn't distinguish the make or color.

Linda felt a growing sense of unease, verging on panic.

On the ridge, there was a glint of windshield under the moon.

The sound of a truck door opening echoed down the mountain to her.

There was no sound from the top of El Bizcocho.

Her grandfather probably couldn't see or hear the truck.

Then there was another glint up on the ridge, and a second sound that was unmistakable to the ears of a girl for whom a ranch was a second home: it was the decisive clack of a bolt on a rifle.

"Grandpa!" Linda screamed. Taco's front legs rose in a half-buck. She fought him to keep control. "Grandpa! Hunters!" And then she turned her face to the ridge. "No! Don't shoot! That's a man up there!"

There were three shots in succession.

Even as the second and third rounds rang out, a terrified whinny echoed down from the top of El Bizcocho and bounced off the canyon walls. Linda heard her grandfather's voice raised in fruitless command to Patches. Taco tried to bolt. Linda exerted all her strength to keep him restrained to moving in small, tight circles. She listened in horror to the terrible sound of Patches slipping on the rocks above, and actually saw part of their fall as they tumbled down the steep, murderously rocky sides of the mountain. She heard her grandfather cry out once. And then there was only the noise of horse and rider plunging to their certain deaths down the rocky slope of El Bizcocho to the bottom of the canyon, where Linda still fought to control her own panicked horse.

"Grandpa!"

She started to gallop in his direction. She was heedless of the danger-strewn path through which she wanted Taco to race. She had to reach her grandfather and Patches and help them, had to hope they were still alive, had to get there, get there . . .

Over the sound of her own ragged breathing, and Taco's, she heard the truck once more, and glanced up.

She was blinded by headlights that were focused on her.

Stunned, she brought her confused and stumbling horse to a halt.

She heard the rifle go off again, heard the slug strike a boulder not five feet from her, felt a shard of rock strike her pant leg, and realized she was the new target.

Por Dios, por Dios!

My God, my God!

If she turned and ran, her grandfather might die. No, he was already dead, she'd seen him fall and she knew there was no chance he could have survived it; she had to face that terrible fact, she had to. And Patches was dead too. There wasn't hope. They hadn't had a chance. If she continued toward them, the rifle would catch her, and the shooter couldn't allow her to tell what she had just witnessed. . . .

Sobbing, crying heartbroken apologies to her grandfather, Linda abandoned him and Patches. She did as she knew he would have instructed her: she wheeled Taco around and they ran out of the spotlight, stumbling over the same sharp rocks they'd so cautiously navigated coming into the canyon. *I can't ride home! They'd find me on the open range! Got a good look at me in their headlights.* She glanced back over her shoulder, up at the ridge, but the headlights were descending now, so whoever was driving clearly knew the terrain, knew there was a dirt road down from the top. And then, in a moment of horrible truth, she caught a glimpse of the truck in profile, and gasped her recognition of it. Linda turned her face into the wind again and urged Taco to go faster. "*Por Dios!* Please! No! It isn't possible!" Her grandfather's voice spoke to her sternly over her anguish: *Run, my granddaughter. Escape. Hide.* Linda obeyed. She guided Taco into the deep shadows on the western edge of the mountains, where nobody coming down from the ridge could see her, and then she raced, raced for the only shelter she could think of, a place that practically nobody else knew about, where almost nobody could find her, if she could get there, if she could make it, if she could only get out of sight long enough to fool the truck's driver into losing her for the time it would take her to reach the favorite hiding place of her childhood. . . .

Taco raced as if from demons, with Linda hunched over his neck.

The wind dried the tears from her face, even as they fell.

Grandpa!

CHAPTER 4

There was no one to meet Mrs. Potter at the Nogales Airport when she arrived there early Sunday evening.

She waited an hour and a half, but no one came for her.

For the first twenty minutes, Mrs. Potter stood outside the terminal with her suitcases at her side, expecting Ricardo's red Ford pickup truck to pull up at any moment. It was a pleasant wait and she luxuriated in the feeling of the warm, dry air on her face, although she immediately put on her sunglasses and shielded her nose from the sun by donning a collapsible canvas hat she had carried with her in her purse. (In Arizona, as Mrs. Potter confided to her friends, she ran through moisturizer the way some cars ran through motor oil. The air seemed to inhale every drop of water. She also made it a practice to drink lots of water, for her skin's sake. It wasn't just wrinkles she was worried about; she was careful to wear sun block, too, and long sleeves and pants. Mrs. Potter saw nothing attractive about leathery skin or melanomas.) Here, the sun was as dangerous as a rattlesnake and potentially just as deadly.

It was good to hear Spanish being spoken again—Nogales was perched right on the border—and it was fun to read the bilingual airport signs and watch the passers-by who looked so much like their Indian ancestors that they could have been statues come to life from the archaeological museum in Mexico City.

"Are you coming, Ricardo?" she muttered.

After a while, Mrs. Potter shed her jacket and folded it over one arm, marveling at how two climates as different as Maine and Arizona could exist in the same country, and how fortunate she was to be able to experience both of them. In one day, she'd gone from an ocean and chilly rain and spruce trees in the morning to the desert and fading sunlight and cactus in the early evening! At the airport in Boston she'd been surrounded by New Englanders in Rockport shoes and Eddie Bauer jackets, people whose complexions were, like hers, still pale from winter; here it was all tanned skin and shorts, T-shirts and sandals and the loose *guayubera* shirts that were designed to be worn outside of, not tucked into, men's trousers. *And I might have taken it all for granted,* she thought, *if not for this enforced wait* (of the sort that tended to give rise to philosophical musings).

"Did you forget me, Ricardo?"

Finally, feeling so hot she wished she could remove her panty hose, Mrs. Potter got help carrying her bags back into the terminal. She called Ricardo's house, but reached only the answering machine. No luck reaching Bandy Esposito or Ken Ryerson, either. As a last resort, Mrs. Potter checked at the counter, but the airline held no message for her.

"He couldn't, wouldn't have forgotten me."

She found a seat near her luggage and pulled out the paperback mystery she had been reading on the plane. When she reached the next to last chapter, where the detective gathered all the suspects into a room and one by one eliminated them until he revealed the murderer, she recalled Ricardo's odd remark about her reading mysteries. Did she read Agatha Christie? Was that what he had asked? Well, of course, Mrs. Potter thought with a smile, as she and the fictional detective uncovered the truth at the same time, didn't every sensible person? What could he have meant by that question? When she finally looked up from her novel, she saw that all the cars pulling up to the curb outside had their headlights on.

"Where are you, Ricardo?"

Surrendering to the inevitable, Mrs. Potter leased a car.

The rental car, a little brown Subaru like the one she drove in Maine, sped down the six-mile stretch of main highway that paralleled the quiet back road leading to Las Palomas Ranch. Mrs. Potter regretted this necessity—not so much because of the expense or even for the bother of having to return the car, but because she hated to drive this highway at night. In fact, she'd rented the Subaru because it was exactly—even down to the brown color—like the car she kept in Maine, and at least she'd feel at home behind the steering wheel. Her night vision wasn't very good anymore, she had to admit. Even worse, she felt like a pawn in an endless game of tag being played by the huge produce trucks carrying tomatoes from Mexico.

Like great beasts of the night, the trucks passed and repassed each other, jockeying for position in what seemed to her to be a contest of machismo among the drivers. Her car was often sandwiched between two of the behemoths. Knowing that a third truck was approaching from the rear and would try to pass in spite of headlights up ahead on the curve, and knowing that the third driver could not realize (or did not care about) the position of her small, vulnerable vehicle, Mrs. Potter had to drive rapidly and well.

"And they aren't even *good* tomatoes!" she protested.

Finally, she gained the turnoff into the tranquility of the ten-mile back road leading to Las Palomas. At last now she could relax.

Her stomach growled.

"I know, I know," she shushed it.

She felt ravenous after surviving the "Nogales 500," as she dubbed that deadly stretch of highway. The strain of driving it always seemed to drain her body of its vital reserves, leaving her craving a juicy steak and baked potato.

Well, Ricardo would have warned Juanita she was coming home, and if she knew Juanita, that superb cook would have toddled over to Mrs. Potter's house this afternoon with *"una cosa pequeña, no es nada"—a little something, it's nothing*—for her arrival supper.

Mrs. Potter made a wish: "Chili rellenos."

Let it please be Juanita's scrumptious chili rellenos, that heavenly, quick and easy Mexican one-dish meal that Juanita made by pouring eggs, condensed milk, and flour over layers of mild green chili peppers and grated Jack and longhorn cheese, which she topped with a mild taco sauce and baked. Oh, it created such a pretty sight in a glass casserole, rather Christmasy, special enough to take to anybody's potluck dinner, and always popular. The condensed milk lent it an unexpected sweetness that took first-timers by surprise. Yes, please let it be Juanita's chili rellenos. . . .

Or maybe her perfect cheese-and-onion enchiladas . . . or her yummy sopapillas, those deep-fried pillows of puff pastry coated with fine grains of sugar and dripping with honey . . . or her creamy guacamole salada, into which she stirred the juice of fresh Florida limes whenever Mrs. Potter could persuade one of her Palm Beach pals to mail a few of those sweet little emeralds to Arizona. . . .

Mrs. Potter's rumbling stomach informed her it would be happy with a bowl of canned pea soup and a grilled cheese sandwich, thank you very much.

She naturally still wondered, but was trying not to be overly worried about, what had become of Ricardo. He would never leave her stranded unless a true emergency had arisen, so where was he, and why hadn't he been able to get a message to her at the airport? A flat tire, perhaps, many miles between telephones? A sudden vision of his pickup truck crushed under the wheels of one of those demonic produce trucks came unbidden to her mind.

"No," she said aloud, decisively. If anything like that had happened she would have seen the aftermath along her route home. Unless they'd already cleared it away. . . . "No."

Still, she felt eager to get home for more than mere sustenance. Mrs. Potter pushed a little harder on the gas pedal. She wanted to hear Juanita tell her "that man" had called from the highway to report a broken fan belt, or somesuch.

She was eager to get home, period.

Mrs. Potter pulled up to her own ranch entrance and rejoiced as she always did at the sight of the sign of the two doves to the side of her main gate. They were sculpted of wrought iron, and seemed to beckon to her with their outstretched wings: *Bienvenidos*. Welcome. She rattled slowly over the cattle guard, which was horizontal bars set into a shallow, rectangular hole in the ground to keep livestock from wandering out the open gateway. They obviated the necessity of keeping the gate closed all the time. There ahead of her was the beautiful, winding final two miles of road that led to the base of the small mountains—the Rimstones—which were backdrop for Las Palomas. Even from that distance, she saw welcoming lights turned on at her patio gate.

"How fortunate I am," she whispered, at this first sight of home.

She and Lew had been living in Philadelphia when they decided to move to Arizona and buy Las Palomas. Some of their friends had snootily claimed there were only two places to go in Arizona: the Grand Canyon for vacations with the children, and Scottsdale, the upscale suburb of Phoenix, if "you absolutely insist on living down there."

But the Southwest had seduced Lew and Eugenia Potter in ways that most of their friends could not fathom. What they both desired, it seemed, was something extraordinary that could not be found in either the Grand Canyon or Scottsdale. Miracle of miracles, they'd discovered it: their beautiful, honest-to-goodness cattle ranch twenty miles north of Mexico. When Lew died, people seemed to expect her to sell the ranch and move back to Philadelphia, or to move permanently into the Maine cottage, but those ideas didn't even occur to her. By then, there was only one real home for her.

This was it, straight ahead of her, with its lamps shining. . . .

Too many lights. Mrs. Potter sat up straighter behind the wheel. Headlights, some of them.

Her driveway was filled with vehicles and people.

Mrs. Potter's first thought was: *Ricardo.*

She knew something had happened to Ricardo as clearly and as irrevocably as she had known that Lew was dead before anyone had actually said the words. She felt it in the same way she had sensed some of those days when one of her children would be sent home sick or injured from school:

a certain paleness to her son's complexion that she didn't even know she'd noticed; a clumsy quality to her daughter's walk that morning, an argument, a spilled bowl of cereal, a forgotten homework assignment. It was as if at an intuitive level, certain facts stuck together to form one inescapable conclusion that propelled itself to the surface of her consciousness. She'd learned to trust—if not always to welcome—those feelings that were stronger than hunches.

Her mind flashed back on the produce trucks. She thought of her own, perhaps prescient preoccupation with death the day before, and of how she'd made a point of saying "adios" to Ricardo, because only a few moments before she'd felt so sad that she hadn't said it to other people she had lost. A great lump of dread and grief and fury rose from her heart into her throat. She wanted to scream protests. She wanted to inform the universe, as she might a willful child, that she wouldn't allow this, it simply wasn't acceptable! No!

"The meeting . . ." she whispered, suddenly feeling enormous relief. It was as if someone had let the air out of an overstuffed balloon. She felt limp and happily deflated.

That's what this was; the meeting he had called at her house!

Mrs. Potter nearly wept with relief; she felt wonderfully, happily foolish. How silly of her to jump to such morbid conclusions. These were her friends and neighbors, gathered in front of her house, waiting for her to come home and open her front door to them. They must have only just arrived, or they'd have used her "hidden" key to let themselves into her house, as easily and as comfortably as she could have let herself into most of their homes. She saw Che Thomas, the Steinbachs, the McHenrys, Charlie Watt, the young Amorys, all here, just as Ricardo had said they'd be.

Mrs. Potter was so hungry that even looking at *them* made her think of food. . . .

There was Gallway Steinbach, who made her think of a beef Wellington, all crusty and pretentious on the surface, but basically just a plain old piece of roast beef underneath. Beside him stood his wife, Lorraine, who brought macaroon cookies to mind: soft, round, and sticky-sweet. Che Thomas, on the other hand, although she was nearly twenty years older than either Steinbach, was one of those chic, spicy new sauces—pureed avocado, perhaps, decorated with elegant lines of pureed tomato and yellow squash, and making a lovely presentation. Che made quite a contrast to sixty-five-year-old Charlie Watt, who was chicken fried steak and gravy, all the way. Marj McHenry, with her British accent, was fish and chips, of course, and Reynolds—Rey—McHenry was unadorned brussels sprouts. "Now why," Mrs. Potter wondered, "does Kathy Amory make me think of a McDonald's hamburger, of all things?" Her husband, Walt, with his quiet, earnest demeanor and his horn-rimmed glasses, also made Mrs. Potter think of a sandwich; she suddenly pictured him sitting at a table, designing his computer software. There'd be a half-eaten sandwich beside him, and he wouldn't know if it was peanut butter or liverwurst.

Mrs. Potter forced herself to stop visualizing her neighbors as food. She'd heard of dying people seeing mirages in the desert, but this was ridiculous. Next thing, she'd be seeing the sugar plum fairy.

Mrs. Potter didn't have to force a smile to her face as she stepped out of her car.

"Hello, folks," she said.

CHAPTER 5

There was a rush of movement toward her and a babble of voices as her neighbors all started talking at once.

"Genia?" Lorraine Steinbach reached her first, with a soft hug and a fulsome murmur of her name. In Mrs. Potter's returning embrace, Lorraine felt as puffy as a fresh doughnut; her face was flushed and damp against Mrs. Potter's cheek, and the back of her cotton dress felt moist to Mrs. Potter's hands, even on this chilly night. "Oh, my dear, I know you're so worried. We all are, I just can't imagine what—"

But then Lorraine gave way to Che Thomas, whose bony embrace was quicker, fiercer, stronger. "My God, girl, how'd you get here so soon?" Mrs. Potter felt herself clamped against a hard necklace of silver and turquoise, which bit into her clavicle, and was enveloped in a delicious fragrance of some perfume that Che had probably picked up on her last trip to Paris. Che's elegant silver rings bit into Mrs. Potter's flesh, but the thin, strong arms that encircled her were warm with affection and welcome. From behind Che, an unctuous bass voice demanded, "How did you know, Genia? Did somebody call you?" Che released her so abruptly that Mrs. Potter reached out a hand to her car for balance, as Che retorted to the man who'd spoken, "Don't be ridiculous, Gallway. How could she know? *We* only just found out!"

That prompted an equally sarcastic response from the tall man with the oily voice and the paunch, as he stepped out of the shadows to shake Mrs. Potter's hand.

"Well, then, why don't *you* tell us what she's doing here, Che."

"I don't *know*, Gallway."

"Found out what?" Mrs. Potter asked, but he didn't answer.

Gallway Steinbach wore a long-sleeved gray flannel shirt tucked into white trousers, with a yellow kerchief tied jauntily around his neck, its two ends sticking out like a butterfly's wings. His too-black hair was slicked back off his extended forehead; he had slightly bulging pale-blue eyes and a mottled complexion reddenèd by high blood pressure. *Well,* thought Mrs. Potter, as she always did upon seeing him, *I guess Lorraine loves you.*

The round, pretty face of Kathy Amory materialized at Mrs. Potter's right hand, which the young woman lifted and gently squeezed. "Oh, Mrs. Potter, it's awful, isn't it?" In her blue jeans and denim jacket, with her frizzy red hair pulled back into a ponytail, Kathy looked about eighteen years old instead of the twenty-eight or thirty that was more like it. She raised a wide-eyed blue gaze to the man on Mrs. Potter's other side. "Isn't it just terrible, Gallway?"

Aware that Lorraine Steinbach had slipped out of the light and turned her face away from the crowd, Mrs. Potter tactfully withdrew her hand from Kathy's. What this young woman did with Gallstones was her own business, but it hurt Mrs. Potter to witness the pain in Lorraine's face as the older woman slipped out of the light when the younger woman came near. Mrs. Potter couldn't help but shoot a quick glance at Kathy's husband, Walt Amory, but his handsome young face was unreadable behind his horn-rimmed glasses, except for the concern it seemed to express for Mrs. Potter, a concern she didn't want to see there. Mrs. Potter looked away. Once again it was Che Thomas who was first with the quick retort: "Not *yet,* Kathy, it isn't awful *yet.* There's still hope, girl!"

"But Mrs. Thomas, I only meant—"

"Have you heard anything, Genia?"

"Genia, is there any word?"

They buffeted her with questions she couldn't answer, demanded explanations she couldn't give. They held her at arm's length to look at her, shook her hand, patted her, hugged her, kissed her, but in a funny way ignored her, so busy were they with reacting to one another. Even Rey McHenry gave her shoulders a stiff squeeze. His wife, Marj, remained outside the circle of swarming neighbors. The rest of them all seemed to her to be speaking in foreign tongues from which she could make no sense at all.

"*Patrona?*"

Mrs. Potter turned toward the sound of that single word as if toward a lifeline. It was Bandy Esposito, standing beside his little truck, on the shadowed fringe of the crowd. The old hired hand was lame now, from a cowboying accident a few years back, and admittedly not much good for jobs around the ranch anymore, except for tending her flowers and keeping her swimming pool clean. Many of her neighbors—including some of those gathered there at that moment—considered her profligate for continuing to employ him at full salary. But it had never been much of a salary anyway, she considered, even if it did come with free room and with feed for his horse and gas for his truck. If she'd retired him, she'd probably have paid him nearly the same in benefits, and this way he got to feel—and be—useful for a few more years. She turned to him in relief, because she knew that people *could* turn to Bandy, because he was utterly dependable in many things, even when those "things" declined in number and importance through the years. He had his straw cowboy hat in his hands, respectfully waiting for her attention, but there was a dark urgency in his eyes and in his voice when he uttered the single word again.

"*Patrona.*"

Mrs. Potter excused her way through the crowd to reach him. She paused a few paces away from the old cowboy, in the gravel of her driveway, and said quietly, "*Dígame*, Bandy, *por favor.*"

Tell me, please.

"*Patrona*, we do not know you are coming."

"Ricardo knew."

Bandy shrugged slightly, an expression of futility. "He go out early this morning, *patrona*, and he no come back. Linda, she is missing too." Through the years, she and he had managed to communicate nicely, with their own mixture of his poor English and her poor Spanish. But now she tilted her head as if she hadn't understood him. Missing? she thought. And Linda? Yes, this was bad—*might* be bad—but it wasn't the worst she had anticipated. Not yet. She wanted to quiz Bandy, to get all of the facts. But not with this crowd at her back.

Mrs. Potter turned away from him, to face her neighbors again.

"It's thoughtful of you to be here . . ."

Che Thomas walked up to her, as if by right of age she had been appointed spokeswoman for them all. Mrs. Potter instinctively reached out her hands, and Che firmly grasped them. "Thoughtful has nothing to do with it, Genia. We're here because Ricardo called each of us last night and asked us to meet him here at seven this evening. He didn't say why, and he didn't tell us you'd be here too. But you know how we feel about Ricardo. If he says jump, we all jump. So, like good little children, here we all are. Only to find out that he's missing"—Che released Mrs. Potter's hands and lifted her arms in a wide and elegant sweep as if to embrace the entire ranch—"somewhere out there in the wilderness. What's going on, Genia?"

"My dear, I don't have any idea."

Che, ever the organizer—of rodeos, of hunting trips, of great fiestas at her dude ranch—clapped her hands, as if to startle everybody into action. "Well, then," she said, "let's all go down to Juanita's and see what she can tell us."

"No," Mrs. Potter said quickly, and persuaded them that the proper course of action was for them to go home and for her to go alone, with Bandy, to her foreman's house to call on his wife. Che meant well, she knew, but the last thing Juanita needed right now was this troop of high-powered types stomping into her house and demanding answers! *She* would find out everything she could from Juanita, Mrs. Potter promised her neighbors, and then she would call them to let them know.

Che Thomas warmly embraced her, as did the other women—except for Marj McHenry—as they walked with the men toward their ranch vehicles, their pickups, and four-wheel-drive cars.

"If you need us . . ."

"Thank you so much, let's hope I won't," Mrs. Potter told each of them.

As she drove away, Che Thomas braked long enough to lean out her driver's-side window and to motion Mrs. Potter over. "This may not be the best time to tell you, but I've got a surprise for you, Genia, back at my place."

"I don't want any more surprises, Che."

"You'll like this one." Then surprisingly, considering the circumstances, Che smiled and winked at her friend. "Trust me. I'll see that you get it later tonight."

"Can it wait, Che?"

"Well, it's already waited forty years," was the mysterious reply. "I guess it could wait a while longer. But I don't think it wants to."

Mrs. Potter gave up trying to figure out what anything meant. People were talking in riddles to her this evening, saying nonsensical things—like that Ricardo was missing. Impossible. And Linda. Even more impossible. And forty-year-old surprises were waiting to be unwrapped. Improbable.

"Don't worry about Ricardo," Che commanded as she slipped her gear shift into first. "He's fine, I'm sure of it. And when he's back, I want you all to come over to my place for my Wednesday tostada spread; you, Rico and Juanita, and Linda—if she wants to, you can never tell about these teenagers." Her smile was enigmatic. "And maybe my surprise will be there too."

"Che!"

Her protest was dismissed with a wave. "Hell, if Ricardo can't take care of himself, there's no hope for any of us, Genia!"

And then Che rode off in a small, dramatic cloud of dust in one of the black Ford pickup trucks that were the trademark of her business, along with matching black Jeeps. Each vehicle had the ranch's brand and address emblazoned on its doors: C Lazy U, Wind Valley, AZ.

Mrs. Potter stared fondly after her, even as she coughed on the dust. She hoped with all of her heart that things would work out so that she would indeed be able to go with the Ortegas to Che's on Wednesday night. The tostada spread was famous throughout the valley, and a coveted invitation, because Che always loaded a huge buffet table with an incredible array of food, some of it mundane but some of it quite exotic, from which her guests could build their own, highly inventive, tostada creations. It was also known as Leftover Night, because most of the delicacies were left over from the culinary masterpieces that Che's professional chefs had cooked for her "dudes" the previous week. The lucky guest on tostada night might create something as simple and traditional as ground beef with shredded lettuce, cheese, and onions, or something unique—and possibly awful—like a caviar tostada or even a liver pâté with spinach and hazelnuts tostado. You never knew what to expect, and that was half the fun of it. Ricardo loved to attend them, and Juanita liked to spy on other people's recipes. As for Mrs. Potter, she'd be content just to know that Ricardo and Linda—

"Genia?"

She squinted into the darkness. "Oh, hello, Charlie."

Charlie Watt had remained behind after all the other neighbors had driven away. "I know what's happened to Ricardo and Linda," he said.

CHAPTER 6

Charlie Watt made his dramatic pronouncement in that quiet, unassuming way he had, which had grown even more so since the death last fall of his wife, Helen. In the bustling, noisy crowd of all of those strong personalities, he'd been practically invisible.

Mrs. Potter held out her hand and he took it in both of his own work-roughened hands, before bending down to lay a gentle kiss on her right cheek. She could feel that his lips were chapped and his face was closely shaved; she smelled the lime fragrance of his shaving lotion and was suddenly, unexpectedly swept with a sharp, vivid, particular memory of Lew getting dressed to go out to dinner. Looking so handsome, so distinguished. Moving with that peculiarly male energy of his, as if he always had a purpose, a goal in mind. She still missed having that male energy in her life, and no amount of working with sweaty cowboys could make up for its loss. She still occasionally—maybe more than occasionally—missed the fragrance of a clean, well-dressed man, the comforting, flattering feel of his arm around her as they walked out the door to a dinner party. . . . She blinked Lew away, and gazed at Charlie Watt, who'd been a friend of her late husband's.

In his dark brown cowboy suit with its embroidered jacket, and his cowboy-cut cotton shirt and bolo tie, and with his brown felt cowboy hat in his hands, Charlie looked ever so much the part of the archetypal Arizona rancher. And he was, actually, one of the few ranch owners left in the valley who lived and worked full-time on his place. Whereas the others, and even Mrs. Potter, were absentee ranchers much of the time, leaving the care of their land and cattle to other hands, Charlie Watt was the genuine article, all year round.

Now they had both, Mrs. Potter and Charlie, lost a spouse. Her heart ached in compassionate understanding for him. The first year was so hard, and he wasn't half through it yet.

"What do you mean you know what has happened to them, Charlie?"

"It's those wetbacks of Bandy's."

"Charlie, please . . ." She glanced at the old hired hand who stood in the shadows.

"All right, illegal aliens then, whatever you want to call them. I've told Ricardo a thousand times to keep out of that damned business. You know I have."

"Why, it's not a business for him, Charlie. He doesn't make any money from helping them, in fact I suspect he gives them money out of his own pocket, he and Bandy. You know perfectly well that it's personal with them, more like a mission."

"That don't make it right. It's illegal, plain and simple. He's been going against the law of this land, and doing it for years. I've threatened to report them both to immigration, and I may yet do it, especially if I'm right about this. It's not only illegal, it's an immoral practice, you ask me, encouraging those poor people to risk their lives coming over the border. And it's dangerous for all of you, which I've tried to hammer into Ricardo's thick skull, but he always thinks he knows better. Not every man who comes over those mountains is a nice fella, Genia. Some of them are pretty damned desperate. They could be criminals, robbers or murderers, just as likely as not. They could have caught Rico and Linda out on the range, took 'em for likely robbery victims, or God knows what else, killed 'em on the spot, and buried their bodies where we'll never find 'em. Maybe they wanted Rico's wallet. Maybe they wanted the horses. I hate to say it, but maybe they wanted *her*. Old man and a girl, they'd look like easy pickin's. Hell, I hate to say it, but they'd *be* easy pickin's. Ricardo thinks he's tough as he ever was, but I know how I feel when I get up in the morning, and I'm still a few years younger than him. Unfortunately, and you know I mean this sincerely, Genia, I think this business is going to prove I'm right, much as I wish I wasn't."

Somehow, he'd managed to say all that without sounding self-righteous, which was why it was easy for Mrs. Potter to reach out again to squeeze one of his big, callused hands. "I also hope you're wrong."

"Well, hell, I didn't mean to frighten you, Genia."

"I'm already scared to death, Charlie."

"Well, I'm sorry, but I've got to say I'm glad to see you, Genia. You're early. Said you'd be gone six weeks and here you are. Only been four." And then he inquired politely, "What brings you back so soon?"

She looked up at Charlie Watt—in his cowboy boots he was a good six inches taller than she—and thought, *How like you, Charlie, to ask the one question that nobody else thought to pursue because they were all too busy talking while you were over there just listening.* They'd known each other a long time. Lew Potter had respected Charlie's ranching wisdom and used to say that the best piece of advice he ever took was to hire Ricardo Ortego on Charlie Watt's say-so. Mrs. Potter had been a regular visitor to Helen's hospital room in Tucson before that kindly woman died of cancer. So Mrs. Potter started—easily and naturally—to tell Charlie the truth.

But then a hesitancy, a reluctance, came out of somewhere, and she held her tongue.

Mrs. Potter knew from experience that she couldn't lie worth a darn. And certainly not to the paragon of probity who stood so tall and quiet in front of her. Charlie was reknowned throughout Wind Valley as an honest man, just like Ricardo. If you counted out too much change to either one of them in the grocery store, they'd return the excess to the penny. If you dropped a bale of hay on the highway as you were trucking it home, they'd load it up and chase you down until you got it back again. Peas in a pod they were, in many ways, although they were never close friends. Mrs. Potter had wondered why, observing their natural and matching affinities for honor and efficiency. She'd put it down to a surplus of tact on the part of Ricardo, his way of respecting the one enduring difference between them—which was not that one was Latino and the other Anglo, but that Ricardo was a ranch employee, albeit an honored one, while Charlie Watt was a ranch owner. In the social strata of the valley, that still made a difference to some people, and she guessed that Ricardo—courtly, old-fashioned Ricardo—was one of them.

She didn't know if it mattered to Charlie.

"It was time," she said simply.

"You're gone too much," he said, as if agreeing with her.

"Maybe you're right, Charlie—about *that.*"

When he loped off to his truck, she wondered why she had prevaricated. What possible harm could there be in telling Charlie—or anybody —that she'd flown home on the spur of the moment because Ricardo asked her to?

But Mrs. Potter suddenly knew that she wasn't going to say a word about that, at least not yet. She only wished she knew why. Every now and then her own impulses were something of a mystery even to her. She'd learned to trust them, however, which is what she did now. Although, she reminded herself, she'd also trusted her intuition about Ricardo, and look: he wasn't dead, he was only missing.

Only missing.

"Thank you for waiting, Bandy," she said to the man standing off to the side.

Silently, he escorted her into the passenger's seat of his own truck, and got her settled before he slammed the door. Had he understood any—or all—of what Charlie Watt had ranted about? Mrs. Potter suspected Bandy had. But other people's opinions had never seemed a major concern of his —or he'd never have continued to care for those "nephews" everyone around here worried about.

When Bandy walked around the front of the vehicle, Mrs. Potter noticed that he was limping badly. He had to pull himself up behind the wheel, and his breath whistled through his teeth as he lifted his injured leg into the cab. She knew better than to express sympathy, but she felt it for him, nonetheless, particularly as her own arm was aching too.

What a pair we make, she thought, *the walking wounded and the* barely *walking wounded.*

As he started the pickup, she wondered if he missed riding horseback; did he ever long for a rough gallop across the range? It would be agony for him now. This truck—she patted the green vinyl bench seat—was probably as good as things could get for him. Ricardo had seen to it, by suggesting that the ranch purchase one of the small, tough new models for Bandy, the kind ordinarily favored by teenage boys. It had an automatic gear shift, so he wouldn't have to press in a clutch with his crippled left leg. Disabled though he was, this truck meant that Bandy could still navigate roads and pastures. So he had his apartment, his truck, and of course, the obligatory rifle in its rack in the back window, which was all he ever seemed to want. If there'd been anything else he lacked, Ricardo would have managed to obtain it for him, she felt sure. Especially as there was still a little guilt there, she guessed, because it had been on Ricardo's orders that Bandy had roped the calf that pinned and crippled him. Mrs. Potter still felt sick at the memory of Bandy's poor knee, twisted and broken unmercifully, along with his left hip. Undeserved though the guilt might be—such injuries were an acknowledged and accepted risk of cowboying—Ricardo would still feel it, and hoist its responsibility onto his own shoulders. Without Ricardo, what would become of old Bandy? Mrs. Potter didn't even want to consider that thought, not yet. She waited until they were moving back down her driveway, toward Juanita's house, before she spoke.

"*Qué pasa*, Bandy?"

It was the old sixties refrain that her children had repeated until she finally got over thinking of it as rude: *What's happening? What's happening, man?* This time it wasn't a casual inquiry.

"*No sé, patrona.*"

I don't know, he told her.

"Ricardo left home this morning, and hasn't returned?"

"*Es la verdad.*"

That is the truth.

"And Linda?" The enormity of these potential twin calamities threatened suddenly to bear down on her like a freight train. She thought of her own children, her own grandchildren. "She's missing too?"

"*Sí, señora.*"

"*Comprendes Charlie?*"

Did you understand what Charlie was saying?

The old man pulled down the corners of his mouth and shrugged as if to say he hadn't. But Mrs. Potter wondered. Where his "nephews'" safety was concerned, Bandy had ears like a desert rabbit and a miraculously improved grasp of the English language. She wondered if the tense set of his grizzled jaw had only to do with the missing Ortegas, or maybe a little to do with his feelings about Charlie Watt's accusation.

"Oh, Bandy." She reached over to touch the old man's arm. He glanced over at her, and she thought she saw an awful sadness in his eyes, and a dread that surely matched her own. "What shall we do?"

"*Es terrible,*" the old man said.

As he drove her to the house where Juanita and Ricardo Ortega had raised their five children, his little truck bouncing over the dirt road, Mrs. Potter reflected that only the sea was comparable to the desert for the utter blackness of its nights. It seemed ironic to her that the driest and wettest topographies on Earth could engender profound feelings of loneliness. And what if one were hurt, alone and defenseless in this wilderness? It would be like being adrift in a rudderless boat on a great dark sea.

Her heart ached for Ricardo and his granddaughter.

She hoped they still had one another's company for comfort.

CHAPTER 7

Mrs. Potter was thankful for Bandy's company on the short ride, quiet though he was. He turned into Juanita's drive. At the end of it was a two-story white frame house to which small bedrooms and bathrooms had been added by the Potters to accommodate the growing Ortega clan through the years. Juanita and Ricardo rather rattled around in it now, except when the children and grandchildren came to visit, which was satisfyingly often, and a pointed contrast, Mrs. Potter thought, to grandparents like Gallway and Lorraine Steinbach, whose offspring rarely visited Lost Dutchman Ranch.

Mrs. Potter tried not to judge people, but it was difficult not to draw . . . conclusions from the relationships that her friends had with their respective (but not always respectful) grandchildren. Che Thomas, for example, who was long-widowed from Frank Thomas and the mother of two sons, boasted of having her grandkids happily underfoot every summer and Christmas at the C Lazy U. It was hard to tell, though, whether it was their glamorous grandmother the kids adored or her fabulous Disneyland of a home—with its horses and cowboys, buckboards and rodeos.

To Mrs. Potter's knowledge, no one in the valley had ever laid eyes on the descendants of Marj and Rey McHenry. Mrs. Potter couldn't even have said how many little McHenrys there were in the world. Trying to be charitable, she thought, well, it's a long way from England to Arizona. A little less charitably, she thought, *my* babies would love the adventure of it all.

Charlie Watt's late wife, Helen, had been childless, but Mrs. Potter had been quietly pleased to meet many young nieces and nephews at Helen's bedside at the hospital in Tucson. She didn't know if they had kept up the contact with their uncle now that Charlie was alone at Section Ranch.

As for Walt and Kathy Amory, they were still in their late twenties or early thirties and hadn't started a family yet. Mrs. Potter suspected that

was just as well, if there was any truth to the rumors about Kathy and old
Gallstones.

The Ortegas had offered Bandy a room and a bath in their house, now
that the kids were gone, but he'd refused, evidently still preferring the
privacy and independence of his little apartment above the garage.

Mrs. Potter jerked out of her reverie.

"Bandy, I see a light in Linda's room."

"Pero no veo sus caballos."

He was right: she didn't see their horses in the corral either. So they
most likely hadn't come home yet. Juanita must have turned on Linda's
light in anticipation of their return, or perhaps she'd been up there looking for some hint as to where they might have gone. The porch light was
on, too, but overall there was no blaze of illumination such as one finds at
a home where there's an emergency. There were no extra vehicles in the
driveway. There was no appearance of urgency to the scene at all.

"Will you come in with me, Bandy?"

"Si tú quieres."

It was said in a reluctant tone: *if you want me to.*

Juanita Ortega met them at the door, looking no more than mildly
surprised to see visitors on her stoop at a time when most ranchers were
getting ready for bed in order to rise at dawn. A rich smell of onion and
garlic wafted out to the front stoop and Mrs. Potter's stomach gurgled
embarrassingly in response.

"Heard you coming down the road," Juanita said from behind her
screen door. For a light-headed moment, Mrs. Potter thought Juanita
meant she'd heard the stomach rumblings. Juanita looked as always—her
plain, stern face was austerely framed by her usual thick coil of silver hair.
She didn't smile, but that wasn't unusual for Juanita, whose thin lips held
a naturally compressed line even in repose. Mrs. Potter knew that many
people thought Juanita was frowning when she was really only thinking
about something. "Didn't expect it to be you, though. Welcome home.
How come you're back so early?"

"Any word from Ricardo, Juanita?"

"Not yet. Come in, both of you. I have coffee on."

"Cerveza?" Bandy asked.

"Yes, there's beer, but not for you, old man, not if you're chauffeuring
the señora. There's iced tea if you want something cold. Or buttermilk.
Get it yourself."

He followed the direction her finger pointed—into the kitchen—and
walked past the two women, who remained in the living room. It was
furnished, as was the entire house, with inexpensive but attractive Mexican pine furniture. The chairs and couches were upholstered in practical

brown leather, but pretty southwestern print fabric covered the throw
pillows that adorned the room. Colorful saddle blankets and Indian blankets hung on the walls in lieu of paintings, along with handwoven baskets
and hammered tin artifacts. In Mrs. Potter's opinion, Juanita had the
same knack in interior decorating that she had in cooking: to take humble
ingredients and create from them something original and special. That
was, as Juanita would have been the first to say, also evident in her personal appearance. By nature a plain woman, she was a good five inches
shorter than Mrs. Potter and as thin in her sixties as she had been when
Mrs. Potter first met her almost twenty years earlier. Her black hair, gone
completely silver now, was wound around her skull in a thick braid that
looked more Swedish than Spanish in its styling. But the cinnamon skin,
the liquid eyes, the bits of turquoise jewelry at her earlobes and neckline,
the hammered silver combs that held her braid in place, the long, full
orange skirt and matching long-sleeved cotton blouse with its hand-em-
broidered Aztec pattern, the huarache sandals on her bare feet, all declared her heritage and her pleasure in it. In the same way that she could
take basic hamburger and dress it up for company, or take simple pine
furniture and decorate beautifully around it, Juanita Ortega used style and
color to transform herself into a striking, if not exactly comely, woman.

Still, Mrs. Potter knew that Juanita had always born the cross of a
basically plain woman married to a naturally handsome man: other people, seeing the Ortegas together for the first time, tended to whisper,
"What do you think he sees in her?" Or worse, "How'd *she* ever catch
him?"

Some people suspected it was because Juanita had one day simply or-
dered Ricardo to marry her. Others, who knew the Ortegas, knew better.
For one thing, nobody ever told Ricardo what to do, not even Juanita, and
for another, there was real love there. You could see it in the solicitous-
ness with which he handed her up into his pickup truck and in the scold-
ings she gave him when he ate too much rhubarb pie at the café at the
crossroads. But most of all, it was apparent, if indirectly, in the close and
loving family they had created together.

"*Siéntese,*" Juanita instructed her employer, who did as she was told by
promptly sitting down. If Mrs. Potter hadn't felt so concerned about
Ricardo and Linda, the cooking smells in the house would have had her
wandering into Juanita's kitchen to peek under lids to see what was cooking. "So, *dígame.* Why are you back so soon, señora?"

The two women, so close in age, had known each other so well and for
so long that it would have been natural under other circumstances for
each to call the other by her first name. But Juanita wouldn't allow that
familiarity, insisting on that last remaining symbol of division and respect.

Mrs. Potter stared at Juanita in surprise at her question. This was one person from whom she couldn't withhold the truth.

"Why, because Ricardo asked me to come, Juanita."

"No!" His wife looked indignant, baffled. "When?"

"Why, yesterday afternoon. He called me at the cottage in Maine. Didn't he *tell* you?"

"Ah, that man! *Por Dios*, I haven't even cleaned your house for your arrival—"

"Oh, goodness, Juanita, I'm not worried about that, and please, don't you be either. Listen, I don't suppose he told you why he invited a small party up to my house tonight either, did he?"

She got a blank, angry stare in reply.

"No, I'm sorry, I see that he didn't. Well, Juanita, when I arrived, I found the Amorys, the Steinbachs, and the McHenrys at my front gate . . ."

Juanita had arched her eyebrows at the first two names.

"Along with Charlie Watt and Che Thomas. They claim that Ricardo called them, last night I guess, and asked them to come."

"No comprendo."

It was exceedingly rare for Juanita to be so at a loss for English words that she lapsed into Spanish when speaking to an Anglo. The fact that she'd done it several times already was a clue to her real state of mind, Mrs. Potter thought.

"I don't understand it, either, Juanita."

"Oh, *por Dios*, I haven't gone to the grocery store for you, there's not a thing in your refrigerator—"

"I'll go tomorrow, please, don't—"

"Your sheets need changing. I haven't dusted since last week. I was going to wash down the kitchen cabinets next week. And the week before you came home I was going to wax those tiles in the foyer—"

"Juanita, stop. None of this matters—"

"Well!" The other woman slapped her skirted thighs vigorously, as if there was nothing wrong but that there was work to be done. "I'm glad you're back, señora, early or no. You must be starved, if all you've been eating all day is airplane food. I made capirotada today, I'll heat it up for you. . . ." She looked over her shoulder, toward the kitchen, while Mrs. Potter's mouth watered at the mere thought of capirotada, which was Mexican bread pudding. "Bandy! You get your drink and then you stay out of my refrigerator! Don't you be stealing any of my food for those 'nephews' of yours! You feed them on your own salary, old man. If you're hungry, I'll give you some pudding. . . ." She turned back to Mrs. Potter and lowered her voice to a stage whisper that could, Mrs. Potter feared, probably still be heard in the kitchen. "Ricardo says it's time for Bandy to retire. He's going to talk to you about it, and recommend that you pension him"—she gave a jerk of her head, toward the kitchen—"at quarter pay. We'll move him out of the garage, get him settled in Nogales. . . ."

Mrs. Potter wasn't entirely surprised to hear it, but it saddened her all the same. It had been, she supposed, only a matter of time. Still . . .

"Why now, Juanita?"

The other woman shrugged. "Because he's useless, that's why, and you know it, señora. What's he good for anymore? To fertilize your roses? Put chlorine in your pool? And for that you pay him and room him and give him a truck? You could pay a young man only a little more and get a lot more work out of him."

"But it's been like this for quite a while, Juanita, why—"

She heard Bandy moving about in the kitchen, and subsided. This was something she'd have to debate with Ricardo, but she had a feeling there must be more to it than Juanita was telling her, otherwise Ricardo would surely have recommended retiring Bandy a long time ago. It didn't seem to her the old man deserved firing any more today than he ever had. Surely, he was still as dependable and conscientious as ever, even if his jobs were only modest ones. Mrs. Potter wondered what Juanita's role was in this, and whether it was her influence that turned the tide against the old man.

But that didn't answer a more immediate concern.

Mrs. Potter left her chair and walked across the room to sit on the couch beside Juanita. She touched Juanita's hands, the briefest of contacts, but it was enough to get Juanita to face her employer.

"My dear, why are you pretending everything is normal?"

"Because it is, of course, why else?"

"Is that why none of your family is here?"

"Why should they be here?"

Mrs. Potter sighed, feeling a very familiar frustration. Juanita Ortega had an amazing capacity for bending the world to her will, whether it was to wrest scholarships out of fine universities for her children or to wring lush flowers and vegetables out of a desert garden. Her modus operandi was simply to refuse to acknowledge what the rest of the world perceived as truth. "You'll never get that kid in that school" was a truth she had refused, five times for five children, to hear. "Nobody can grow lettuce at this altitude in this soil" was another truth she didn't even bother to scorn. She simply created her own vision of how her world should be, and turned it into the truth, while turning conventional wisdom on its head. Mrs. Potter admired her enormously. She also found Juanita Ortega frequently infuriating—as had school admissions officers, neighbors with weeds in their own gardens, and regularly, Juanita's own family. Now she gazed into those stern, steady brown eyes, and her heart sank.

But this was a truth Juanita was going to have to face.

So Mrs. Potter stared right back at her longtime cook and housecleaner and friend with what she hoped was a will to match Juanita's. She reminded herself that she was, after all, *la patrona.*

"Why should they be here? Because he's their father, or grandfather, or uncle. Because she's their daughter, or niece, or cousin. Have you tried to contact Linda's parents, Juanita? There must be ways of reaching them in Brazil. You simply cannot keep this from them. They will never forgive you if you delay any longer. I wouldn't, if Linda were my daughter, and neither would you. This isn't fair of you. *That's* why you should call them." She took a breath, watching Juanita's lips narrow into an even more stubborn line. Juanita always thought she knew best. But Mrs. Potter recognized this obstinacy as being born of fear. "And they should be here because you need them."

"No, I don't. Why should I? There's nothing wrong. Those two fools have gone off to a cattle sale, or something, and I forgot to remember. So I'm the fool, okay? They told me, and I forgot, that's all."

No, Juanita, Mrs. Potter thought, *I'm going to win this one.*

"Did they take his truck?"

"No, but—"

"Is any vehicle missing?"

Juanita shook her head mulishly.

"They took their horses, didn't they? And yet surely you don't think they rode horseback to a cattle sale, do you?"

"They could have ridden over to somebody else's ranch, and then hitched a ride with them."

"With whom? You've called around, to inquire?"

"People can't answer their phone if they're not there."

"Ricardo took a suitcase? And Linda did too?"

"If he's only going overnight, sometimes he just stuffs fresh underwear and a razor down in his spare cowboy boots."

"So there's an extra pair of boots missing?"

"Or sometimes he stuffs them in a plastic bag."

"Is his toothbrush gone?"

"He could buy one when he gets there."

"Where, Juanita? When he gets where?"

"It's also possible that I'm wrong about that. They may not have gone anywhere. I think they probably went out early—"

"How early?"

"Before sunup, is all I know. When I woke up, they were already gone.

Probably to check on those heifers up in the northeast pastures, so they needed an early start."

"And they're not back *yet*?"

"Well, I think, yes, I think it's possible, that one of them had an accident, don't you, Bandy?" The old man had come back into the living room with a glass of buttermilk and sat down in an easy chair opposite the women. He didn't respond to the question, but only stared impassively back at Juanita. "And they're having a hard time getting back home. Bandy, do you want something to eat? Señora, I can put together some delicious enchiladas, your favorite cheese-and-onion ones, in a jiffy, if you'll help me shred the—"

Mrs. Potter tightened her grip on Juanita, to keep her seated.

"One minute you say they've gone off to a cattle sale with somebody else, and the next minute you say that Ricardo has fallen off his horse."

"I didn't say any such thing! If either of them had an accident, it was Linda—"

"Why do you say that?"

Juanita jerked her hand out of Mrs. Potter's grasp and shot to her feet. "So, it's tacos for you. . . . Bandy, *los quieres, tambien*?"

Mrs. Potter, feeling a desperate sadness for her, looked up at her.

"I'm organizing a search party, Juanita."

She thought she saw terror flit through the dark eyes.

"We will also locate an aerial search service and get them out here to start looking. Frankly, I think that's our best bet, but we'll also need volunteers on horseback and trucks. If Linda and Ricardo have had an accident, they could be hidden down in some arroyo or under a ledge and be hard to see from the air." Mrs. Potter contined in the same gentle but firm tone, "I can arrange things from here, if you'll let me. Or I can do it from my house. Where's Ken? We need him."

She meant Ken Ryerson, their regular part-time hired hand who also filled in at other ranches in the valley whenever an extra cowboy was needed, or the owners were away.

"He's out . . ." Juanita set her mouth in a trembling line.

Mrs. Potter completed the sentence for her. "Searching for them. Good for him, although I suspect there's not much he can do at night. I presume he's in his truck, and not on horseback?"

Juanita nodded once, violently, as if Mrs. Potter had jerked her hair.

"Good, safer for him that way. I'll want him to take charge of the search tomorrow, so when he gets back, no matter what time it is, I want you to send him up to me at my house. Right now, you and I are going to get on the phone to recruit volunteers. And you have to call your family.

Do you have an emergency number for Linda's parents? Have you talked to the sheriff, Juanita?"

The other woman stood stiff and still, refusing to answer.

"No?" Mrs. Potter swallowed her remonstrances. "Then I will. He will probably treat this as a missing persons case, so he won't commit to an official search for seventy-two hours, but maybe we'll get lucky, and he'll pitch in with people and expertise. Especially as it's Ricardo who's"—she took a breath and then said clearly—"missing."

It hurt to see Juanita flinch at the word, but Mrs. Potter persevered, feeling as if she were plowing a rocky, resistant field. She stood up so that they faced one another.

"So, Juanita. What's it to be?"

She waited in silence, while across the room Bandy stared at them over the rim of his glass of buttermilk.

Finally, Juanita spoke, though she wouldn't meet Mrs. Potter's eyes.

"You're wrong, señora, but I suppose it won't hurt to take precautions. If it'll please you. Come into the kitchen. I'll heat the capirotada while you make your calls." Her mouth pursed and her eyes briefly closed, so that it appeared that she was forcibly holding back tears. But then she opened her eyes and nodded once, decisively. *"Bueno. Venga."*

Good. Come.

Behind Juanita's back, Mrs. Potter glanced at Bandy.

He shook his head, seeming to share her feelings about Juanita's behavior. There was also a glint of something else in the old man's eyes, and Mrs. Potter had an uneasy feeling that it was a deep, deep anger. Did he think that Juanita was endangering Ricardo's and Linda's lives by refusing to face the facts? Or had the old man heard them talk about his forced retirement?

How helpless Bandy must feel, she thought.

The old man limped after her into the kitchen.

CHAPTER 8

Juanita started pulling covered bowls out of her refrigerator.
"Before you do that," Mrs. Potter said to her, "call your family. Please."

"After you've finished with your calls."

Well, that was capitulation of a sort, Mrs. Potter thought.

Mrs. Potter began with the county sheriff, as the valley itself had no police force. She'd met Sheriff Ben Lightfeather only once, but he had impressed her as being smart and practical and she knew that Ricardo thought well of him. Many Arizona sheriffs still looked wonderfully the part of nineteenth-century lawmen, complete with ten-gallon Stetson hats, handlebar mustaches, and gold stars pinned to their vests. They were still capable of jumping on their horses and rounding up an actual posse, though they might have a helicopter circling overhead and a cellular telephone at their hip. To look at one of these rugged, handsome sheriffs, you might think that the only thing that had changed in a hundred years was the rifle in his hands: these days, Mrs. Potter had been informed, it could be an Uzi instead of a Winchester. Ben Lightfeather was one of these, a good man by all accounts. Unfortunately, his headquarters was miles away, and he had a lot more territory and population to cover than merely Wind Valley.

At first he reacted as she expected by pretty much refusing to take seriously that Ricardo Ortega—"of all people"—could possibly be missing on ranchland he knew as well as he knew the back of his horse's neck.

"I told you," Juanita muttered, at the stove.

The sheriff found it particularly unlikely that both the old man and the young woman were missing. He espoused Juanita's theory—one of them —that they'd had an accident and were still trying to get back home. "If they're not back by morning, you go ahead with your search party, Mrs. Potter. My guess is, you folks can do it better than I can, knowing that valley better than I do. You going to organize it yourself, Mrs. Potter, or who?"

"My part-time hired man, Ken Ryerson."

"Well, have him give me a call tonight, and don't worry about how late it is, either. If I can't be there, I can still advise him, and I'd be happy to do that. If they haven't shown up by noon tomorrow, Mrs. Potter, I'll try to see about getting you some help out there. But I can't promise much. We've got budget and manpower problems—what else is new, right?— and a whole lot of other situations on our backs right now, including three bank robberies and a truckload of Mexican illegals that somebody left to die in the desert.

"I'm sorry about this, because I've got a lot of respect for Ricardo Ortega, and I can tell that you're all mighty worried about him and that girl. I'll tell you what, though, I do think that's probably a good idea you've got about leasing an airplane. Helicopter would be even better, what with those twisty mountain valleys you got out there." Mrs. Potter determinedly closed her mind to the question of cost; it would cost what it cost; she would pay what it took, for as long as she had it to pay. "Obviously, with a plane or chopper, you'll cover a lot more ground, so to speak."

"Can you recommend a service, Sheriff?"

"Funny you'd need to be askin' me that question, Mrs. Potter, because Ricardo Ortega was in here not a week ago, wantin' to know the very same thing."

Mrs. Potter felt a flicker of surprise run down her spine.

The sheriff was saying in his baritone drawl, " 'Where can I find a reliable pilot,' was what Ricardo wanted to know. I gave him the same answer I'll give you, Arizona Aerials. Ask for Tom Fletcher. Or Lucy Dermitt, that's his wife, she's a crackerjack pilot too. They'll charge you an arm and a leg, but at least you'll still have all your arms and legs in one piece when you land. Damn good pilots. Both of them were in the war— Vietnam—he was a chopper pilot, and she flew commercial transport for a while."

"Did Ricardo tell you why he wanted them, Sheriff?"

"Nope. And I didn't think to ask. It's not so unusual a request, Mrs. Potter. I figured he wanted aerial photographs of your ranch, maybe for you. A lot of people want that kind of thing, just to hang on their wall. Like Mrs. Thomas has over to the C Lazy U; only, I think she uses them to map out hunting parties. And I know that Reynolds McHenry got a bunch of them for the whole damn valley back a few years ago, probably even got your ranch in it. Hell of an expensive wall decoration, if you ask me, but then, I'm not paying for it."

By the time Mrs. Potter hung up from that call, Juanita was bending over the table with wide-mouthed ceramic bowls of steaming bread pudding in each hand, and Bandy was pulling another chair up to the table. Mrs. Potter's mouth watered at the sight and smell.

Juanita's capirotada could pass for either a dessert or a full meal, depending on one's appetite. Made with half a pound of cheese (a quarter pound each of longhorn and Jack), one whole loaf of raisin bread and a full cup of chopped walnuts, it boasted everything from calcium to fiber, especially when made with multigrain raisin bread instead of ordinary raisin bread. Some people ate it straight, Ricardo liked it with real whipped cream, Lew Potter had preferred ice cream, but Mrs. Potter was always happy to slosh it around in plain old milk.

Juanita opened a white paper napkin and spread it on Mrs. Potter's lap as if she were a child. "I'll bring you a drink. Iced tea all right? You want some milk to go on that pudding?"

"Please. Why would Ricardo want aerial photos?"

Juanita didn't answer until after she had poured milk into a ceramic pitcher, which she set on the table between Mrs. Potter and Bandy. "Photos of what?"

"Well, I suppose that's a good question too."

"I don't know about aerial photos. He did buy us a new thirty-five-millimeter camera the other day. One of those fancy ones that shows the time and date on each picture, you know? I said to him, we have a perfectly good camera the kids gave us two Christmases ago, what do we need with this new one?"

"What did he say?"

"He said now I wouldn't have to label our pictures of our grandkids. I said, What? You mean that camera can print their names on the pictures too?"

"And he laughed?"

"Oh, yes. That man! He said, no, now we'll have a permanent record of the date, so we can always tell when the picture was taken, so we'll know how old the child was. I don't need a camera to tell me that, I said, you think I can't tell my own grandkids' ages by looking at them?"

Bandy had waited politely for *la patrona* to pour the cool goodness of the milk over the hot, rich pudding, and then he emptied the rest of the pitcher into his own bowl, until his pudding looked like a brown island floating in a sea of milk.

Juanita glared at him. "What do you know about this?"

Bandy only shook his head, hunched over his bowl and dipped his spoon into it.

"How come you didn't hear them ride out this morning?" Juanita demanded of him.

"*Dormiendo.*"

I was asleep.

Mrs. Potter became aware of a low rumbling noise outside, louder even than her stomach (which she appeased with a bite of delicious pudding). At that sound, Bandy lifted his gaze to hers.

Silently, they acknowledged that a storm was brewing, maybe one of those sudden Arizona downpours that flushed the mountainsides and poured into the dry washes as if God had turned the cold water tap on full.

Juanita didn't appear to have heard it yet.

To distract her so that she might have a few more moments of freedom from this new fear, Mrs. Potter blurted the first thing that came into her mind: "I'll bet Ricardo got bucked."

She wasn't prepared for Juanita's volcanic reaction to that innocent surmise. Neither, to judge from his agape mouth, was Bandy.

"Are you loco?" Juanita's face was fiery with rage. "Ricardo get bucked? *Nobody's* as good a horseman as he is, *nobody* can control a horse the way he can, I can't believe you said that, it's an insult to that man, and I resent—"

"Juanita, good gracious—"

"*El es un viejo,*" Bandy muttered, but both women heard him.

He's an old man.

Juanita turned her furious glare on him. "You're the *viejo . . . y loco!*"

You're the old man, and crazy to boot.

Bandy lowered his gaze to his bowl and began to eat again. But Mrs. Potter saw that the gnarled, walnut-colored hands that held the spoon were trembling. And suddenly she saw them all, including herself, as if the light in the kitchen had altered, throwing deep lines onto their faces and painting shadows under their eyes. She saw herself as part of this quartet of people, if you counted Ricardo, who had known each other for so many long years. She saw, as if she had never noticed it before, the wrinkles and creases, the swollen blue veins on the tops of their hands, the eyes that held the wisdom and fear that comes with advancing age. Goodness, was it true, were they *old* now, all of them? Bandy, all right, yes; but she and Juanita, and Ricardo? A minute ago, she'd felt no more than middle-aged, and their faces, even Bandy's, had appeared merely comfortable, familiar and loved, but now . . .

Mrs. Potter shook herself of the dismaying vision.

All the same, when she looked back at Juanita and Bandy, she didn't see them quite the same as she had before. And she was suddenly quite loathe to look in any mirror, for fear it might all be true.

"Ah, señora." Juanita looked stricken. *"Lo siento."*

"It's all right, Juanita, I'm sorry if I—"

Bandy noisily pushed back his chair and got up. The scrape of the chair legs against the tile was accompanied by a crack of lightning that hit close enough to flicker the overhead lamp.

"Mi Dios!" Juanita nearly dropped the glass she held.

Bandy grabbed his straw hat from off the back of his chair, and with a nod to both women, limped out of the kitchen. Shortly, they heard the front door slam.

"Viejo," Juanita muttered as she picked up his dirty bowl and spoon.

Mrs. Potter brought the telephone to the table.

"Shouldn't use the telephone during an electrical storm, señora."

Mrs. Potter ignored her and the danger of lightning coming through the wire. She began calling around the valley to recruit volunteers for the next day's search party. As she expected, nearly everybody said yes, and those who didn't expressed sincere regret and good excuses. In between calls, she consumed another helping of bread pudding and a cup of brewed decaf coffee, which Juanita flavored with a pinch of nutmeg. Her last calls were hard to hear because of static, but she didn't have any trouble with the party line, because everybody cooperated once they knew what she was up to. When she finished eating and phoning she shoved back her bowl, folded her hands on the table in front of her and gazed across at Juanita, who now sat in the place Bandy had vacated.

"I want to tell you that you and Ricardo have lots of friends in this valley."

There was no reply to that, so she took a deep breath, and said, "All right, Bandy's gone. I'm finished. Now, *mi amiga*, do you want to tell me what's going on with you?"

For a moment, she didn't think Juanita would tell her.

But then the other woman broke, in a torrent of words and indignation. "That man wants to retire! Do you believe that? Him and me both, he says, we ought to retire! He says he's no good anymore, that he's not doing the job for you that he used to do, that you need somebody younger and more able. I tell him, if he'd get rid of Bandy he could hire somebody to do the job that Bandy's supposed to do! I tell him, he's doing his job and Bandy's and Ken's too. I tell him, why does he let Ken take on all those jobs at other people's ranches when we need him here? I tell him, what does he mean *we* ought to retire? *I'm* not too old to cook! *I'm* not too feeble to clean house for you, señora. *Por Dios*, I'll still be cooking and cleaning for that man when I'm ninety years old. But no, he wants to move *me* out of *my* house, move us clear off the ranch, into town or some retirement village, or someplace, maybe with one of our children. *Por Dios!* What does he think I'm going to do, ride around in golf carts in Sun City with the rich Anglos—no offense? That man is not old! He's not feeble. He's a strong, virile man, I can tell you that, and there's nothing wrong with his brain or his body, I'm telling you. I tell him that. Over and over, but no, that stubborn man only hears his own voice saying, retire, retire, retire. . . ."

"When he called me yesterday, Juanita, he didn't sound like a man who was ready to give up."

"No? He didn't?"

"No, he sounded like the old Ricardo."

"Old!" Juanita raised her hands in the air. "I hate that word!"

"What makes him think he can't do the job anymore?"

"I don't know! He's been so secretive lately. . . ."

When Juanita didn't go on, Mrs. Potter prodded her. "How's that?"

But Juanita seemed to wrap a cloak of privacy—or secrecy—around herself, and would only say, "I don't know, he won't talk about it."

And neither will you, Mrs. Potter thought.

"Could it have anything to do with his disappearance?"

"He hasn't disappeared, I keep telling you. Could *what* have anything to do with it?"

"These secrets of his."

"I didn't say he had secrets."

"You said he's been secretive."

"He just won't talk to *me,* that's all."

"Has he talked to anybody else?"

"Well, he talked to you, yesterday, didn't he?" And suddenly, there was deep hurt in Juanita's voice. "And you say he talked to the Amorys and Charlie Watt and Che and the Steinbachs and even the McHenrys. He talks to all of you, but not to me, not to his own wife—"

They both jumped at the sound of a truck horn outside. Mrs. Potter was surprised at Bandy, at the rudeness of his summoning her back outside by blowing his truck horn. He, who'd never been other than the soul of Latin courtesy, honking for her? Juanita, calling her loco? Ricardo, claiming he wanted to retire? What had gotten into everybody while she was absent? Had *they* all gone loco?

But it was late and Juanita looked exhausted.

Before Mrs. Potter trotted out into the rain with a borrowed umbrella, Juanita said, "I make them carry full canteens. He laughs at me, but I make him do it anyway. Linda too." At the sound of her granddaughter's name, Juanita's voice cracked and her eyes filled for the first time. Mrs.

Potter ached to embrace her, but waited instead for this proud woman to win her struggle to control her emotions. When Juanita spoke again, Mrs. Potter couldn't detect so much as a tremor in her voice. "This time of year, I make them carry rain slickers with them all the time, rolled up behind their saddles. Tonight, *por Dios*, they will be thanking me." She looked out at the rain, not appearing to hear Mrs. Potter's hurried "adios."

CHAPTER 9

"Lo siento, patrona."

As soon as Mrs. Potter climbed into his truck, Bandy apologized to her for honking. His hand slipped, he told her.

"I hate to leave her alone tonight," Mrs. Potter confided to him, over the metallic sound of the rain on his truck. They pulled out of Juanita's drive and into the dirt road—rapidly becoming a mud path—that led back to Mrs. Potter's compound. Five fingers of lightning crackled in the sky east of them, illuminating the entire range of Rimstone Mountains for a dramatic moment. The sandstone formation known as El Bizcocho stood out as if in bas-relief.

Bandy nodded his understanding, but kept his usual silent counsel.

"I feel as if I'm abandoning her," she added.

After another few silent moments, in which Mrs. Potter felt a need to bridge the night with words, even if he didn't, she asked a question she rarely voiced. "Is anyone staying with you, Bandy?"

She meant, as he knew, illegal aliens. His "nephews."

"No, patrona, no ahora."

No, not now.

"Bueno," she said. Mrs. Potter rarely inquired about the thin, dark, frightened young men she glimpsed now and then hurrying along a back country road, trying so pathetically hard to be invisible. Ricardo had long ago hinted it was better not to ask. As far as Mrs. Potter knew, no women had ever taken refuge with her old hired hand. She thought about those women who fled north, and wondered whether they left children behind or brought them along. Who provided shelter for those "nieces" of the road? They were so vulnerable, men, women, and children alike. Vulnerable to the weather, to illness, to their own empty bellies. Vulnerable to unscrupulous, even murderous operators who promised jobs that never materialized. Vulnerable to the border patrol who were charged with an impossible task, like trying to plug a leak with a cotton ball. Mrs. Potter

knew that she didn't make the border patrol's job any easier with her tacit approval of Bandy and Ricardo's activities, but she and Lew, when he was alive, had always tended to view it as humanitarian aid, like the underground railroad that sheltered runaway slaves during the Civil War. And so the Potters had never interfered with what was obviously a moral imperative for their ranch manager and their hired hand.

She could just hear Charlie Watt's objections!

When Bandy pulled up in front of her patio gate again, he indicated that he would retrieve her luggage from her rental car. Mrs. Potter opened the truck door, letting in a small gale of rain and wind. She struggled to get Juanita's umbrella raised, then trotted over to the wrought-iron gate, left it open for Bandy behind her, and scooted along her flagstone walk to her own front door. Once under the shelter of the long veranda, which was known as a "ramada," she propped the umbrella against the house. Mrs. Potter didn't try to fish for her keys in her purse, but grabbed the "secret" key under a potted cactus, instead. "Some secret," as Ricardo frequently said. Practically every repair person and tradesperson as far as Tucson and half the hired cowboys in Wind Valley knew where to find it and had probably used it at one time or another to fix the toilets, or wallpaper the bedroom, or to wander into the kitchen to pour themselves a cup of coffee while they waited for her to show up for a conference on cattle prices or part-time employment. "Has anybody ever abused the privilege?" Mrs. Potter always demanded of Ricardo when he challenged her "open door" policy, and he had to agree that nobody ever had. The key was handy, that was all, but no secret.

Mrs. Potter stepped into her house and fumbled for the hallway light switch. There wasn't time to appreciate the view it illuminated. She crossed quickly to the hall closet, slipped out of her wet shoes and located a pair of fleece-lined moccasins to put on. At least her stockings were still dry. She heard Bandy wiping his feet on the mat outside. When he brought her luggage in, she directed him on down the long hall to her bedroom.

"*Gracias,*" she said when he returned.

"*De nada. Buenas noches, patrona, y bienvenidos.*"

Good night, Mrs. Potter. Welcome home.

"*Hasta mañana,* Bandy. Pray for them."

"*Sí, patrona. Es la verdad.*"

Yes, ma'am. That's the truth.

A crack of lightning and a rumble of thunder punctuated his exit. Mrs. Potter glanced up at the sky, feeling as if God had exclaimed: *You can say that again, old man.*

And so she did pray again, briefly, standing there in her slippers with eyes closed, listening to the rain outside the dark house.

Mrs. Potter opened her eyes to a sight that warmed her worried heart. Despite Juanita Ortega's protests to the contrary, Mrs. Potter's home looked beautifully maintained, right down to the orange Mexican tiles at her feet, the ones Juanita had said she planned to wax next week before her scheduled arrival. Mrs. Potter suspected that Juanita had been up to the house at least once a week to dust the furniture and plump the pillows, to run the rust out of the faucets and swish a wet rag around the sinks and bathtubs, the appliances, countertops, and toilets, and probably to perform special little tasks without even being asked—like polishing Grandmother Andrews's good silver, washing the windows, pulling the books out of the cases one by one and dusting them, or vacuuming the draperies.

Mrs. Potter's Arizona home was a rambling one-story structure of adobe painted white to match the wall and other buildings outside. If Mrs. Potter had stepped back outside her front door, she could have stood on her trellis-covered ramada and looked around what was essentially a compound surrounded by a white adobe wall. One step down from the ramada was her small green square of irrigated lawn, and a short walk across it was a much smaller one-story building, that one a guest house with two big bedrooms, baths, and walk-in closets. When Lew was alive, they had entertained often. The guest house had been as seldom vacant as a popular motel. Against the inside wall of the compound, and beside the front gate, lay one of her two small rose gardens, which were Bandy's responsibilities. The second rose garden lay to the other side of the guest house, facing the swimming pool. If Mrs. Potter had stood on her ramada and turned right, she could have walked up onto a covered patio that looked out onto her swimming pool, which she kept at a constant 90 degrees—being more and more sensitive to cold as she got older—and where she took her afternoon swims for exercise. There was just enough room to walk entirely around the rectangular pool. To the east, beyond the outside wall, rose her beloved Rimstone Mountains.

But all of that lay outside her home.

At this moment, she was looking within.

There, in the foyer where she stood, was the carved wooden chest that held the serapes she offered to visitors who came unprepared for cold Arizona evenings. They'd warmed the shoulders of many a guest, some of whom she had dearly loved, others of whom she could have happily strangled with one of those serapes.

She turned her head and looked to the right, into her dining room, where literally hundreds of guests had sipped and supped during the years when she played hostess for Lew and her children. Mrs. Potter could almost hear the sound of silverware clinking against china, of ice cubes rattling in drinks, of laughter, and of the bass, tenor, and soprano notes of the chords of conversation. From where she stood, she could see Grandmother Andrews's dining room furniture: there was the hutch and the sideboard of glowing walnut with polished brass hardware; there was the infinitely accommodating walnut dining table, which had been at home in every house she and Lew had ever owned; and the carved walnut chairs with their supple black leather upholstery. Here in Arizona, the General Grant provenance seemed comfortable, serene within white brick walls warmed by a fireplace bordered by Mexican tiles. Swedish ivy spilled luxuriantly from a Chinese bowl in the center of the table.

Beyond the swinging door on the far side of the dining room was her roomy kitchen, with its cool tile floor and big center rug, and a cozy corner fireplace with a stainless swing-out grill for cooking steaks over mesquite. It had old but reliable appliances and lots of counter space and a round wooden table—on which she liked to place a yellow-and-white checked linen cloth and the soft light of an old-fashioned shaded kerosene lamp for entertaining casually.

Every room in the house had a fireplace, including the spacious living room, which was down two broad steps from where she stood in the foyer. It was Bandy who kept the log buckets and kindling baskets filled. As she gazed down the steps, her imagination filled the living room with her favorite guests who had gathered there on various occasions over the years for drinks before dinner and then for dessert, if the weather didn't allow her to shoo them outdoors to the patio or the ramada. She saw Ricardo, dressed in his casual best, answering with grave courtesy even the dumbest of questions that her city-slicker guests might ask him, such as which was the front end of a cow . . . while Juanita stayed in the kitchen, putting the final flourishes to dinner, and Mrs. Potter fetched refills from the liquor pantry. She'd always been grateful that Ricardo was willing to make himself available to her guests, as they did so dearly love to get a gander at a real live American cowboy. It pleased her to present to them one who was so gallant, so handsome, articulate, and gracious. And it was always generous of Juanita, Mrs. Potter fully appreciated, to allow Ricardo to bask in the glory while she performed the unsung work in the kitchen. Her praises were always sung to the heavens in hallelujah choruses once a meal began. Theater guests—actors and director friends— had even been known to applaud and shout "author! author!" until Juanita appeared, flushed and tight-lipped, but clearly pleased to receive their "good reviews."

"*Gracias, mis amigos,*" Mrs. Potter whispered.

Mrs. Potter looked into her living room at her wonderful old black grand piano with its collection of family photographs on its broad, reliable back. She glimpsed edges of her own large needlepoint works, which Lew had insisted on having beautifully framed and hung alongside their favorite paintings. Mrs. Potter had always greatly appreciated his pride in her creative endeavors, whether it was cooking for a party of his business associates or designing her own needlepoint patterns rather than buying them ready-made. At first, she'd been embarrassed to have her own work displayed on a wall. But when visitor after visitor complimented them—before knowing she was the artist—she had eventually accepted the surprising fact that they seemed to afford almost as much pleasure to the people who viewed them as they did to her when she was creating them. Now they were a source of modest satisfaction to her, not least because they represented Lew's confidence in her.

The far southern wall of the living room was solid windows. If it had been day instead of night, Mrs. Potter would have been able to see a grand expanse of prairie rolling all the way to the mountains that formed the border with Mexico. It was a view broken only by her horse barn and corral and by the Ortegas' home and the garage where Bandy lived. At this time of year, the grass was tall and thick and a lovely platinum color that reminded her of Marilyn Monroe's hair.

From the foyer, to her left, was the long hall that led to her small office/study and then to a bathroom and then on to her own large bedroom and bath and a guest bedroom and bath.

"Genia's home on the range," her friends called it.

But with Ricardo and Linda gone, that word "home" felt as if it were missing some letters. On this night, the ranch felt too large for just Juanita, Bandy, and herself, and the house felt too big for one woman living alone. Which was why Mrs. Potter felt awfully glad at that moment to hear the doorbell ring.

CHAPTER 10

The tall cowboy who stood under her porch light didn't smile when she greeted him. He was clad in a dripping black rubber rain slicker that covered him from his neck to the ankles of his denims, below which the feet of his cowboy boots showed, their light tan leather darkened to brown by the rain. His cowboy hat was covered in a plastic rain wrap, of a kind manufactured especially for the purpose.

"Ken! Any luck?"

"No, ma'am. Juanita sent me up here, okay?"

"Yes, I told her to. Come in, come in."

Ken Ryerson, the part-time hired hand on Las Palomas, slouched through her doorway as if he carried the weight of the ranch on his broad young shoulders. He was thirty years old, but the years of working cattle in the sun and wind had carved lines into his good-looking face that added at least five years to his appearance, and on this night he looked as if he'd aged a few more. If someone had told Mrs. Potter that this six-foot, blond-haired, mustachioed cowboy she had employed for twelve years was actually fifty years old, she'd have been tempted to believe it. Ken didn't work only for Las Palomas, but also filled in at other ranches in the valley, keeping an eye on things for owners like the Amorys and the Steinbachs, who were often more absentee than resident. Mrs. Potter knew without asking that he'd had a long, hard day of performing chores for them and for others, even before setting out on his fruitless search for his main boss.

Ken hung up his slicker on the coat tree in the foyer. When he removed his hat, Mrs. Potter could tell by his matted, sweaty hair and by the ground-in dirt where his hat pressed into his forehead that he'd been outside for hours, long before it started to rain. Her imagination gave her a quick, vivid picture of Ken in his blue stretch pickup truck, his driver's window rolled down, and him leaning out, squinting through his sunglasses into the countryside, looking for some telltale sparkle of metal, or some other sign of the missing pair. What with the caked dirt on his face and his customary dark tan, Ken Ryerson, the son of hard-shell Southern Baptists from Kentucky, could have passed for one of Bandy's "nephews" that night, she thought. Until, of course, you got a glimpse of the white-blond hair under the hat. Even his Fu Manchu mustache drooped from the rain, and instead of looking its normal blond with platinum streaks, it was soaked to a dark and nondescript shade of brown. Ken Ryerson looked, in the lingo of the valley, as if he'd "been rode hard and put away wet."

"Come on into the kitchen, Ken."

He trudged after her, his boots dragging on the tile floors, clearly too tired to talk unless he had to. She motioned him into one of the chairs around the big round kitchen table, and he sank into it like a man on the edge of a bed, and placed his arms on the table, up to his elbows. He leaned his head forward and laced his fingers together at the back of his neck, and groaned. Then he stretched, and finally sat up about as straight as a tired man could be expected to do.

"What will you have, Ken? Would you like a beer? Coffee? Coke?"

His lips barely moved. "Beer."

Mrs. Potter crossed her fingers that there would be at least a Dos Equis lurking in the recesses of her refrigerator. She sighed in relief when she found an entire six-pack, and she slid a bottle out of it.

"In a glass?"

"Bottle."

She removed the cap the old-fashioned way, with an ancient Coca-Cola bottle opener that was attached to the underside of one of her cabinets. As she passed the beer to him, she asked, "Are you hungry?"

He shook his head, slugged down some beer.

Mrs. Potter sat down at the table with him.

After a minute, he stopped swallowing beer. His chest lifted in a sigh. He glanced at Mrs. Potter, then looked down at the beer bottle and he began to roll it between his palms, back and forth, back and forth. "Well, I been every place I could think to go ever since Juanita told me they was missing. Hell, I honked, I hollered. I kept looking even when I couldn't see past my goddamned, excuse me, headlights."

"I know you've tried hard."

"I ain't seen a sign of 'em."

"Juanita says maybe they've gone to a cattle sale."

His mustache twitched in a brief display of scorn. "She don't really think that."

"Or she says, maybe one of them is injured, and the other one is trying to get both of them back home."

This time he looked up at her and held her glance. "If Ricardo got bucked, Linda'd've come on back here to get me, 'cause she couldn't've lifted him by herself. No way she could get him ahorseback once he fell off. And what's she going to do otherwise, build her a Indian pallet?" His quick frown of scorn flickered again, then disappeared.

Mrs. Potter decided quickly that a man this tired had to be hungry as well, and that he was just too cowboy-polite to say so. She got up while he was talking and quietly rummaged in her cupboards until she located some canned soup she felt pretty sure he might like: black bean. Maybe she wouldn't have fresh onion to dice on top of it, but she could add a little sherry and maybe a touch of garlic salt and onion salt from the seasoning bottles she kept in the refrigerator door. Cold beer and hot black bean soup with a plate of oyster crackers. . . . Surely *they* were fresh in their tin . . . yes . . . and at least it would give him something to do besides dwell on his failure to find his boss and Linda. She poured the canned soup into a chili bowl and set it in her microwave to warm. While she moved about efficiently, she listened and asked questions.

"If it was her got injured," Ken was saying, "Ricardo'd've had her back here by now."

"What do *you* think has happened to them, Ken?"

He took another swig of beer before saying, "Hunters."

"Oh, no." Mrs. Potter involuntarily raised both hands to her heart. She discovered in that moment that Ken wasn't the only exhausted person in her kitchen: her own brain had failed to kick in that most frightening possibility. Hunters! They were always a hazard on a ranch, on practically anybody's ranch, anywhere. The mountains were often full of them, in legal season and out. There was *never* a season for hunting within the fences of Las Palomas, not even for pleading, cajoling, crack-shot friends of the family. Lew hadn't approved of the danger to livestock or people, and neither did Ricardo. As for *la patrona*, she understood the thrill of a chase, but she figured it wasn't quite so exciting for the animal on the other end of it, and so she happily upheld her late husband's stern dictum: No hunting; violators will be prosecuted. Or fired, as had been the case with a couple of part-time hired hands a few months back. There'd been harsh words between Ricardo and those two men. There were always those hunters—like those quickly unemployed cowboys—who didn't bother about such niceties as hunting seasons or licenses or even fence lines that were clearly posted.

"Hunters are the most likely bet, seems to me," Ken said. "But if that's what happened, we'll never find 'em. Some hunter ever shoots me by accident or otherwise, he's going to hide my body so he don't get found out. Lots of places to hide a body out there, Mrs. Potter. Caves, for one.

Stick 'em way back in one of those little caverns, hell, nobody's ever gonna know, nobody's ever going to find 'em."

The bell on the microwave went off, causing them both to jump like a hunter's startled prey.

Mrs. Potter removed the bubbling soup from the microwave and put the bowl on a matching plate. Around that, she arranged oyster crackers. They looked far too dainty for the brawny cowboy at her kitchen table, but they were all she had. She poured a generous dollop of sherry into the soup, sprinkled on the onion and garlic salt, mixed it all together, and sniffed. Yes, that would do. Mrs. Potter slid a soup spoon from the silverware drawer, grabbed a paper napkin from a holder atop the refrigerator, and put it all down in front of Ken Ryerson. Seeing that his bottle was empty, she fetched a second beer. By the time she had it opened, he was crumbling oyster crackers into the soup.

"Careful, Ken, it's still hot."

"Got any jalapeños, Mrs. Potter?"

"Of course, how could I forget them?" *Indeed*, Mrs. Potter chided herself, *I have been away too long if I've forgotten that you don't serve a ranch hand a meal without plunking down jars of jalapeño peppers, Tabasco sauce, and ketchup on the table.* It didn't matter if the meal was a hamburger supper or a breakfast of fried eggs, a cowboy was sure to want to "hot it up" some more. She fetched all three and then watched Ken utterly destroy the careful balance of her delicate seasonings. *So much for expensive sherry*, she thought, *I may as well have used vinegar!*

He curved his back and shoulders over the soup and commenced to eat as if hot or cold didn't matter; what counted was getting food into his stomach.

Mrs. Potter eased back down into her chair and watched him devour the snack. "I've been on the phone tonight, Ken, organizing a search party for tomorrow. Soon as the sun's up. I want you to be in charge of it. Sheriff Lightfeather may be here to help, but I don't think we ought to count on it. He says he's got bank robbers to catch and he has to deal with some illegal aliens that somebody left to die in the desert. We can't wait for him to take our missing persons report seriously. I don't think he really believes anything has happened to Ricardo and Linda. I hope he's right, but that didn't stop me from rounding up a good number of volunteers to help look. I want you to map out this ranch, and assign sections for them to search, in some sort of organized manner that covers every inch of this place."

"You think they're still here, ma'am?"

"If they're not, I don't know what we'll do."

He wiped his mouth with the napkin. "Spread out over the valley, get people asking at gas stations, ranches, what-all. Find out if anybody's seen 'em. Put up posters, I guess. Don't know what else."

"Those are good ideas I hope we won't need, Ken."

"We'll find 'em, unless it's hunters. Even then, they might've got scared and careless, left the bodies."

A feeling of terrible grief began to well up inside Mrs. Potter. *Not again*, she thought, *not still other dear friends*. "Oh, Ken." She couldn't get any other words out.

"I'm sorry, *patrona*, I'm too tired to be tactful, I guess."

She stood up to remove his empty soup bowl and carry it to the sink, where she ran water over it. "I've arranged for an aerial search."

"How'd you find somebody to do it?"

"Asked the sheriff for the name of a company. Arizona Aerials, out of Tucson. When you find Ricardo I *am* going to dock him for the cost of *that*."

"What?"

"Oh." Mrs. Potter laughed a little. "Nothing." With her back turned, she dried her wet hands on a tea towel and then brushed her fingers under her eyes. "I've just thought of something the sheriff told me . . ."

Mrs. Potter used the phone in the kitchen to dial Highlands Ranch, the home of Marjorie and Reynolds McHenry.

"It's Genia Potter, Rey. I'm sorry to bother you again, but I need to ask a favor in addition to the search party tomorrow. I do appreciate it so much that you and Marj are going to bring some of your men over to help us. I understand you have aerial maps of this valley, possibly even including this ranch, is that right?"

She listened for a moment.

"Oh, I can't remember who told me, Rey, but the point is, do you have such maps and do they include Las Palomas, and may we borrow them to help us plan our search party?"

Mrs. Potter was in no mood for his evasions or equivocations, but she wasn't above using those tactics herself. The man was so secretive, she thought, that he would hedge before telling you the sun was up! *Why, I ought to give him a piece of my mind for invading my privacy with his airplane and photographer!* She decided instead to be grateful for unlikely blessings; the maps would help, if he'd ever admit he owned them, and then if he'd release them to her.

She gave him no quarter.

"If you'll find the maps and leave them with your guard at your front gate, I'll send Ken Ryerson over to pick them up on his way home to-night. Thank you so much, Rey."

Mrs. Potter was almost smiling when she hung up the phone.

"I can't think of anything else to do, can you, Ken?"

He shrugged. "Pray, I guess."

"I've been doing that."

"Uh."

Mrs. Potter recognized that sound as the preliminary to something he wanted to say to her, and so she waited patiently for him to get it out. She had many years' practice of waiting for cowboys to speak their minds. Finally, he seemed to do that: *"Patrona,* there's something I want you to know. Nobody else does, except Linda. Her and me, we've got plans. To get married."

"Oh, Ken!" Two young people, working together for months at a time, it was perfectly natural. But poor Ken, she thought, feeling fresh compassion for the tired cowboy seated at her kitchen table. Not only his boss was missing but his fiancée as well. He dug his wallet out of his jeans and removed from it a tiny photograph that he slapped down onto the table. "Haven't told anybody yet, like I say." He stared down at the picture as he spoke. "Thought we'd wait to tell her parents till they get back from Antarctica or wherever the hell they are. Haven't told Ricardo or Juanita yet." He glanced up at her, but his glance was quickly pulled back down to the little photograph. "Don't know if they'll approve, me not being Mexican and all."

Mrs. Potter thought it far more likely that they'd disapprove if marriage meant postponing college for Linda, or if they were concerned about the disparity in the ages of the couple. Ken and Linda both seemed very young to Mrs. Potter, but she recalled that there could be a vast chasm of experience lying between an eighteen-year-old and a thirty-year-old. The older people got, the closer they drew together in maturity; at those ages, however, a difference of a decade could make a difference.

But, Mrs. Potter thought, *I guess it doesn't to them.*

"I know my folks won't like it, but I don't plan on ever goin' back to Kentucky, so that don't matter much." Ken ran out of words, and just gazed down at the photograph.

"Ken, I'm so sorry."

She was suddenly acutely aware of just how many impending tragedies were in the making here, affecting so many lives. The outlook for the morrow seemed bleak at that moment, especially when she looked at the picture of dejection and frustration sitting across from her.

Mrs. Potter straightened her spine and her resolve.

"We'll just have to find them safe and sound, that's all there is to it," she said as firmly as she could, as if that could make it come true. A friend's sarcastic voice echoed in her head: *"Clichés are such a comfort, aren't they?"* To which she silently rejoined, *"Oh, do be quiet."* They would all take their comfort wherever they could find it right now, even in bromides.

Ken pushed back his chair, which creaked as he stood up.

"Yeah. Thanks, Mrs. Potter. I'll stop by Highlands for the maps. Where should I be at sunup?"

"You'll be lucky to get any sleep. I told everybody to meet at the old windmill."

"What do you want me to do about the regular chores, Mrs. Potter?"

She slapped her forehead. "Oh, Lord, Ken. Life does go on, doesn't it, with cows to check and calves to be born? Well, you obviously can't be organizing a search party and doing ranch work at the same time. Bandy can't manage it. I guess that leaves me, Ken."

It seemed to her that he made a manly effort not to look skeptical.

"Tell you what, *patrona*. When I'm divvying up the ranch for the search, I'll assign myself those pastures that need to be checked for new calves. As long as I'm looking behind rocks for newborn babies, I might as well look for Ricardo and Linda too."

Mrs. Potter nodded her agreement. "Yes, that'll do for tomorrow, but then you're going to have to have help." Aghast at the implications of her own statement, she stared up at the tall cowboy. "Oh, Ken, how would we ever manage without him?"

"Won't have to," he said, tightening his jaw.

"Yes, of course, that's right."

She followed him as he walked out of the kitchen, his spurs jangling, back through the dining room and into the hall, where he put his slicker and hat back on. "I hope this won't inconvenience your other employers too much, Ken." She was referring to people like the McHenrys, who shared his services with other ranchers in the valley besides herself.

"They'll just have to understand that I'll get to them later."

"I'll make up for any lost pay, Ken."

He turned a less-than-friendly stare on her, and Mrs. Potter stepped back a bit. "This is Ricardo," he stated flatly. "And Linda. Don't want no pay for it."

"All right, Ken. It'll be a long day for you."

He shrugged.

This is what Wind Valley is all about, Mrs. Potter thought as she watched him button his rubber coat: being neighborly, doing for one another as we might need done for ourselves one day. The wheel had turned her way this time; now it was her turn to take hold of the strong, helping hands that reached out to her. She attempted an encouraging smile for him. "Maybe Ricardo and Linda will show up tonight, Ken, as Juanita keeps saying they will."

"Juanita says a lot of things." He tipped his water-stained hat to her. "No disrespect intended. Thanks for the soup. Sorry about the mess. Good night, ma'am."

"Good night, Ken."

He turned back. "You won't say anything about Linda and me?"

"Not if you don't want me to."

"We want to be the ones to say."

"Of course you do. I won't breathe a word of it. But I'll be praying for both of you." *And for your future grandfather-in-law,* she thought.

Ken Ryerson stepped outside onto her ramada and then walked down the flagstones into the darkness beyond the wall. Mrs. Potter's heart ached for him as she listened to his steps fade. The rain drummed on the plastic cover on the swimming pool. Her hanging plants rocked in the wind. Mrs. Potter breathed deeply of the sweet scent of rain in Arizona. Moisture blew in at her through the screen, forcing her to close the door. After locking it, she returned to the kitchen to clean up Ken's dirty dishes and there she noticed that he'd left his little photograph behind.

Mrs. Potter sat down at the kitchen table.

She held the picture in the cup of her right hand, and stared at it.

Linda "Ortega" Scarritt. Daughter of Francesca and Les. Les's Anglo blue eyes and her mother's Latino dark hair. It wasn't a very good picture of her, didn't begin to do her justice. She had the high-planed cheeks of her Indian ancestors, but also the thinner nose and lips of her European forebears. It was an odd combination of features, not pretty exactly, but interesting. An intelligent child, if not as academically inclined as her family would prefer. Quick to laugh, even quicker to learn anything that had to do with a horse. Mrs. Potter sighed. She was very fond of Ricardo's granddaughter and felt deeply concerned about her. The child was young for an eighteen-year-old, almost naive in the way a horse-struck adolescent girl was, not sophisticated at all. It was probably a good idea to keep her out of college for a year. Could this sweet child, she wondered, survive any truly rough encounter with the world? Mrs. Potter folded her fingers carefully over the little face, intending to return this treasured memento to Ken Ryerson in the morning.

"Find her, Ken," she said as she got up and switched off the lights in the kitchen. "And please do it soon."

CHAPTER 11

Mrs. Potter padded in her moccasins to her small office/study off the foyer and sat down at her desk. There was a telephone there and one of the ubiquitous yellow pads with which she organized her life. (And everybody else's, too, her children, Louisa, Emily, and Benji, claimed.) She spent the next few minutes engaged in listing the activities for the morrow: they included inviting the volunteers back for supper, which meant shopping for groceries, which meant selecting a menu so that she could make a list of things she needed to purchase.

"What can I fix," she asked herself, pencil eraser tapping her chin, "that's easy and can be expanded to serve a lot of people, will satisfy both the men and the women and maybe even take their minds off their troubles for a while?"

The answer came in a flash, literally, of lightning outside her windows: 27-Ingredient Chili con Carne.

Perfect.

Not only was it delicious and filling, but the riddle of the ingredients kept guests happily occupied in competing with one another to guess all twenty-seven.

Quickly, from memory, she jotted down her shopping list, starting with ground beef.

The telephone rang at her elbow.

Her heart in her throat, she picked up the receiver, hoping to hear Ricardo's voice, saying, "I'm so sorry to have worried you, *patrona*."

"You *promised* you'd call me," accused a contralto voice.

"Oh, Che! I did, didn't I? I'm sorry, I forgot."

"Understandable," said her old friend. So vivid was Che Thomas, so full of enthusiastic life, that Mrs. Potter could practically smell her signature perfume wafting through the party line. Surely all that anybody in the valley had to do was pick up their receiver and sniff. "It's Che

Thomas on the line," they'd declare, "talking to that Genia Potter again."

"Well?" Che demanded.

"No news."

"I don't like this, Genia. What are you doing about it?"

Mrs. Potter told her about the arrangements for the next day, and got in response a heated protest because Mrs. Potter had not called Che to request *her* participation in the search party.

"Don't be silly," Mrs. Potter said rather sharply, she feared; but then, she was awfully tired. "I don't expect you to get out there on horseback, any more than I expect to get out there myself. I don't think we'd be much help, Che, darling."

"At our age, you mean?" was the indignant response. "We'll see about that, Eugenia Potter. Maybe you think you're too old to be of any earthly use to anybody, but I certainly am not. I'll be there, four-wheel drive and all, and I'll have as many guests and employees as I can roust out of bed in the morning. If they can get up before dawn to go out on hunting parties to shoot poor defenseless little mountain lions, they can darn well get up to go look for Ricardo."

"Che, this is very good of you."

"Ricardo," was the tart reply, "has been very good to all of us here in the valley. He's always there with the wisest advice this side of Solomon, and always ready to help out with everybody else's roundups—"

"Which everyone repays by helping *us*—"

"Makes no never mind, Genia Potter. He's a special man. And that grandchild of his is the apple of his eye and he'll never forgive me if I didn't go look for her myself. I'll be there with a crowd, count on it."

"Thank you, Che," was Mrs. Potter's humble answer.

"Now. I promised *you* something too. A surprise."

"And I asked if it could please, possibly, wait?"

"No, it's waited long enough, and if this chance goes by, it may not come again. Hold the phone, dear, your surprise is coming on the line."

"Che!"

She wanted to find out if there'd been a C Lazy U hunting party out on the morning when Ricardo and Linda disappeared, but it was no use. Mrs. Potter couldn't call her friend back to the phone. She could only wait in weary frustration, kicking her moccasins off under her desk and raising her feet, one at a time, to massage her toes. She wanted with all her heart to plod off to a shower and then to bed. Morning could not come soon enough—

"Is this Mrs. Potter?"

"This is she."

It was a man's voice, eerily familiar. Had that been a hint of Boston accent as he began, asking for Mrs. Pottah? He started to introduce himself just as the thunderstorm took momentary charge of the telephone lines, so she missed his name.

"I'm sorry, who did you say?"

"Andy? *Andy? Is that you?*"

No one called Mrs. Potter Andy anymore. Christened Eugenia Andrews, known generally to family and friends as Genia, no one called her Andy. Except, *except* . . .

Could it be . . . after forty years? Jed? Jed White? *He* was Che's surprise?

Mrs. Potter took a deep breath and tried to manage a cordial, social response, the proper response due a friend of one's youth. *Not* the answer of her suddenly eighteen-year-old-again heart. The answer, instead, of respectable middle-aged widowhood.

"Yes." She took another breath. "Yes, Jed, it's me." And then another breath, until she felt quite dizzy. "It's just that I haven't been called Andy for so many years, and we're having a bit of a thunderstorm, and I couldn't quite hear you. But then I guess you know it's storming, if you're at Che's. My word, you're at Che's!" She paused, scrambling for composure again. "How *are* you, Jed?"

There, that sounded quite calm and friendly, she hoped, with no betrayal of her quickened pulse.

"I'm fine now that I have you on the phone. When I couldn't reach you yesterday, I began to think I wouldn't manage it—"

"I've been in Maine—"

"So I hear. When I told Mrs. Thomas I have an old college friend living in the vicinity, she told me she knows you very well, and she was kind enough to let me know you got in tonight." He paused. Mrs. Potter suddenly wondered if he, too, might be having trouble finding sufficient composure and just the right words. "I'm spending a week or so here, Andy. It seemed like a good idea to call you to say hello."

"I think it's a wonderful idea, Jed," she said warmly. "But what in the world is an Eastern boy like you doing there at a dude ranch?"

His voice, deeper and more authoritative than she remembered it, held great warmth, too, and his reply had a friendly, teasing quality that instantly bridged forty years and made her feel like a girl again. "I'd like to say I came out here just on the off chance of seeing *you* again, Andy."

She laughed lightly. "But the truth is . . ."

"But the truth is that I have business here as well."

Mrs. Potter wondered what sort of business could possibly bring him to Wind Valley, where the only commercial enterprises that she knew of were ranching and the mom-and-pop cafés and shops in the town at the crossroads.

"All right, but how did you even know I live in Arizona, Jed, much less on a ranch in this valley? It's been so many years. I have to admit that I haven't known a thing about you, where you were, or what you were doing. How *could* you have known I was here?"

"But I've always known where you were, Andy. No matter what, you must have known that. I've always known where you were. Every year, every move, every child. I've always known."

It was said so simply, so straightforwardly.

And it left her speechless.

"Say, what's that noise I'm hearing?" he asked, rescuing her from her own silence.

"That clicking?" she managed to blurt out. "Party line."

His reply made him sound as incredulous as *she* was over his previous comment. "In this day and age?"

"Yes. Welcome to the past, Jed."

There was a moment of silence as they both seemed to weigh the double meaning of her quip. With no further interruptions on the line as the rain squall passed by, and no further clicks, she managed to invite him to visit her ranch the next day.

"That's very kind of you, Andy, but Che—Mrs. Thomas—has told me something of your troubles there. I'd be in the way."

"No, you'd be doing me a favor, Jed. Che must have told you that my ranch manager and his granddaughter are still missing. I can't be much help in the actual search tomorrow, and if I stay around here all day by myself, I'll go crazy. I would appreciate your company."

"Really?"

"Really."

"Well, then, yes, of course I'll come."

"Ordinarily, I'd suggest a time," she went on. "Lunch or dinner or somesuch. But there's no telling what tomorrow will bring, so my best advice is to come when you feel like it, as long as it's any time after noon. I have to run into town before that. Che will give you directions, and probably a car if you need one, or even one of the ranch pickups. I'm afraid that if we don't have good news by the time you arrive, I may not be the best of company. But I will be here. And I *would* like to see you, Jed."

"I'll admit this isn't quite the reunion I envisioned."

"No."

"And I know the reunion you'd really like to have tomorrow is the one with your missing employees."

"Yes." She thought it sensitive of him to acknowledge that. "I must tell you they're much more than employees; they're friends, very nearly family."

"I'm so sorry. Are you sure . . . ?"

"I'm sure."

"Tomorrow, then."

"Good night . . . Jed."

Mrs. Potter hung up the receiver and then got up and wandered into her bedroom in a bit of a daze, hardly feeling the carpet on the soles of her feet. She sank down on the edge of her bed, and felt a transformation take place inside herself. . . .

Suddenly, Mrs. Potter, *la patrona* of Las Palomas, was Eugenia Andrews of Harrington, Iowa. And it was no longer early May in Arizona, where she was faced with horrifying, heartbreaking adult responsibilities. It was October in Massachusetts and she was a freshman at college, and a voice she had not heard since then was speaking to her as if the years between them had not existed. . . .

Andy.

It had always sounded like An-day when he spoke it.

Her bedroom in Wind Valley disappeared in a mist of memory.

Suddenly, the world was new and she was eighteen again and in love, or so she thought, with a clear, slightly nasal, upper-class Boston accent.

Jed and Andy.

They had met one sunny Saturday in early fall, introduced by her roommate, Gussie, and her roommate's brother. From the time of their meeting, both the brother and the roommate had been ignored and forgotten. All during that magical autumn, she and Jedders H. White had spent as much time together as their college schedules permitted, sailing on the Charles, walking hand in hand on Boston Common, strolling rain-wet brick sidewalks, feasting on steamed clams and lobsters—which he had shown the girl from Iowa how to eat—and on White Tower hamburgers when their allowances ran low.

In a daze of first love, Eugenia Andrews spent that autumn in a dream. "I'm in *love!*" she awoke each morning to remind herself. "I'm in *Boston!* I'm in *college!*"

And then the dream, the dazzlement of first love, the thrill of city life, the first excitement of intellectual challenge, lost some of its wonderment. Mrs. Potter could scarcely recall now just what had happened between her and Jed. Some misunderstanding, she supposed, which perhaps one of them had thought trivial, and the other had thought important, and then almost as suddenly and magically as they had fallen in love, they had fallen out of it.

It had been painful for both of them, she remembered, but then spring came and there was another, though much less electrifying, young man, and then another. And then she had returned home to the summer joys of her own Blue Lake, and then off to another fall at college. And then Lew. She never had a regret during all the long good years of their marriage, and almost never had even a fleeting thought of that first love. *Except when I fly into Boston*, Mrs. Potter corrected herself. Sometimes at Logan Airport she might suddenly imagine she caught sight of that tall, thin figure, might sometimes imagine she heard that mixture of softness and twang that New England had given to his speech.

All right, she admitted, there *was* a folk song (or was it the Beatles?) she never heard without thinking of Jed. Something about seeing fire and rain, I always thought we'd meet again. Something like that. To be honest now at last, she knew she really had always expected that sometime they would meet again.

But not like this. . . .

Mrs. Potter felt herself transported back into the present again, along with all of its attendant weariness and worries, aches and pains. And age. Ah, but for a few moments there, she'd found that magic elixir in memories of her own youth. She told herself to stop being absurd. She was seated on her double bed, not on a narrow cot in a college dormitory. And the man who called was not the boy she had loved. This man, nice as he sounded, would prove to be happily and appropriately married to a wonderful woman and the doting father of several children, pictures of whom she would see when he pulled them out of his wallet tomorrow. He would be a lawyer by now, possibly a partner in some old Boston firm; or maybe a doctor. He probably played squash at his club twice a week, and jogged the other days, and he would—should—be on the phone right now telling his wife about the nice old college friend he'd managed to find "way out here in the sticks, could you believe it?"

Mrs. Potter glanced at her watch.

Well, no, it was later in the East, so he had probably either already called his wife this evening, or he would talk to her in the morning, and why was she, Mrs. Potter, concerned about that anyway?

It would be nice to see him tomorrow; she and he would have a nice, reminiscent chat, that was all.

Mrs. Potter got up from the bed and went to stand beside one of her bedroom windows that looked out on the Rimstone Mountains. At least it had stopped storming, but she knew the spring winds whipped cold and harsh through the arroyos. She thought of Linda and Ricardo being somewhere out there, who knew where, and in goodness only knew what condition. It was *those* two dear people whom she'd give nearly anything to see tomorrow, and not, with all due respect, some long-lost boyfriend of hers.

"*Dónde están?*" she murmured.

Where are they?

Before she went to bed she remembered to put two pounds of dry pinto beans in water to soak so that they'd be ready for the chili the next day.

CHAPTER 12

Worry could have kept Mrs. Potter awake all night, but sheer exhaustion drove worry to its knees, defeating it. She slept without stirring, until her alarm sounded at 5 A.M.

When she opened her eyes, it was to a dark bedroom.

She felt unaccountably happy and didn't know why until the name "Jed" floated into her consciousness. But that immediately brought with it a recollection of the rest of yesterday, like a movie played backward, and the happiness instantly gave way to fear. There had been no phone call from Juanita to wake her during the night, no jubilant voice reporting, "They're home!"

Mrs. Potter didn't reach out a hand to press the "snooze" button to give herself an extra five minutes of rest. Nor did she allow herself her usual pleasure of a prolonged gaze out the window at her beloved Rimstone Mountains. She rose immediately from bed and padded across the carpet to the bathroom.

There were many things to be done this morning.

Moving briskly, impatient with the morning stiffness of her own fingers and legs, Mrs. Potter shed her nightgown and slipped into a pair of light wool navy-blue trousers, a rose-colored cotton turtleneck and a navy cardigan. Navy-blue stockings and good, comfortable walking shoes went on next. Mrs. Potter did up her silver-blond hair in its customary neat knot, selected small gold ball earrings, and then applied a dab of gray eye shadow on each lid, and a touch of color to her mouth. Giving a quick thought to the idea that she might be seeing Jed White that day before she ever had a chance to freshen up, she applied a dab of perfume behind each ear and at her throat and wrists.

"I would do this anyway," she defended herself to her mirror.

Mrs. Potter stepped back to take a look at herself.

"My, dear," she recalled her grandmother saying, "thanks to the blessings of paint and powder, it is nearly always possible for a woman to look better than she feels."

Mrs. Potter decided her mirror gave certain proof of that.

Her yard was still dark when she walked to the carport. She kept to the flagstone path and then to the gravel, as she'd never quite conquered a fear of snakes literally in the grass. Arizona sheltered several poisonous varieties—rattlers, for one—and millions of rocks for them to hide beneath. They were one of the dangers she preferred not to think about in regard to Linda and her grandfather.

She backed out of the carport and then headed southeast on a well-worn dirt road that wound through several pastures and required her to open and close a few gates. By the time she'd climbed out of her car for the sixth time, and closed the third gate, she was as wide awake as only exercise and cold morning air could make her. She was also regretting the fact that she hadn't paused long enough for her usual cup of hot tea, or brought along a Thermos of coffee.

She never would have guessed it had stormed the night before. Several hours of dry desert wind had absorbed the puddles like a sponge. By now, she thought, our excess moisture is on its way to Kansas. The dirt beneath her tires was dry and the little arroyos she crossed were exactly what their name meant in English: dry washes. If Ricardo or Linda had been soaked by the deluge, they'd be dry by now, but cold. The morning was very crisp, and that wonderful fleece-lined jacket of Linda's wouldn't protect her fingertips or her toes from the chill. Ricardo, Mrs. Potter knew, had a habit of going out in almost any weather with only chaps and a fleece-lined leather vest for protection. Both of them had probably worn long underwear for their early-morning ride, and Ricardo wore kid gloves for riding—most cowboys did—and he'd have on his hat. Mrs. Potter could see it in her mind's eye: a glorious battered black work hat, a Stetson with its side brims rolled high and a hammered silver band. Juanita claimed that band was big enough to blind cows when the sun hit it. Ricardo only laughed at that and agreed it *was* his secret technique to get cattle and people to obey him: blind 'em and hypnotize 'em. Mrs. Potter's eyes filled with tears as she smiled at the memory of their marital banter.

The sun had barely begun to frame El Bizcocho when she drove over a small rise and saw the now-defunct windmill, which sat down in a hollow with a strange topographical characteristic: although steep hills rose around it, there were narrow passages through those hills, which formed wind tunnels that still whipped the broken vanes around like a child's top in a cyclone. When she and Lew bought the ranch they found more efficient access to water, so they let nature turn the windmill into a picturesque artifact that their amateur-artist friends adored to capture in water-colors. Mrs. Potter found it amazing that the windmill still stood, but she knew it was set deep and built of a nearly indestructible hardwood back in the days when people built things right the first time. Sometimes she entertained the notion of restoring it to its original use, partly for ecologi-cal reasons, but mostly as a sentimental tribute to its good old days.

She'd selected it as the gathering place because it was situated nearly dead-center in the ranch. From there, the searchers could fan out effi-ciently in every direction.

The wind was whipping good this morning, as the locals said, and even in her closed car she could hear the windmill creaking, moaning like something alive. She saw Charlie Watt talking to Ken Ryerson. Both men had their hands on their Stetsons, to hold them on. Other volunteers were showing up early, and either staying in their vehicles or huddling in small, quiet groups in the lee of the hills. Most of last night's visitors were present this morning. It looked to her as if everybody had come equipped for any eventuality, whether that be traversing rough country in a truck or going cross-country on horseback, or even the possibility of violence, to judge by the number of firearms attached to back windows. It was also true that under many of those driver's seats a person would find a hand-gun if she were inclined to look. Guns were a way of life out West, where ranchers liked to be prepared to shoot varmints, particularly the danger-ous wild dogs that threatened livestock. Mrs. Potter herself had resisted all efforts—by Lew, by Ricardo, even by women like Juanita and Che—to tote her own pistol. "There is no boot leather thick enough to guard against the probability that I would shoot myself through it," she told them, "and no side of a barn so big I can't miss it."

Marjorie McHenry waved at her, stiffly, and she waved back.

She noticed that Marj and Rey had brought along three burly men who provided security for them on the ranch. Mrs. Potter was grateful for the extra help, but she did wonder whether it was intended for Ricardo's benefit or to protect the McHenrys while they were out in the open. What an awful way to live, she thought, and wondered why on earth they needed bodyguards. What did they fear could happen to them? That was something everybody in the valley craved to know and nobody ever seemed to find out. All they ever got out of the tight-lipped McHenrys was a cryptic cliché along the lines of "You can't be too careful." And all they got out of the Highlands employees, almost all of whom appeared to be imported from out of state, was a vague "I wouldn't be able to say" or "I wouldn't know about that."

Mrs. Potter waved at Lorraine Steinbach, but didn't see Gallway.

Rattling noises coming from behind her startled her. Mrs. Potter checked her rearview mirror and spotted a small parade coming her way, an all-black cavalcade of pickups and Jeeps, each with the C Lazy U brand painted on its doors. Che Thomas, true to her word and bless her heart, appeared to have sent a small army of her dude ranch guests and employees.

Mrs. Potter hoped that Jedders H. White wasn't one of them.

Granted, it would be nice of him to help.

But it would be awkward to hold a forty-year reunion under the eyes of her curious (not that she'd blame them) neighbors. Mrs. Potter held her breath a bit until every black vehicle had parked in the grass and every occupant had alighted and not one of them appeared to be a tall, thin, handsome college boy forty years later.

She saw Ken suddenly walk away from Charlie, looking as if he was mad about something. The younger man stomped over to the covey of vehicles, while Charlie, still holding on to his hat, followed at a more leisurely pace. The older man noticed Mrs. Potter, and waved, a gesture she returned. Several of the other volunteer searchers raised their hands in greeting to her, too, and she returned their salutations, although her own right arm felt as heavy as her heart.

She drove on toward the cluster of vehicles, passing Ken en route.

As soon as she parked, between two ocotillo shrubs, there was a knock at her window. She turned to see the tanned and handsome visage of Che Thomas smiling in at her. Che was dressed in layers, as if she expected to be out all day from the chill of the morning on toward the peak of the afternoon. Above the window line Mrs. Potter saw a black down jacket with the C Lazy U insignia over a black sweater, over a black shirt, and she expected there were black pants and black socks and black boots below the window line. All that black made a dramatic frame for Che's short-cropped white hair, the huge turquoise brooch at her neckline, her turquoise-blue eyes and the high color of her cheeks and lips. Mrs. Potter rolled down her window, letting in a dusty gust of cold wind and a breeze of perfume.

"Told you."

"Thank you, Che, I really appreciate the help—"

"No, no." The other woman laughed. "I mean to say, I *told* you that you'd like my surprise. My God, Genia, you're blushing. I can't believe it, at your age. I thought maybe he'd come with us this morning, but he said he'd wait to see you this afternoon." Her elegant white eyebrows arched inquisitively. "This afternoon, hmm?"

"What's he like, Che?"

Che grinned. "Ugly as sin. Fat as a marshmallow. Face like a javelina pig. Gets around with a walker. Talks about his prostate all the time. Can name every game show host on television." The grin widened. "You'll just love him, Genia."

"I may kill you for this, Che." Mrs. Potter experienced a sudden, overwhelming desire to change the subject. "You're not really going out there, are you?"

"You bet I am, kiddo. I may be as old as these hills, but I've still got eyes that can tell an eagle from a hawk, and even shoot the right one when they're flying a thousand feet up. Don't you forget I was raised here. I'm a tough old country broad, Genia, not like you sissified Philly types." Che smiled at her with eyes full of mischief. "Besides, I've known Ricardo longer than anybody else here except maybe Charlie. The three of us were working cattle or going to parties on this ranch a long time before you and Lew ever bought it, you know. These youngsters"—she indicated the other searchers, several of whom were over sixty, with a dismissive wave of her beringed left hand—"don't know this terrain like we do. So who better to look for him than Charlie and I?"

The door on the passenger's side opened and the high voice of another woman interrupted them.

"A person could die out there!"

Mrs. Potter turned her head, and Che craned hers to find Kathy Amory staring in at them with big, round eyes. "*Anything* could have happened to them! The desert's just the most dangerous place! Why, they could have been bitten by rattlesnakes or attacked by mountain lions. I was wondering, Mrs. Potter, can you die from a scorpion bite?"

It was Che Thomas who answered her, in a tightly controlled voice.

"Not usually, Kathy. But maybe they got attacked by hundreds of scorpions all at one time."

"Oh, my God, can that happen?"

"No," Mrs. Potter said gently. "Che's kidding."

Kathy and Walt Amory were relatively new to Arizona in general and to the desert in particular, and Kathy obviously had yet to accustom herself to the normal everyday hazards that natives took more or less for granted . . . scorpions lurking in the toes of bedroom slippers, Gila monsters sunning on rocks (or chaise lounges), rattlesnakes slithering across highways (or patios), stinging ants that built mounds as big as moguls on a ski slope, or black widow spiders, brown spiders, centipedes, and coral snakes, not to mention your run-of-the-mill bees, wasps, and four-legged predators. You learned to be alert and hope for the best—much as city dwellers kept their eyes open for stinging bullets and two-legged predators.

Kathy shivered in her neon-orange ski jacket with matching waterproof pants and brimmed cap. "Maybe they got mauled by a pack of those awful javelina pigs. Gored to death, you know? Or coyotes. Walt says it could have been coyotes, although I didn't know they'd actually kill a man."

"They don't," Che said in a voice as tart as a slice of lemon. "They only kill women—they prefer juicy young girls best, not scrawny old hags like Genia and me, well, like me, at least—so they might have gotten Linda, but Ricardo's safe—"

"Che!" said Mrs. Potter, under her breath.

But Kathy was wide-eyed. "Really?"

Che nodded, looking preternaturally wise. "Maybe you'd better not go out there, Kathy." She arched an eyebrow. "What with being young and female, and all."

"I wish I could talk to Walt!"

"Where *is* he?" Che demanded, as if she felt every able-bodied soul in the valley ought to be on hand and she wanted to know why this one wasn't.

"He's not here," was the reply, offered with a bright smile.

Che exchanged a look with Mrs. Potter, as if to say, "Well, that's a big help."

The young woman said good-bye quickly and slammed the car door, leaving Mrs. Potter to stare in mock disapproval at her friend.

Che shrugged. "She looks like she got outfitted by a road maintenance crew . . . what the trendy young person will wear for her next search party. Oh, well, let's look at the bright side. Maybe *she* will get eaten by coyotes."

"Che! What's the matter with you?"

"Lorraine Steinbach is my friend—and yours, may I add? And where the hell is old Gallstones this morning, I'd like to know?"

It was Mrs. Potter's private opinion that Lorraine Steinbach could only benefit from the loss of the execrable Gallway from her life, but saying it would be akin to telling a recent widow, "That's all right, dear, you'll find another one."

"Speak of the devil," Che said, as she and Mrs. Potter both waved at Lorraine Steinbach, who now stood talking to several other women. "Or, I should say, the devil's wife."

All the volunteers were climbing out of their cars and trucks by now and walking toward Ken, who stood waiting for them to gather around him. Mrs. Potter opened her own door. Che got out of the way and then the two of them walked over to join the gathering, where Ken was starting to issue instructions.

"Got maps here that I made last night. Hope you can read 'em. They're assignments. I've divied the ranch up in pie slices radiating out from this point. Let's see a show of hands, how many of you are actually goin' out there . . ."

He counted thirty-two hands, including himself, which was everybody there except Mrs. Potter. They were all going. Bless them. She swallowed a lump in her throat, and listened carefully to Ken.

"Okay, I'm going to hand these maps out to groups of you. I expect you all know this area well enough that you can tell who's goin' by vehicle and who's going to have to go ahorseback. But if you're not sure, check with me, and I'll tell you how I think you ought to do it."

Che Thomas called out, "What if we find them, Ken?"

Grim-faced and weary-looking, he turned toward her.

"Make sure there's a rifle among the group of you. Let off two shots if you find either one of them, give three shots if you find something you want some of the rest of us to come take a look at."

"Like what, Ken?" asked a cowboy from the valley.

He shrugged helplessly. "Damned if I know, Shorty. But like a piece of their clothing, maybe, or some sign of their horses, some track looks like they been there, I don't know. I guess if you find something, you'll know it when you see it. And listen, I expect some of you got two-way radios or car phones, I want to talk to you, see if we can set up some better communication system that way. Oh, and another thing, folks, don't y'all be doin' anything dangerous, don't y'all be takin' any chances make the rest of us come lookin' for you, you hear?"

"Sound like a Kentucky boy, Ken," teased another cowboy.

"Ain't no joke, hoss," was the short-tempered reply, as Ken Ryerson began walking among the crowd handing out his hand-drawn maps. The offending cowboy muttered apologetically, "Didn't mean nuthin' . . ." But Ken ignored him, and the hapless cowboy got a few cold looks from some of the other volunteers. Mrs. Potter noticed that Charlie Watt winked at him in a kindly way.

Tempers are already short, she noted, and the day has only just begun. It's not a good sign. It means these people are already feeling hopeless and frustrated.

Mrs. Potter stepped forward and raised her voice.

"I just want to say how deeply Juanita and her family and I appreciate your doing this. I know that Ricardo and Linda are your friends every bit as much as mine, probably more in some cases, for those of you who've known Ricardo for so long. . . ." She nodded at Che Thomas and Charlie Watt, acknowledging their lifelong ties to Ricardo. She held Bandy Esposito's glance for a moment, too, out of respect for his special relationship to Ricardo. "I'll be praying that you find them." She smiled and tried mightily to keep it from wavering. "When you *do* find them"—

scattered applause broke out and a couple of "hear hears," as her neighbors valiantly tried to help her cheer them on their way—"I hope you'll come back to my house for chili."

Che Thomas said in a bold voice, "I know Rico loves chili, Genia."

"That's right," Charlie Watt answered in an equally strong and steady voice, "so make him a big hot bowl of it, Genia, 'cause he's going to need it after this tomfool adventure of his."

Mrs. Potter nodded her agreement, because she was suddenly unable to speak another word. Lorraine Steinbach was quickly beside her, wrapping her in a warm hug, which she returned gratefully.

As the volunteers formed themselves into small groups, according to Ken's instructions, Mrs. Potter walked around shaking hands and personally thanking them. In return, she got clasps and quiet words of encouragement and sympathy, as well as firm instructions to transmit those same feelings back to "poor Juanita and her family."

Finally, feeling both bolstered and shaken, Mrs. Potter returned to her car and just sat still for a while, watching these good people begin the work of doing what had to be done. She stayed long enough to wave the searchers off and to watch them disperse over her fields. Then she climbed back into her car and drove home in the rapidly lengthening shadows of morning.

CHAPTER 13

On her way to the kitchen to finally fix her morning cup of tea, Mrs. Potter detoured into the living room. She stood in front of the windows that looked toward Mexico and stared down the hill past the barn and corral, past the big garage where Bandy lived, to the two-story white frame Ortega home.

There were cars she didn't recognize in Juanita's driveway.

"Good, her family's here."

She was willing to bet that all the available Ortega children had hopped in their cars as soon as their mother called with the news. There was an unmarried son who was a social worker in Phoenix; in Tucson there were a married son who was an assistant grocery store manager and a married daughter who was an accountant; there was an unmarried daughter who owned a candy shop in Santa Fe; and there was Linda's mother, the anthropologist, now in Brazil. She wouldn't have been surprised if the various sons- and daughters-in-law, not to mention the grandchildren, had been packed up and brought along too. Ricardo and Juanita were the matriarch and patriarch of a close and loving clan; the children would drop everything to come help search for their father and support their mother. Not that Juanita would make it easy for them. Mrs. Potter shook her head in sympathy for all of them, mother and children alike. They'd see no tears from their mother and Juanita wouldn't tolerate many from them, at least not as long as there was still hope. Seeing them reminded her to call her own three children, but then she thought: why worry them unnecessarily? Ricardo and Linda would show up any time now, and then she could write Louisa, Emily, and Benji nice long chatty letters all about these "tomfool" adventures. The voice of Louisa, her eldest and a psychologist, spoke in her ear: *"That's called denial, Mother."*

She took a moment longer to draw strength from the view.

"I call it hope, Louisa."

Now that the sun was fully risen, it revealed the beauty of the rangeland that stretched to the foothills of the mountains on every side. In the distance, she spied her favorite signs of spring: mother cows and their calves. Tears sprang to her eyes at her sheer pleasure and gratitude at seeing this favorite vista again. *And may there be many, many more,* she thought, *for all of us.* Red flowers were budding on the tips of the long, thin stalks of ocotillo shrubs, and she saw thistles that had sprouted white flowers looking as soft and delicate as a lotus. Pretty little yellow flowers, and purple ones, too, whose names she could never remember, dotted the range and softened it. At this time of year the native grass grew as tall and thick as it ever got in this part of the country, and this morning it looked like the thick and heavy platinum mane of a palomino horse. Some people preferred the greener month of June, but Mrs. Potter loved the way the long grasses of May undulated in graceful ivory waves. They seemed to be waving to her now . . . welcome home, Genia.

"Thank you," she whispered back to them.

In the kitchen, she put the water on to boil for tea while she rummaged through her cupboards for something to eat until she could get to town for groceries. She found oatmeal, dry cereals, and biscuit mix, but there was no milk for them. At last she came up with pancake mix that required only water, no eggs.

"Please, please let there be a sliver of butter . . ."

Thank goodness there was, half a stick, on a plate in the fridge.

Well! This was better than she'd any reason to hope it would be.

Mrs. Potter drank a cup of English breakfast tea while she fixed "five bucks' worth" of dollar pancakes and also put the water-logged pinto beans in big pots of water to simmer on the stove until they were tender. When the pancakes were golden brown—a hot-enough griddle was always the key to perfect pancakes—she slathered them with butter, poured on some maple syrup that she had brought back from a previous trip to Maine, and placed the plate on a tray. She added knife and fork, napkin and another cup of tea, and carried it all to her desk in the study off the hall. Mrs. Potter wanted to peruse her list of "things to do" while she ate breakfast.

She lifted her yellow writing pad to make room for her tray.

When she did, its top sheet fell over on top of the page on which she had listed her groceries. The first thing she recognized was that the writing on it was not her own. The second thing she realized was that it was Ricardo's.

Mrs. Potter sank down into her desk chair, pancakes forgotten.

KR, he'd printed, and placed a check mark by it.

Then *Mrs. P.*, with another check.

Under that, he'd written in a vertical line the letters *J* (with a question mark beside it), *B* (crossed out), *CW*, *A*, *S*, *Mc.* Included in that cryptic list was a capital *C* with a capital *U* written sideways.

"C Lazy U," Mrs. Potter deciphered.

And then suddenly the rest of the list was easy too:

Charlie Watt.

The Amorys.

The Steinbachs.

The McHenrys.

And Che Thomas from the C Lazy U.

They were all of the folks who'd been in her driveway last night, the people whom Ricardo had summoned to a mysterious meeting at her house.

KR had to be Ken Ryerson.

And there was herself, of course, *Mrs. P.*

He'd placed a check by every one of them.

And the question mark beside the letter *J?* Mrs. Potter thought that might mean that he wondered whether to include Juanita. By crossing out the *B* was he eliminating Bandy from the guest list?

Was this his calling list? If so, the check marks appeared to indicate that he'd successfully reached everyone he had telephoned.

That wasn't all, however.

He'd written the number *7:30*, and circled it.

And in an upper corner, he'd written *Elb: 5*, and circled *it.*

Mrs. Potter wasn't so curious about the actual notes—she guessed that 7:30 merely indicated the time that last night's meeting of the neighbors was to take place, so *Elb: 5* was the only thing she couldn't immediately decode.

But she was awfully puzzled about something else. . . .

"Why did you call us from *here*, Ricardo?"

From her desk, she meant, from her house, her private domain, while she was away. It gave Mrs. Potter an uneasy feeling to think of someone besides her sitting at her desk, looking at her papers, which were scattered on it, staring at her pictures in her study. Even if that person was Ricardo, whom she trusted implicitly. Still . . .

"Why?" she asked him.

With no answer to that easily forthcoming, Mrs. Potter ripped off her own list and drove to the grocery store with it.

They were lucky, she thought, to have a grocery store at the crossroads, which was just that, and not even a real town at all. Without Ryan's Grocery, she and everybody else in Wind Valley would have had to drive as far as Nogales in one direction or Tucson in another for anything fancier than the packaged bologna, potato chips, and candy bars that were sold at the corner gas station at the crossroads. Besides Ryan's and the gas station, there was Sally's Café, and a tiny shop that sold locally made crafts, and a rambling, messy, greasy, absolutely indispensable garage for repairing cars, trucks, tractors, and just about anything else on wheels, including the bicycles of the children of Wind Valley.

Outside Sally's, where Sally herself made the best rhubarb pie in Arizona, Mrs. Potter noticed a silver Mercedes with California license plates parked in the dirt. It was Walt Amory's car. And now that she thought about it, Mrs. Potter remembered that Walt Amory hadn't been at the windmill this morning. Kathy had been there to endure Che's tormenting, but not her husband. And there he was, seated at a window table inside Sally's, with . . .

Conveniently stopped at the crossroads stoplight, Mrs. Potter stared, and very nearly rubbed her eyes in disbelief.

With Gallway Steinbach, the very man with whom Kathy Amory was rumored to be having an affair? She squinted in spite of herself, in an unabashed effort to get a good look at the expressions on their faces. Why, Gallstones was shaking a long, bony finger at the younger man, who was looking abashed. This was not at *all* how one might have expected such an encounter to proceed.

My goodness, she thought, this was sufficiently intriguing gossip to keep valley tongues busy! Mrs. Potter, no friend to mean gossip, had to admit that she would love to be a fly on that particular windowpane. Not, of course, that Sally ever permitted any such thing as a fly to darken the interior of her immaculate café—as immaculate as a place could be, that is, where the customers regularly trooped through in cowboy boots.

Mrs. Potter glanced up at the second floor of Sally's, where the curtains were pulled against the sun. That was where her own part-time hired man, Ken Ryerson, rented a single room with a bath down the hall. Or so she'd been told by Sally, who also informed anybody who asked, and a few who didn't, that Ken wasn't any too neat, and he wasn't always on time with the rent, but by gracious, he didn't cat around or take women upstairs with him. Sally, who was a mainstay of a local church, seemed to think that was "right proper" behavior for a man of thirty-odd years, and Mrs. Potter was glad to hear that Ken wasn't, apparently, behaving irresponsibly in this sexually dangerous age. She had wondered however, whether a young man like Ken might be working too hard and playing too little. His room at the crossroads put him right in the middle of all his many odd jobs, making it convenient for him to get to the ranches where he helped out in the owners' absences. But Mrs. Potter worried that by feeding his ambition with lots of hard work, Ken might also be starving his heart, which was how her own grandmother used to describe the type of man who found all of his pleasure in making money. *Type A's, we'd call them now,* Mrs. Potter thought. She'd been glad, really almost relieved, to hear from Ken himself that he was engaged to Linda Scarritt.

Mrs. Potter, curious though she was about the two men in the window, virtuously drove on to the grocery store when the light turned green.

By the time she bought her supplies and greeted everyone she knew and fielded their questions about the search party and whether or not it was true the National Guard was being brought in and was it true they found a mutilated corpse of a cow in one of her pastures and did she think they'd been kidnapped for ransom and did she have a ransom note yet . . . by the time she dealt with all of that, and then drove back home, and stopped for her mail at the front gate . . . and paused at Juanita's to hear "no news" and accept a cup of cinammon-flavored coffee and apple strudel and then drive on up to her own home . . .

By *that* time, it was lunchtime.

As she prepared a bacon, lettuce, and tomato sandwich to go with a glass of orange juice and potato chips, Mrs. Potter glanced out her kitchen window to watch a single-engine, high-wing airplane traverse the air above her fields. The sign on its fuselage, when it passed close enough for her to read it, said ARIZONA AERIALS.

Mrs. Potter was watching the plane disappear to the east, over El Bizcocho, The Biscuit, when she became aware of a small cloud of dust visible out of the corner of her right eye. She turned fully toward it, and squinted. It appeared somebody was coming up her road in a pickup truck. Maybe one of the searchers, with news. . . .

Her heart was already pounding with nervous anticipation when she saw that it was a black truck with a capital *C* and a "lazy" capital *U* on its side, painted on its doors. C Lazy U.

"Oh, good heavens, it's Jed."

Her stomach did a double back flip.

Mrs. Potter dropped the crusts of her sandwich into the sink and quickly washed them down the disposal. Her hands seemed to work—or not work—independently of her as they rinsed out her glass, put her dishes in the dishwasher, sponged down the counter, dried themselves on a towel. The towel slipped from her hands and she had to pick it up once and then twice before it stayed on the towel rack. Her hands flew to her hair to tuck in stray strands.

She raced out of the kitchen and back down the long hallway to her bedroom to check her appearance—"Oh, dear, isn't there any makeup to erase the years?"—and to apply a fresh dab of lip gloss. "You'd think I'd never met a man before!"

In fact, there had been only two men in her life with whom she had considered herself to be in love, and one of them was walking up to her front door this very minute. The other one was Lew. Since his death, there'd been infrequent escorts, even a blind date now and then—usually a disaster!—and once or twice a mild romance. But none of those men had inspired in her the same depth of feeling she'd experienced with her husband or with her first love. Compared to all those good years of marriage to Lew, those few months of infatuation with Jed White ought to seem as nothing, she reminded herself. That being the case, her heart must be pounding so hard only because she'd practically run down the hall to her bathroom.

"I wonder what he'll look like?"

He'd been such a slim, strikingly handsome boy.

Was he slender still? Certainly he would have filled out in the way that men did starting in their early twenties, and it would be unfair to expect him still to boast the erect carriage and slim torso of an eighteen-year-old. Mrs. Potter touched her own hips, clad in their dark trousers, to remind herself that times pass and figures change. . . .

She heard the doorbell ring.

A terrible thought occurred to her.

What if he'd been lifted and tucked and spa'd into skinny, golden perfection?

"I'll look like his mother!"

Mrs. Potter, with her heart still doing its infuriating imitation of an eighteen-year-old in love, went to answer the door.

CHAPTER 14

"Hello, Andy."

Why, he looks like himself, she decided, having only at the moment of seeing him suddenly remembered him clearly. Tall, slightly stooped, yes, and maybe a hint of a paunch on an otherwise thin frame, and his hair a fairly even mixture of brown and gray, as her own was rather evenly blond and silver. His features were somewhat bony, just as she remembered him, and there was that lovely patrician nose, long, sharp, pinched at the end. His hazel eyes were still water-clear, sharp and keen. *Those eyes were one of the reasons I first fell in love with him,* Mrs. Potter thought with a start. All the boys in Harrington, Iowa—all those Dutch, Anglo-Saxon, German, and Scandinavian boys—had blue eyes. A young man with hazel eyes and with that strange and wonderful New England accent, one who had gone to an honest-to-goodness prep school, had bowled her over. He had seemed a beautiful alien being, she thought, and so he rather appeared now, standing there on her doorstep, as if it were the most natural thing in the world for his spaceship to have landed in Arizona.

He held out both of his hands to her, and she took them.

"I always hoped you'd look like this," he said.

Almost as quickly as it took her to say, "Come in, Jed," he was seated casually at her kitchen table, one long leg crossed elegantly over the other, his hands clasped easily in front of him on the table, his well-groomed head turning as he watched her begin her preparations to make chili. It all seemed as easy as if it were, indeed, only yesterday. In that short time, she had already promised him a tour of the compound and the ranch if he wanted it—which he eagerly seemed to—but for now, she told him, she had to think about company coming, and thank goodness he was here now to keep *her* company!

At first, their questions and answers tumbled over each other like clothes in a dryer.

"I just can't believe you're here, Jed."

"My excuse really *is* business. But how'd *you* end up here, Andy?"

"So funny to be called Andy again! Well, as to how we got here, it's a long story, but basically we fell in love with the valley . . . what businesss is it that you're in, Jed?"

"Electrical design. So you bought this place, what, about twenty years ago?"

"I'm just amazed that you know that. Are you an engineer, Jed?"

"Yes, we design electrical systems. It's a company I started a few years back. J. H. White Research. You know, I can't take too much credit for the investigative work of keeping track of you, Andy. Your husband was so successful, I couldn't help but follow his career path—as they say—in the newspapers. There were times when it seemed as if Lew Potter's name was in the *Wall Street Journal* every other week. I felt awfully bad for you when I read he had died, almost sent you a note then, but I didn't want to intrude, wasn't sure you'd remember me—"

"Oh, Jed, you didn't really think—"

"Well, I just didn't know."

"What about you? Are you married, widowed, divorced? I suppose that's none of my business, but it feels like we're old friends—"

"You think so too? It's wonderful how we—how people can just take up where they left off years ago. Well, I'm divorced. About five years now. I wonder if you knew her family, her maiden name was . . ."

At first she felt self-conscious under his gaze. It was equally difficult to resist the temptation to stare at him. A small point, but she liked the way he dressed. Brown flannel shirt and some kind of neat, serviceable tan trousers and good walking shoes. And what if he'd come in a plaid Western shirt, polyester pants, fancy cowboy boots, a turquoise bolo in place of a tie, all this after a few days on a dude ranch? she wondered. Would it have mattered? Soon, she was so busy cooking and chatting and reminiscing that she utterly forgot how she might appear in slacks from behind, or whether every strand of her hair was tucked into its knot, or whether either of them was recalling the lithe, firm-skinned youths of their past.

Jed expressed astonishment at the very idea of her chili recipe.

"*How* many ingredients, Andy?"

"Twenty-seven, believe it or not."

"That's amazing. And here, I always thought chili basically had about four ingredients."

"It usually does, the way most people make it if they're not real chili aficionados. Chili *nuts*, some might say. What are your four ingredients, Jed? Beans, I suppose?"

"And hamburger."

"Oh, good, you're a hamburger man; not everybody is, you know. Some folks just seem to want beans and grease with crackers and hot peppers to wash it down. What's your third ingredient?"

"Tomato sauce."

"And chili powder?"

"Uh-huh, I do like chili that's hot enough to fire a missile."

"Well, I'm going to fix two batches of this, so I'll make one pot hot enough for the likes of you, and the other pot a little milder for the rest of us. Am I getting the impression that you cook, Jed?"

"Nothing over four ingredients."

Mrs. Potter laughed and he did too.

"Here." She walked across the kitchen and handed him her *Country Friends' Cookbook*. "If you'd like to make yourself useful you can read all twenty-seven ingredients to me as I set them out."

Mrs. Potter practically knew them by heart, especially as she had shopped for them that very morning, but she also knew from experience that participation made cooking fun, whether your cooking partner was a grandchild or a gentleman caller.

"Ahem." Jed cleared his throat in an amusingly officious manner. In a dramatically sonorous voice, he announced, "One pound of dry pinto beans."

"Check! Actually, they're not dry any longer. I soaked them overnight, and then I cooked them this morning until they were tender."

"Why"—Jed feigned an impressed astonishment—"that's just what it says to do with them, right here." He thumped the open cookbook with the flat of his hand—which had, Mrs. Potter couldn't help but notice, the same long, thin, aristocratic-looking fingers she had admired so when she was eighteen years old. "It seems to me," he said, reading on, "that calling water an ingredient is stretching this 'twenty-seven' thing a bit far."

Mrs. Potter laughed again, and thought what a pleasure it was to have the company of an intelligent, amusing man in her kitchen. "Just read the ingredients, Jed. There'll be no editorial comment, please."

"Yes, ma'am. Half a cup of butter or margarine."

"Check."

"Which?"

She glanced up at him. "Butter."

His pleased smile was its own editorial comment.

"Two medium onions, chopped."

She murmured "check" to all the next twenty-three ingredients, and then doubled all of them in order to make two batches.

"One seven-ounce can of diced green chilis.

"Two cloves of garlic, minced.

"Three pounds of chopped sirloin.

"One pound of pork sausage.

"Two tablespoons of flour.

"One one-pound can of baked beans.

"Why do you need two kinds of beans? The beans in baked beans are pea beans, aren't they?" When she affirmed that, he said, "Do they really taste all that different from pinto beans?"

"You *are* a research scientist, aren't you? I don't really know, Jed, but I don't believe I care to run that experiment today."

"One four-ounce can of pimiento.

"Two thirty-ounce cans of tomatoes.

"Three quarters of a cup of chopped celery.

"A half pound of sliced fresh mushrooms.

"A half cup of chopped sweet red pepper.

"A half cup of chopped green pepper."

As she listened and "checked," Mrs. Potter decided that he had just the *nicest* voice for reading aloud, one of those voices of which it was said the owner could read the phone book and be entertaining.

"One nine-ounce can of pitted ripe olives, chopped.

"A half cup of minced parsley.

"One twelve-ounce bottle of chili sauce.

"One tablespoon of salt.

"One tablespoon of garlic salt.

"Two teaspoons of black pepper.

"One tablespoon of chopped cilantro.

"What's cilantro, anyway?" Jed inquired.

"Funny you'd ask." Mrs. Potter smiled to herself. "It's coriander."

"I see. What's coriander?"

"An herb. Here, smell."

She held a leaf under his nose, and he sniffed. Then he took it out of her hand and stuck it in his mouth and chewed it.

"Hot," he commented. "But cool."

Mrs. Potter handed him a napkin so that he could spit it out, but then saw that he'd swallowed it. She rushed to the sink to fill a glass of water, which he gratefully accepted and drank. This was fun, she thought, and wasn't it amazing that his curiosity seemed to be snagged on some of the same odd little edges of life that amused her?

"One tablespoon of oregano.

"Two to four tablespoons of chili powder, to taste.

"One pint sour cream.

"*Sour cream?*"

"Yes, I'll spoon a dollop onto each helping when I serve it. It cuts the spiciness and the heat, and adds a lovely tang. You'll be surprised how refreshing it is."

"I'll be surprised all right."

There was a little silence as each of them seemed to absorb the rather natural fact that she had apparently just invited him to stay for supper and he had apparently and just as easily accepted.

Mrs. Potter said, or rather, blurted, "You'll try it, though?"

"I don't know." He acted doubting, teasing. "Sour cream?"

"I tried steamed clams, remember."

"Certainly an act of greater courage."

"It seemed so at the time."

He closed the cookbook with a decisive slap. "All right, I'll do it."

"There's a brave lad. But don't close that yet, Jed, we've only put the ingredients out on the counter. We still have to *make* this chili."

Mrs. Potter melted butter in her favorite cast-iron skillet, then sautéed the onions, chilis, and garlic until the onions were soft. She added the chopped sirloin and cooked it all over a moderate heat until the meat browned.

In a separate pan, she browned the sausage and poured off the fat.

She added the sausage to the steak and vegetables.

Over that, she sprinkled the flour, and stirred to blend.

"The best chili tip I ever heard came from a friend of mine on Nantucket, of all places," she told Jed. "She said to add a little fresh grated orange peel to chili con carne, so now I always do. Most people seem to like it."

"And that's the twenty-seventh ingredient?"

"It is. All good cooks add a mystery ingredient to their best recipes. So when somebody asks for the recipe, they somehow neglect to include that one little extra ingredient. Which means, of course, that nobody can ever exactly duplicate their successes."

"So *that's* why I always hear people say"—Jed mimicked a woman's voice so well that Mrs. Potter laughed out loud—"Why, Julia, I made lemon meringue pie from your recipe the other night, but Claude said it just didn't taste as good as *Julia's*. I *know* I followed your recipe exactly. What do you think I did *wrong*?"

"To which Julia will innocently reply, 'Why, I can't imagine, Gertrude, I'm sure I wrote down everything that goes in it! I know *I've* never had a bit of trouble with it myself.' "

"Trade secrets."

"Industrial espionage," Mrs. Potter rejoined, in a stage whisper.

Jed held up his right hand, palm forward. "I swear not to tell about the orange peel."

"Unless you're tortured, of course."

"Well, yes, if they stick needles under my fingernails, I'll squeal."

"That's what I used to say to Lew when he'd talk to me about *his* trade secrets."

"He was a lucky man, Andy."

She turned her back to hide her pink face, and transferred the meat mixture to a cast-iron Dutch oven into which she poured the pinto beans, along with the remaining ingredients, except the sour cream. She brought it all to a boil and then left it to simmer for a half hour.

"Come on, Jed, you can help me put things out, if you will. Let's see, we'll need bowls for the chili, and we'd better stack those in the kitchen, along with the soup spoons, and we'll need my extra-large napkins. I have some that my friend Susan made especially for me, and they're big enough even for cowboy-size laps . . ."

He followed her into the dining room as she thought out loud.

"Serving bowls for crackers, tall glasses for beer and iced tea, iced tea spoons, mugs for coffee, creamers and sugar bowls, salt and pepper, and we might as well go ahead and set a couple of extra bottles of Tabasco right out on the table, along with a bowl for extra jalapeño peppers. I know it's hard to believe, some of these men will want their chili even hotter than I made that pot for you, the missile-launcher pot. . . ."

Soon they had Grandmother Andrews's trestle table in the dining room and the round table in the kitchen all set for a buffet.

And through it all they talked . . .

And talked, and laughed, and talked, and there were a few moments when Jed said something so amusing or so interesting that he almost made her forget about her worries and her fears.

"Cynthia," he told her, when Mrs. Potter asked him to repeat his ex-wife's name. "Her maiden name was Satherwaite, an old family from Boston. Remember when things like that used to matter?"

"Do you mean the 'old family' part or the 'Boston' part?"

Jed laughed. "Both, I suppose."

"Yes, there was a time when things like that impressed me, and I guess they still might if I were still eighteen." She paused, in the laying out of her friend Susan's gigantic print cotton napkins, and smiled at him. "You, for instance, seemed so very sophisticated to a little girl from Iowa. Your accent, your appearance"—Mrs. Potter raised her eyebrows dramatically —"your *prep* school."

"I'm afraid I was a little overimpressed with that myself."

"It didn't show, Jed."

"Oh, you were just blinded by love, Andy."

She smiled at him again. "I was, it's true."

"So was I. For my part, I was bowled over by your Iowa farm girl honesty and your openness, not to mention your big innocent blue eyes." He smiled back at her. "Never quite got over it."

Mrs. Potter suddenly found a napkin that needed her full attention to refold. Jed started telling her what he hadn't gotten around to earlier, about his marriage, his family, his divorce.

"I met Cynthia about three years after graduation, and we married within the year. We had Haj a couple of years later."

"Haj?"

"Harry J."

Mrs. Potter was just on the verge of saying, "So he'd be about thirty-six by now?" when Jed hurried into speech again, and she was relieved she hadn't had the chance to inquire. Jed and Cynthia's only child had died in Vietnam in the closing days of the war. He'd gone straight from Harvard Medical School to the army surgical corps, and had served only two months of his duty when the helicopter in which he was riding with wounded soldiers on board had crashed in the jungle.

"We were lucky," Jed said, in a quiet and steady voice. "His friends recovered his body and we were able to bury him at home. Cynthia blamed me for his death, because I didn't try to dissuade him from enlisting. I think she finally divorced me when she just couldn't stand the sight of me anymore. Being a reminder of Haj, you see. She may be right. At the time, I thought he was a grown man who had earned the privilege to make his own decisions."

"You couldn't have stopped him, Jed."

"No, and I couldn't have draped beads over him and stuck flowers in his hair and turned him into a hippie, either. I know that. Rationally. But in my heart, I want to go back in time and try to talk him out of going. I want to listen to his mother. Cynthia was terrified when he left, convinced we'd never see him again. It's no wonder she never forgave me. I was so proud of him, my handsome, smart young doctor son going off to war, that I nearly cheered for him on the day he left. Oh, I'd change it all, if I could." He managed a lopsided smile. "I'll even go so far as to say that I wish I had been a radical Democrat in those days instead of a conservative Republican. I wish I had raised Haj in a household that voted for Eugene McCarthy, so there wouldn't have been any way for him to consider going to war. I would change everything about the way I was—the way I am—if it would bring him back again."

"I'm so sorry, Jed, I can only imagine the pain."

He bowed his head for a moment, but when he looked up again his hazel eyes were clear and calm. "It's been rough. Never goes away. Never should, I guess. Breaks my heart every time I read in the newspaper about somebody's child being dead or missing. I know how they feel. It's like reliving it every time."

"Then this"—Mrs. Potter motioned vaguely with her hand, as if to encompass the entire situation at her ranch—"is especially painful for you to witness."

"You have to find that girl, Andy."

"You understand what her family's going through, don't you?"

"It's an unbelievable hell, you can't imagine. No, I take that back, you're one of the few people I've ever known who actually can put yourself in another person's shoes. I always liked that about you, it was like admiring somebody who was really good at"—Jed laughed suddenly, and Mrs. Potter wondered why—"poetry!" Now she understood, and smiled over at him. "One of those talents I didn't have, heaven knows."

"They were lovely poems, Jed." There was laughter in Mrs. Potter's voice as she said it. "At least, I loved them."

"They were heartfelt, I'll say that for them."

"I probably still have them somewhere."

"No! You don't, really?"

Mrs. Potter noticed that in spite of his horrified amusement, he looked a bit pink at the top of his lovely, aristocratic-looking ears. *Stop that!* she said to herself. *Leave the man's ears out of this.* "Anyway, it sounds to me as if you have learned to put yourself in another person's shoes, judging by your sympathy for Linda's family."

"Andy?"

"Yes, Jed?"

"Wouldn't you really rather be out there helping to look for her?"

Mrs. Potter admitted it with a nod.

"Well, you did promise me a ranch tour . . ."

"Oh, Jed," she exclaimed, having instantly comprehended his meaning. "Thank you. I haven't wanted to go out by myself because I'm always afraid that if the car breaks down I'll be in a real fix out there in the pastures, miles from home. And I thought I could truly be of more help by staying here to field phone calls and fix the chili. But yes, I hate being so passive. I really want to get out there and look for them everywhere I can think to look. Would you really go with me?"

"It would make me feel better too."

Mrs. Potter understood what he meant, and that it had something to do with his own lost boy.

CHAPTER 15

In her four-wheel-drive vehicle, with Mrs. Potter driving and Jed in the passenger's seat, he said it was her turn to talk. He wanted to know more about Lew and about her children; he wanted to know "the long story" about how she'd ended up in Arizona.

"And Maine and Iowa," she added.

"So tell me everything you've done every minute of the day for the last forty years. Don't skip anything. Tell me what you love, tell me what you hate, tell me what interests you and makes you laugh and what you do with your spare time, and whether you have any spare time, and tell me what you read and did you do those beautiful needlepoints in your house, and—"

Mrs. Potter took her hand off the gear shift long enough to hold it up, as she laughed, to halt his flow of questions.

"One of my daughters writes," she teased him, "and she tells me that a cardinal rule of writing is 'show, don't tell.'"

"I can't wait that long, Andy. You're going to have to tell me. We've wasted too many years already. You'll just have to tell me some things, to catch me up to this moment. In the meantime, you *are* showing me"—he suddenly turned his face toward the window. Mrs. Potter thought, but could not be entirely sure, that the phrase with which he ended that sentence was—"what I've missed."

"I wish," she said, abruptly, "we could climb to the top of El Bizcocho."

"El what?"

She pointed. "See that sandstone formation, how it looks like a big round biscuit? I'm told that from the top of that, you can see all of Wind Valley in every direction. Ricardo says it gives you a perspective on things, shows you the topography in its proper scale . . ."

"That's what I'd like to have, all right, perspective. Actually, I think age has imparted a bit of that to me, although—Andy?"

Her thoughts elsewhere, she didn't answer him.

"Andy, what's the matter?"

"It isn't '*Elb*,' it's '*El b*.' And what was the number beside it? Five, I think. *El b: 5*. Circled. As if it was important. I wonder if Ricardo was supposed to meet someone at El Bizcocho at five o'clock. And would that be morning or evening?"

"I suppose you know what you're talking about, Andy? It's all Czechoslovakian to me."

"Morning, I'll bet. And that's why he left so early, with Linda following him." She turned toward her passenger. "Jed, who did my foreman make an appointment to meet at El Bizcocho at five o'clock on the morning he disappeared? Did he ever get there? What happened to him there, if he did?"

"Croatian."

"What?"

"The foreign language you're speaking, which I hope you're going to translate so that I may continue to converse with you."

Mrs. Potter put the car in reverse, backed it up, wheeled around to the east, and said, "Sorry. I'll explain as we go there."

"Go where?"

"An old Czechoslovakian landmark, Jed. Better known to you tourists as The Biscuit."

Jed insisted on opening and closing all the gates for her.

"They're called Texas gates," she told him, when he asked about the triple strands of barbed wire strung between two light end poles. All he had to do was drop the gate to the ground while she drove through and then pick the gate up again and refasten it before climbing back into the car with her.

"You'll get your exercise today, Jed."

"Good. I need it," he said, with a hand on the paunch that seemed to Mrs. Potter virtually to have disappeared in the last couple of hours. Maybe she'd only imagined it. He really was wonderfully slim and vigorous for a man of his—their—age, she thought, and was glad there wasn't any roll of flab at her own waistline in spite of the fact that it still felt too tight after her weeks away from the ranch. "I've never seen white cattle before, what are these fellows?"

"A mix of Charolais, which is a French breed as you may tell by the name, and Brahman. They get the grayish-white color from the Charolais. The Brahman blood is what gives them that slight hump between their shoulders and that funny-looking wattle under their chins. I think it makes them look rather wise, myself. Or foolish, I'm not sure which.

Rather like some old men I've known. They get those long droopy ears from the Brahman side of the family."

"The old men, or the bulls?"

Mrs. Potter laughed out loud, which produced a pleased smile on her companion's face. She pointed to an enormous white bull who stared aggressively at them from beyond a fence in the next pasture. He had a confident, kingly bearing, a noble brow, and short white curls above wide-set eyes.

"There's our only full-blooded Charolais bull, Jed. I think I keep him just because he's so gorgeous. Ricardo says that Charolais bulls make him think of Roman emperors. He says they only lack a toga, casually tossed over one of those great shoulders, to be hailed as Caesars."

"I'm impressed by your knowledge, Andy."

"Don't be. I have only the most superficial knowledge about cattle and ranching. If you want to hear it from an expert, you'll have to talk to Ricardo." Mrs. Potter paused for a moment, took a breath, swallowed hard. Jed suddenly reached over and placed his left hand on top of her hand on the gear shift. She felt enormously comforted by his sympathetic touch, so much so, in fact, that she nearly burst into tears. Only iron self-control—fueled by a horror of disgracing herself in front of him—kept her from displaying the fear and sadness that had lodged, seemingly permanently, beneath her breastbone. In a few moments, she felt sufficiently in control of her emotions to continue. Jed removed his hand from atop hers, but the warmth of his touch lingered on her skin. "I don't have any illusions about my abilities as a cowboy or a ranch manager. I'll tell you, Jed, I would be at such a loss without him."

"Like losing Lew all over again?"

"Oh, no, not like that, but it would be an awful blow, and to a lot more people than myself." She told Jed about Ricardo's near-legendary standing in the community, about his status as the best cowboy and one of the finest men in the valley, how he knew everything and everybody. She related stories of his generosity to their neighbors, of the helping hand he'd lent to everybody from Bandy's "nephews" to landowners like Charlie Watt and the McHenrys. . . .

"You don't mean Reynolds McHenry?"

Mrs. Potter glanced in surprise at Jed. "You know him?"

He didn't answer immediately. Finally, he seemed to come to some decision. When he turned his face toward her again, there was a bemused smile on it. "He's the business I'm here to do."

"What?" Mrs. Potter felt a stirring of unease. "Are you saying that Reynolds McHenry is your potential client for J. H. White Research?"

"Yes, I didn't dream you'd know him."

"Jed, surely you can see by now that everybody knows everybody else in Wind Valley. I couldn't possibly *not* know Reynolds. Or Marj, for that matter."

"His wife."

"Yes."

She felt Jed's gaze on her, studying her, it seemed.

"Why," he said, "do I get the feeling you're holding out on me?"

Mrs. Potter was taken aback by his perception. But she didn't want to gossip about her neighbors, particularly when it might do them actual harm in terms of a business deal that was none of *her* business. And besides, she didn't have anything concrete to say, nothing she could prove, because nobody really knew what the McHenrys were up to on their exceedingly private property. So she ducked and feinted, saying lightly, "I'd say *you're* the one who's holding back!"

"Well, remember those industrial secrets that Lew used to share with you?"

"Yes."

"The ones you promised not to reveal unless you were tortured?"

"Like the orange peel in my chili, yes."

"I think you're about to hear some more of those secrets, Andy. This business of mine with the McHenrys is very hush-hush. I'd appreciate it if you wouldn't mention the connection to anybody. We're talking about the possibility of a merger, and so it's important that no word get out. White Research went public a few years ago, and so any leak of this might affect our stock. I was hoping to fly in and get this business accomplished and then fly back out again without anybody being the wiser."

"Well, rest assured that I couldn't possibly break this confidence, Jed. If I did, you might tell somebody about the grated orange peel."

"You bet I would."

"Ingrate."

He groaned at the pun, as she'd hoped he would, because Mrs. Potter wanted very much to distract this perceptive, intelligent man from the unhappiness she felt over the knowledge that he might be involved in some scheme with the owners of the mysterious Highlands Ranch, with its guardhouse at the gate and its electrified fence all around. Should she warn him, she wondered? But of what? Anyway, it would be slanderous to do that, as she knew of no ill-doing on the part of the McHenrys.

"That's how you ended up at the C Lazy U, isn't it?"

"Yes, the McHenrys got me a reservation there."

Begging the question, Mrs. Potter thought, as to why they didn't put him up at their own place. Apparently they didn't want Jed around any more than they wanted other visitors.

"They've invited me to their ranch for dinner," he said.

So much for that theory, she thought. "Really? How nice."

He glanced at her, and she was afraid she detected a glint of curiosity in his eyes. He was too *damned* sensitive to the nuances of what she said and how she said it! After an absence of forty years, how could he know her so well?

"Tomorrow night," he added. "Want to come with me?" With a mischievous twinkle, he added, "You'd be my cover. Make it look like a strictly social event, one couple having a simple home-cooked meal with another couple. And the McHenrys will undoubtedly think more highly of me if I show up with you on my arm."

"Well, I don't know about that," said Mrs. Potter, and then added firmly, because she was dying to go, just to get a gander at the inside of the McHenry estate and to eavesdrop on Jed's business with Reynolds, "But yes, I'd love to, thank you very much."

Depending, of course, as she didn't have to say, on Ricardo and Linda.

"Jed," she said as casually as she dared. "What *is* Reynolds's business?"

"I'll get out and get this gate."

And suddenly Jed was out of the car and gone, before he'd answered her. And then he was back in the car, waxing lyrical about the beauty of her ranch, and her great good fortune in having it, and asking all sorts of intelligent questions about the valley, and its economic base and its fertility and its population, so there wasn't any tactful moment for Mrs. Potter to return to the subject of the McHenrys' mysterious business, which seemed to earn them so very much money from no visible source. Maybe she'd find out tomorrow night.

El Bizcocho loomed larger through her windshield.

As they drew near, Mrs. Potter saw that large birds were circling, swooping, and dipping midway down the mountainside.

The arroyo that cut between El Bizcocho and the government-owned mountains to the east was dry in spite of last night's storm, which she knew had probably flooded it. Mrs. Potter was looking down the arroyo, squinting against the glare of the afternoon, when she made out the vision of a man on horseback. At first her heart leapt: *Ricardo?* She braked the car to a stop to await the approach of the man.

"How do you know it's a man?" Jed asked, when she told him why they had stopped. "I can't see that far from here."

"Something about the set of his shoulders, I think, his height . . ."

As the lone rider advanced, his appearance felt familiar to her.

Mrs. Potter recognized the horse first.

"Palo Alto," she said, naming the animal, which identified the man. "It's Ken Ryerson." She explained that Ken was her part-time hired hand, who served as a sort of second-in-command to Ricardo. "When he has time. He also hires himself out to other ranchers to help out or fill in when they're gone. We've got a lot of absentee owners in the valley. I guess most of the locals would count me among them. Ken would probably like to be a ranch manager like Ricardo, but those slots are few and far between."

She was talking too much, she knew, but she was anxious, so anxious, watching Ken ride inexorably toward them.

"His first loyalty should be to us, because we're his primary employer, but Ricardo gives him plenty of leeway to find other work to support himself, too, because a young man with any ambition couldn't possibly hope to have a family just on what we pay him."

Mrs. Potter thought of Ken's hopes of marrying Linda Scarritt, and nearly told Jed about it until she remembered that that news had been imparted to her in confidence.

"He's not like our other hired hand, Bandy Esposito. Bandy gets his lodging free, mainly because he always has, but a ranch this size can't afford to provide that for every employee. So Ken's got the ordinary expenses that everybody has, although he gets more than a few perks— sides of beef, access to our propane gas tank, and I don't know what else from his other employers." Actually, she knew that Ricardo had been growing increasingly exasperated by Ken's other commitments and that the young man was, in Ricardo's view, all too often over helping out the Amorys or the McHenrys or somebody else in the valley, instead of here at Las Palomas when Ricardo wanted him. Juanita had hinted at the same frustration last night.

Mrs. Potter watched Ken riding ever closer to them, and she recalled other conversations with Ricardo.

"You spoil him," Mrs. Potter had chided her manager, and suspected his wife scolded him also. "You let him come and go as he pleases, you let him off to fulfill his other responsibilities, while you take up the slack here —which you're getting too old to do, *compadre*—and now he thinks he can get away with murder."

"I don't want to hold a young man down," was Ricardo's defense, "but all right, if he gets too busy with his other jobs, I'll tell him he'll have to choose, either cut back on his outside employment or quit his job here. I'm not about to hire a second man to help do the job that one man ought to be doing for me." Having Linda on the ranch eased the strain; she was an excellent cowhand and slipped easily into the holes Bandy and Ken left in the operation. Mrs. Potter didn't think that an ambitious young man like Ken Ryerson would be satisfied to continue as everybody's hired hand for the rest of his life. Not like Bandy.

The horseman was approaching slowly, his horse picking his way carefully. When they drew nearer, Mrs. Potter was the first to see they were carrying a burden, one that was wrapped in black tarpaulin and slung lengthwise across Palo Alto's wide rump.

"Oh, no," she breathed, "no, please."

Jed reached out his hand to her, and she grabbed it.

CHAPTER 16

Mrs. Potter got out of her car on wobbly knees, and let Jed lead her by the hand along a narrow path through the cactus and boulders to meet the rider and his burden.

Ken Ryerson pulled his horse to a halt in front of them, without even a curious glance at the stranger. "I found him a couple hundred yards down the canyon."

Mrs. Potter gently freed her hand. She managed to say, "What about Linda?"

Ken shook his head.

"Their horses?"

Again, he shook his head.

Mrs. Potter raised her right arm and pointed midway up the slope of El Bizcocho. The two men turned their heads to look at the birds she had noticed before. They were still swooping and soaring. Ken nodded again as he acknowledged what they recognized: the ugly, enormous black creatures were vultures.

"I'll ride up there and take a look, but I'll have to leave his body here."

Finally, he glanced, incuriously, dully, at the man who stood just behind Mrs. Potter, and she managed to introduce them, though her throat was swollen with grief. Jed moved quickly to help Ken lower Ricardo's body from the back of Palo Alto onto the ground.

"How did he die?" Mrs. Potter wiped her cheeks with the backs of her hands, but tears kept falling, as if she had no control over them.

Ken looked up at her and shrugged. "Dunno. He's pretty beat up from the fall or the flood carrying him down the valley. Hard to tell what got him." He was soon back atop his horse, and heading toward the lower slopes of El Bizcocho.

Mrs. Potter and Jed stood guard over the body on the ground, both of them silent except for the sound of her weeping. She couldn't bear the thought of leaving Ricardo's body alone under its tarp, looking so forsaken, like something of no value tossed aside by people who didn't care. Feeling kin to women through the ages, Mrs. Potter sensed that somebody needed to stand near the body, to guard it, to show some respect for the remains of a great man. Jed waited with her, his neck craned, too, as they watched Ken Ryerson wind up the steep and narrow paths of El Bizcocho.

She felt Jed's hand touch her shoulder.

"Andy, I'm so very sorry."

Her own hand went up to press his and she turned her face gratefully up to his, but didn't speak, as she knew she couldn't yet, without breaking down in tears.

Jed put an arm around her, and she leaned into him.

Ken was out of their sight by the time he reached the vicinity where the vultures circled, but they heard his rifle shot when he scattered the birds, and they saw the vultures lift off and fly away with their great wings flapping, their voices screaming furious protests at being interrupted at their feast.

"Patches is up there," Ken informed them when he pulled his horse up in front of them again. Mrs. Potter's knees buckled and Jed used both of his hands to steady her. She'd been so afraid Ken was going to find Linda's body. Palo Alto moved restlessly, seeming to sense his rider's emotions. "No sign of Linda or Taco. I didn't ride on up, but I took a good look. From the way the rocks are scattered and some cactus are broken, I'd say Patches did a houlihan up there."

"A houlihan?" Jed murmured.

Mrs. Potter found her voice, although it sounded strange to her, weak and far away. "Ranch lingo, Jed, for a fit of bucking. Can we get Patches down from there, Ken?"

"Nope," was the answer, uttered with an air of unarguable finality. "Not worth riskin' another man's life over. The buzzards'll be back. The earth'll clean him."

The earth will clean him. . . .

The homely phrase echoed in Mrs. Potter's heart.

She felt an eerie calm descending on her. Her tears ceased as silently and as abruptly as they'd started. There were things she had to do now. Things they all had to do. Ken must ride on to headquarters with the body. She must return Jed to her own home, and encourage him to drive back to the C Lazy U. She herself must then drive down the hill to inform Juanita and the Ortega children. The sheriff must be called, and she must inform the funeral home that she wished to pay for all arrangements.

"I think you ought to bring the search party over here," she said.

Ken handed the reins of his horse to Mrs. Potter, who took them in her right hand while she began to stroke Palo Alto's soft nose with her left. Ken climbed down from his horse and then loosened his rifle from its moorings behind his saddle. He cocked the rifle back, and propped the butt of it against his right leg. "I gotta tell you, Mrs. Potter, this don't make no sense. If Ricardo got bucked and killed, that's one thing. But that don't answer where Linda is." He walked several yards away from them and they watched him point the rifle high into the air.

At the first shot, Jed put his arm around Mrs. Potter's shoulders. When the second shot echoed through the canyon, Jed tightened his grip and she leaned into his side again. Ken's horse, superbly trained, didn't do anything more than flinch and whinny softly, though Mrs. Potter was only loosely holding his reins. The sound of the shot was still whining in their ears as Ken walked back. Jed helped him lift Ricardo's body back onto the horse and tie it securely behind after it was decided that that would be better than transferring his body to the car. While the men accomplished that, Mrs. Potter trudged back to her car. She got in on the driver's side again, put her hands on the wheel and lowered her forehead onto them.

But when Jed climbed in on the passenger's side again, her eyes were dry and clear and determined as she looked over at him.

"I'm awfully glad you're here, Jed."

He reached over and gave her hand a quick, comforting squeeze.

"There are things I have to tell somebody," she said.

"Tell me, Andy."

She swallowed. "I think Ricardo was murdered, Jed."

CHAPTER 17

Jed looked shocked, but that didn't stop her.

She told him about Ricardo calling her in Maine and asking her to come home two weeks early. She told him about Ricardo calling the Amorys, Steinbachs, McHenrys, Charlie Watt, and Che Thomas. And how Ricardo made those calls from her house instead of his own, in her office, at her desk, with her phone, and how he used one of her yellow notepads to list them. And about the notation that led her to believe he had an appointment to keep at El Bizcocho at five o'clock Sunday morning. And how he must have died sometime between then and Sunday night, because if he got bucked on El Bizcocho it was Sunday night's rain that washed him down the canyon. And how Linda would never have abandoned her grandfather unless something awful had happened to her as well. And how secretive he'd been, not even confiding in his wife, and about how he had leased the services of an aerial photography company. Telling it all to Jed was almost as helpful as summarizing it on one of her yellow pads. He listened intently, without question or comment, until she wound down. Then he simply asked, "What's your conclusion?"

"I think it was one of those people on his list. I believe he was going to meet one of them yesterday morning. Why there, and why five o'clock in the morning, I don't know."

"*Why*, Andy? Why would one of them kill him?"

She wondered if Jed thought she was crazy, or hysterical.

But that didn't stop her either.

"I think Ricardo suspected one of them of something, Jed, or he was a threat to one of them in some important way." She began to recite a litany that felt like a betrayal of her friends and neighbors. "There's Walt and Kathy Amory, for instance, who want to refinance their ranch through a bank in Nogales where Ricardo was chairman of the board, only they weren't going to get the loan because he was going to make sure the bank turned them down."

"So with him . . . gone . . ." Jed said carefully, "they'll get the money?"

"Possibly. I don't know. But that's not all. Kathy Amory is rumored to be having an affair with Gallway Steinbach, and I know that Ricardo made no secret of his disapproval of that relationship."

"But where's the motive there for any of them, Andy?"

"I don't know that either, I'm just throwing it out as one of the convolutions of the situation, Jed."

"Yes, I see, go on."

She glanced at him as she directed the car toward home. "Then we have your McHenrys."

"Not mine, Andy, although I may be theirs before the week is out."

"You mean they want to buy your company, it's that kind of merger?"

He nodded. "What's their motive?"

"Oh, probably none at all! I feel bad even suggesting the possibility. But, you see—oh, Lord, I wasn't going to mention this!—Marj and Rey are rather mysterious, even sinister figures here in the valley. They sit up there on the side of their mountain, surrounded by bodyguards and electric fences, and nobody knows *why*, Jed." She waited, pointedly, for him to offer some bit of inside information that might ease her suspicions. But when she looked over at him again, she saw that he had turned his face to the window and seemed only to be staring at the scenery. *Oh, Jed*, she thought, *are you part of their secrecy, do you know something you're not telling me?* Feeling suddenly alone and terribly sad, she couldn't speak until she forced herself to continue, and her voice quavered as though she might lose control of it at any second.

"I feel so bad saying anything against Che or Charlie, but there is the suggestion that Che appears to have more wealth than a dude ranch could produce. I suppose it's possible that Ricardo knew something incriminating about her source of income. . . ."

He had turned around to face her again once she got the conversation off the McHenrys. "Any idea what that might be?"

"None. And Charlie, well, there's always been his opposition to Ricardo helping shelter Mexicans who came over the border. Charlie would probably say that if anybody killed Ricardo, it was one of the illegals."

"Why would this Charlie person have any motive to kill him?"

"Again, I don't know. It's only another point of contention, if you will, and another person with whom Ricardo crossed swords. It just seems more than merely coincidental that that's true of nearly every person on his calling list, and that he was going to meet one of them the morning of the day he died, or at least, I think he was."

"But Andy, he got bucked off his horse. Not shot, not stabbed, not beaten up—"

"We don't know that, Jed."

He looked startled. "I guess we don't. Is that everybody who was on his list?"

"His wife, Juanita, but he had crossed her out, so I think we can too. And Ken, the cowboy you just met, and Bandy Esposito, who's another of our hands and who's been on this ranch longer than I have."

"Their motives?"

"Ken's very ambitious. And now the obvious thing for me to do is to offer Ricardo's job to him." Mrs. Potter couldn't go on for a few moments. She couldn't get out the words to tell Jed that Ken had another possible motive, too, which was the probability of Ricardo's opposition to his engagement to Linda. "Bandy," she said, after she had dabbed at her eyes and cleared her throat, "may be afraid that Ricardo was going to pension him off. Bandy is an old man who doesn't have any life but"— with her left hand, she gestured as though to encompass all that lay outside the vehicle—"this life."

"But what about the girl? If Ricardo was killed, do you think she's been kidnapped?"

It sounded so melodramatic, stated boldly like that, that Mrs. Potter felt almost embarrassed even to entertain these terrible thoughts. But she plunged on, trusting her instincts. "I have no idea about that, Jed, but I would suspect not, or we'd have heard from the kidnappers by now. No, I'm afraid that she's dead, too, and we'll find her body soon."

"Will anybody else think as you do?"

"If it turns out he was shot they will, although even then they may think it was hunters, and an accident. In any case, it may be better if most people *don't* think as I do."

"Yes, I see what you mean."

"You do?" She looked at him and discovered that he wasn't staring at her as if he thought she ought to be locked up. His gaze was full of intensity, yes, but his thoughts seemed to be right with her, keeping pace with her, understanding her. She began to feel less alone. "Really?"

"Absolutely, so the killer will think he . . . or she . . . got away with it. We'll have to talk to the sheriff, though, won't we? Or the highway patrol, or whatever it is you have around here?"

Mrs. Potter couldn't help but notice how easily he had slid into the plural *"We'll have to . . . won't we?"* and she didn't resist the pleasure of it. She needed a friend at this moment, and Jed was being a wonderful one indeed, sympathetic, attentive, helpful. The black hole inside her shrank back down to a size only big enough to contain her grief over Ricardo and her fear for Linda. Fate was such a funny thing. So odd for Jed to come along again, after forty years, right at this strange and terrible time; and how *right* for him to come along again, after forty years, at this time. . . .

"Yes," she agreed, and hoped she didn't place any emphasis on her next word, "we will. Jed, do you mind if I drop you off at my house? You can drive back to Che's place, can't you?"

"I'll wait at your house, if you don't mind."

She glanced at him. "Wait?"

"For you. You have to tell Ricardo's wife, don't you?"

She nodded, again amazed at his easy understanding. Jed seemed to know what she was going to say, what she was going to do, before she said it or did it.

"And I can't very well go with you," he continued. "They don't know me. I'd be an awful intrusion on their privacy. But I don't want to leave you alone, either, Andy. So I'll wait for you at your house, if that's all right. They're not the only ones who'll need the support of their friends today." He reached over to touch her hand again, only this time she reached out her own hand and grasped his. They clung together for a moment, before she withdrew her hand in order to shift gears.

Mrs. Potter wanted to say thank you, but once again she couldn't speak for fear of all the tears that might pour out with the words. She had a feeling, however, that she didn't need to say it. Jed knew. She managed to be practical instead. "Good. Perhaps you'd like to examine that list of Ricardo's while I'm gone. It's on a yellow pad on top of my desk, in that little study I showed you, to the left, off the front hall. There's still coffee in the pot, Jed." She hesitated. Now here came a test of a man's good intentions: "And if you wouldn't mind, I'd appreciate it if you would check the chili pots. Give them a stir, make sure the burners aren't too hot, I don't want it to stick and burn."

His smile was quick and warm. "I think I can do that."

She let him out at her front door, told him where to locate the "secret" key, and then she bravely drove on down the hill to the Ortegas'.

The search for Linda "Ortega" Scarritt continued all the rest of that Monday. Mrs. Potter stayed for hours with the grieving Ortega family while Ricardo's body was carried away to be examined by police and doctors. "It looks as if he was bucked," Mrs. Potter carefully, gently, informed Juanita. "It appears that Patches fell halfway down El Bizcocho and that Ricardo fell on to the bottom and then the flash floods carried his body down the arroyo."

Once, having stepped outside the house to escape the smoke from the cigarettes of visitors, Mrs. Potter overhead Sheriff Ben Lightfeather say to Ken Ryerson: "Dammit, Ken, I wish you'd left him where you found him, it's against all procedure to move a body like that. You should have left him for us to examine on the site." And she heard Ken's reply: "There wouldn't have been anything left of him if I had, Ben. You saw him. Something'd already been at him, coyotes, probably."

She knew then why Ken had refused to allow anyone—even Juanita, who had demanded and pleaded before she was led back into her house by her daughters—to remove the tarp from around Ricardo's body until the sheriff arrived and took over.

The two men didn't appear to know how close behind them she stood.

"Well, I don't think we're going to find a bullet in him," the sheriff said. "The man died falling down that mountain. But we better get somebody out to examine that damned horse, see if there's a bullet in *him*. Some blind hunter probably took the horse for a deer. This search for the girl has got to get serious now. I'll get you all the assistance I can, Ken. But my personal opinion," the sheriff added, "is that you'll find her body washed downstream too."

Mrs. Potter's heart went out to Ken. She saw his chin come up stubbornly, and his tone was gruff when he said, "Linda was horseback."

"So?" the sheriff retorted. "You know some of these gully washers are strong enough to move boulders, much less a little ol' girl and a horse. They'd float like rafts on a stream. You have your searchers look farther downstream, Ken, that's where you'll find them, sure as shootin'."

The young cowboy stared off in stony silence.

Mrs. Potter slipped quietly back into the Ortega house.

The volunteers—now aided by the sheriff's people—did look downstream, until the sun slid down the far side of the western range of mountains at the other end of Wind Valley. They combed every precipitous inch of El Bizcocho and all the acreage around it on every side. They found what looked like ricochet shots off boulders, right up where Patches had done his houlihan, which confirmed the local opinion about hunters, but they found no sign of Linda or Taco.

It took Arizona Aerials, flying at five hundred feet between two mountains, to sight the young girl's horse in an isolated mountain pasture.

"Ken took five of us men out to that far pasture with him to round up that horse," Charlie Watt quietly told Mrs. Potter after they'd all straggled in for her chili. "We searched for Linda for as long as the light held. We found her saddle and bridle, Genia."

"Oh, Charlie!" Mrs. Potter's hands leapt to her mouth and her heart to her throat. "Where *is* she?"

"I wish I knew. We had to practically drag Ken out of that pasture," Charlie continued, lowering his voice even more, bending over so only she could hear his words. "I swear the fellow would have searched all night if we'd've let him. He was hollerin' like a crazy man—hell, I guess we all were—trying to get her to yell back if she could hear us. But we gave up, we had to. . . ."

She patted his arm as if to say, "I know."

"It's not going to do that girl any good," Charlie said, "to have one of us get hurt up there in those draws and hollers now it's night."

"What did you do with Linda's saddle, Charlie?"

"Dunno what Ken did with it."

"Shouldn't it go to the sheriff?"

"Oh, hell, Genia." His shoulders slumped and he looked old and tired. "The rain washed it clean, you know that. That saddle ain't going to tell any tales."

"Thank you, Charlie, I just can't tell you—"

"Now that ain't necessary, Genia, so you can just stop that right now before you get started." His voice had turned gruff. "You think I don't recollect all those times you sat with Helen at the hospital? You're good neighbors, and that's all that I'm tryin' to be. Now, where's that famous chili of yours, Genia?"

She bit back tears of appreciation as she led him into her kitchen. These valley people were so kind, so good, she reflected: how would she or the Ortegas ever have managed this awful day without them? Mrs. Potter glanced over to where a tall, distinguished-looking man with graying hair was ladling chili out of pots on her stove into the bowls held in her neighbors' hands. *And how*, she thought, *would I have ever endured this day without you?*

As if he'd actually heard her, Jedders H. White suddenly looked over at her and winked. It was a small gesture, probably unnoticed by anybody else, but it bespoke such warmth and understanding that Mrs. Potter had to walk quickly back down the hall and into her bathroom to blink away tears and compose herself for her other guests.

CHAPTER 18

They were curious about him, of course, this handsome older man who just appeared in Eugenia Potter's kitchen, stirring her pots of chili as casually as if he lived there.

"You a friend of Genia's?" inquired Charlie Watt in his blunt way, when he grabbed a bowl and walked up to where Jed stood at the stove.

"I'm staying at the C Lazy U," was Jed's reply, offered with a friendly smile and a ladleful of steaming chili.

"Guest of Che's, then," said Charlie, jumping to a correct conclusion, which was also the wrong one. "Where you hail from, you don't mind my askin'?"

"Around Boston. Beautiful country you've got here . . ."

Which was all that Charlie, a proud Arizona native, needed to get him talking about his business and distracted from Jed's, Mrs. Potter observed. She appreciated Jed's discretion—no need to get her neighbors all atwitter about "Genia's old beau"—but she wondered if it was on her behalf or that of his private business with the McHenrys. Well, she didn't have time to think about that now. . . . Thank goodness, Jed appeared to be the self-sufficient sort who didn't need her to introduce him to people or make sure he felt comfortable in the crowd. She had more than enough to do, without having to babysit a full-grown man in this crowd.

Her chili party, which she had so hoped would be a celebration, was more like a wake. Juanita and her family didn't come up from the house down the hill, but Mrs. Potter didn't expect them to. They needed each other and privacy this evening, she thought. Mrs. Potter hoped she was doing them a favor by keeping these well-intentioned neighbors away from them for a little while.

"I'm concerned about Bandy," she confided to Jed, when she had his ear for a brief moment. "I asked him into the house, but he won't come."

Bandy Esposito was still outside, stoically going about his chores at the swimming pool and the rose gardens. She had watched from her ramada as, one after another, the people of the valley had come into the compound and immediately noticed the old man as he measured chemicals into the sparkling blue pool, or as he mixed fertilizer or bug-spray beside the roses. She had watched a few of them stride toward him, as if to commiserate with him on the loss of his friend and boss, but there was something about the stiff set of Bandy's back, the rigidity of his head and neck and shoulders, the fierceness of his face that discouraged them from taking the remaining steps up to him. Respectfully, often with their cowboy hats in their hands, they had all backed away from the old hired hand, leaving him to his chores and to his apparent grief.

Mrs. Potter did not know who had told Bandy about Ricardo.

By the time she found him, he already knew.

They had simply gazed at each other, the hired man and *la patrona*, and then he had lowered his gaze and turned away first. Mrs. Potter had reached out her hand to grasp his shoulder for a moment, and he had almost looked back at her, but not quite. Instead, he had gently eased out from under her touch and slowly limped away in the direction of his apartment over the garage. She hadn't seen him again that day until he showed up at his usual time to perform his jobs around her house. Like her other guests, Mrs. Potter respectfully left him alone, but her heart ached for him.

Inside her house there was at first no talk of anything except Ricardo and Linda, even in the odd moment when Lorraine Steinbach drew Mrs. Potter back down the hall and into her bedroom. By the time Mrs. Potter had closed the door at Lorraine's gestured request, the other woman had started weeping. Lorraine moved quickly to Mrs. Potter's bed, sat down on the edge of it, and put her face in her hands.

Mrs. Potter sat down and put an arm around her, wondering if these tears were for Ricardo. She hadn't realized that Lorraine and he were close; she'd assumed they were friendly acquaintances. A soft tap at the bedroom door preceded the entry of a third woman, Che Thomas.

"Bastard," breathed Che, as she quickly crossed the room to sit on Lorraine's other side, and took hold of the weeping woman's hands. Her chic black outfit was dusty now, but she still moved as energetically as if the day had only just begun. "You know perfectly well that he's not worth crying over, Lorraine, darling."

No, Mrs. Potter decided, *this was definitely not about Ricardo.*

But, in that, it turned out, she was partly wrong.

"Did you see them?" Lorraine cried to her friends. "They don't even try to hide it anymore. He gives her a peck on the cheek, right out in public, and she giggles at him, like some stupid schoolgirl. Oh, why do they have to make such a fool of me? And of Walt?"

"Because they are fools, my dear," said Che.

Lorraine Steinbach looked up tearfully at Mrs. Potter, who had an irreverent desire to shake the plump little woman until her teeth rattled. "Ricardo told them to quit it, you know. He stopped Gallway one day in the grocery store, right there in the canned soup aisle, and he told Gallway he was behaving monstrously toward me, and if that didn't faze him, then he ought to know that he was ruining that bitch's reputation all through the valley."

"*Ricardo* said that?" Mrs. Potter asked.

"Not 'bitch,' that's my word," Lorraine said, bitterly.

Mrs. Potter knew it was never a word Lorraine would have used before this. She'd never seemed like the kind of woman to know the meaning of certain four- and five-letter words, much less ever to use them.

"What did Gallway say to that?" Mrs. Potter inquired.

"He said Ricardo ought to mind his own business for once, or one day he'd find he didn't have any more business to mind!"

Over Lorraine's head, Che and Mrs. Potter looked at each other.

"What was that supposed to mean?" Che asked.

Lorraine shrugged, as if in hopeless despair. "Oh, you know Gallway, half of what he says doesn't make any sense anyway."

Mrs. Potter glanced at Che again, and the two friends shook their respective heads. Then Che did what Mrs. Potter was only thinking and which she herself might never actually have done. She took hold of Lorraine Steinbach's shoulders and turned her around and glared at her. "Do you hear yourself, Lorraine? Did you hear what you just said about him? He doesn't make much sense, that's what you said. An old fool, that's what you've called him. Along with idiot, moron, and bastard. This is all true, Lorraine. He is all of those things, and more. So the point is, the question is, what the *hell* do you care what he does with Kathy Amory? *Let* him leave you for that little twit. Then *she'd* have to take care of an old fool who doesn't make any sense, and *you* wouldn't have to anymore! Sounds pretty good to me, Lorraine. Doesn't that sound pretty good to you, Genia?"

Mrs. Potter almost smiled, though she was surprised at Che's words. Che had previously maintained that if Lorraine really wanted to stay with the execrable Gallway, then she ought to do just that. With a raised eyebrow, Mrs. Potter silently inquired of Che: *What's with you?*

She didn't get an answer, because Lorraine was protesting, over a fresh deluge of tears, "You never have liked him, either of you. He's my husband, and I love him. Ricardo should never have said that to him, either, because it just made Gallway more determined to do what he wants. I could have killed Ricardo for sticking his nose in—"

Lorraine stopped, horrified at what she'd said.

This time Mrs. Potter did speak up. "Oh, don't be silly, Lorraine, we know what you meant."

But did they, really? she wondered.

Could she and Che, both of whom had been married to nice and normal men who had treated them with respect born of love, could they ever possibly understand what went on in the head of a determinedly mistreated woman like Lorraine Steinbach? Judging by their annoyance and impatience with her, Mrs. Potter—rather sadly—suspected they could not. She was relieved to excuse herself from the tearful scene in the bedroom in order to return to the kitchen to see to her other dinner guests.

"Thanks a *lot*," Che mouthed at her, with a wry smile.

As the first sad hour passed into the second, the twenty-seven-ingredient chili eventually worked its magic, filling stomachs so that people felt less cold and tired, and soothing their emotions by creating a companionable warmth around the chili pots.

It was like gathering around a campfire.

Mrs. Potter's guests seemed to enjoy taking turns serving chili that night, using the long-handled, deep serving spoons she had stuck in the two big pots.

"Brilliant idea, Genia," whispered Che when she returned from the back bedroom. "Takes everybody's mind off their worrying over that poor girl for a little while."

"Don't you mean 'woman'?" said Kathy Amory, who stood close enough to overhear.

"She's still a girl to me," Che snapped, and Kathy blushed like a girl herself. "Even if she is eighteen years old. I watched that child grow up and as far as I can tell she's not done yet. Some females stay girls for a lot longer than others," she said pointedly, and then shifted her gaze to Kathy's husband, Walt. "Like some males remain boys for a while longer than most."

As Mrs. Potter had predicted to Jed, the "hot pot" of chili went down faster with the men, while the women consumed most of the milder version. Each of the "servers" displayed his or her own distinct style of ladling as well.

Walt Amory's style of serving was as quiet and reserved as he was. He merely stood beside the stove and gave people what they asked for.

His wife was another matter entirely. Kathy Amory's style was to serve up flirtation along with a bowl of chili. The question "Could you give me a little more of that spicy variety?" might turn into a double entendre.

"I'll give you spicy," she'd say with a wicked grin. "Hot and spicy, just the way I hear you like it."

Only later would Mrs. Potter realize that it wasn't the *way* they served her chili that was important, but *who* was near the chili at any time during the evening.

Che Thomas dragooned people into third helpings, while Lorraine Steinbach's style was solicitous.

Charlie Watt took over the spoons from Lorraine, and his style was a serious and honest one. "Yes, Genia's chili is always plenty good, but I do believe the best chili I ever tasted was at a little roadside café outside of Houston one time. It was just beans and onions and grease, if I recall exactly. No tomato sauce like this here. Everybody puts tomato sauce in chili, like it was the eleventh commandment or something, but there's no real reason for it. I remember President Harry Truman had a favorite chili place in Kansas City—I ate there one time, called Dixon's Chili— and they never used no tomato sauce that I recall." And to the person to whom he was saying all this: "Nice-looking black-and-white shirt you got on, Gallway, even if it does make you look like a pregnant zebra."

When Bandy Esposito stepped up to the pots, having finally come in from the yard, there was a sudden eager flow of hired hands to the stove, as if the valley's part-time cowboys had been shy of approaching their employers for food. But they didn't hesitate to stick their bowls out to Bandy, especially the ones of Spanish descent, who appeared to be trading jokes and asides with the man who was the oldest one of them in the valley. Ken Ryerson took over from Bandy when the old man slopped chili onto the kitchen floor once too often, and then the younger women in the crowd seemed to find sudden excuses to make their way back to the stove for refills.

Early on in the evening, even Gallway Steinbach took a turn, although he didn't get much business, Mrs. Potter noted. Hardly anybody appeared to be very hungry if it meant they had to approach "Gallstones" for a helping of chili. But the crackers went fast during his reign at the stove, as did the carrot and celery sticks, the coffee, iced tea, and beer. Feeling sorry for him, Mrs. Potter put him to work filling empty marjarine tubs with chili so that any guest who wanted leftovers might take some home, maybe for the children or for a late-night snack, or for lunch the next day. She noted with some exasperation that Gallway didn't bother to put the lids on any of them, but just set them out all over her countertops, a fact that seemed important to her only later. Mrs. Potter would have covered them herself, but she was too busy chopping extra vegetables to refill the crudités trays.

Her guests miraculously recovered their appetites when she retrieved her apron from around Gallway's waist and stepped up to take a turn at serving the chili herself.

Her personal style was to coax her guests gently out of their sad weariness by getting them to tell her about *their* favorite chili recipe, or to encourage them in their wild guesses about the twenty-seven ingredients of her *Country Friends'* recipe.

"Soy sauce?" hazarded Kathy Amory.

"Soy sauce!" Che Thomas snorted. "What do you think this is, Chinese chili? But there's chili sauce, right, Genia?"

"Right, Che."

"And I think you've got two kinds of peppers in here."

"Yep."

Che grinned. "Not going to tell me what kinds, are you? Well, smarty, that's easy anyway. Red. And green. So there."

"That's three out of twenty-seven," observed Jed from the sidelines. "You only have twenty-four to go, Mrs. Thomas."

"I found a bit of black olive in mine," Kathy said, but timidly this time, with a cautious glance at Che. And sure enough, the older woman laughed at her. "Soy sauce and black olives! Now, who in the world would put black olives in chili?"

"I would," Mrs. Potter said, with an oh-so-innocent smile for her friend. "Kathy's right."

Nobody guessed the two different kinds of meats and they only guessed the beans when she helped them along by telling them there were two varieties. They did well on the herbs and spices—Che even guessing the oregano and cilantro. And then Jed made a confession.

"I like the sour cream," he said.

Mrs. Potter smiled at him. "Told you so."

It was the oddest thing, she thought, but he and Marjorie and Reynolds McHenry behaved all evening like total strangers who wanted to remain that way, and not at all like potential business partners looking forward to a dinner together the next evening. Mrs. Potter was extremely curious to know the reasons behind the odd behavior: was their deal as "hot" as her chili, and so secretive that they couldn't even let on that they knew each other? She wondered if perhaps Jedders H. White had been a bit disingenuous, a bit overly modest, about his "little" White Research firm, and about the importance of the electronic gadgets his "little" company manufactured?

Marjorie McHenry didn't even acknowledge Jed's presence when she came up and surprised Mrs. Potter by offering to take over the job of attaching the lids to the little tubs of leftover chili.

"Why, thank you, Marjorie."

Neither of the McHenrys took a turn at the chili pot. They ate theirs standing, alone together—if you didn't count their bodyguard—in a far corner of Mrs. Potter's living room, talking to nobody, approached by no one. A strange pair, Mrs. Potter thought, as she had so often. She didn't know whether she was dreading or anticipating the dinner with them and Jed the next night. Did they know that she was coming too? Mrs. Potter glanced at Jed, who smiled at her again. Had he asked them yet? *Well*, she thought as she returned his smile, *I guess I won't know that until I show up at their door tomorrow night. Unless, that is, I manage to get a few more minutes alone with Jed before the end of this horrible . . . wonderful . . . day.*

"Here, Bandy." She handed him one of the tubs of leftover chili that Marj McHenry had just lidded for her. "Take some of this back home with you."

When he didn't immediately go off with it, but stood there for a long moment, she took the hint. Mrs. Potter lifted two more tubs off the counter and stacked them onto the other one in his hands. Only then did Bandy murmur *"gracias,"* and turn to go. Mrs. Potter knew why: those extra tubs would go into his freezer to feed some thin and hungry stranger who sneaked up Bandy's back staircase under cover of the dark of some future night.

He'd said he didn't have any "nephews" staying with him now.

Mrs. Potter wondered if that still held true.

Did *"now"* mean *now* . . . or only *then*, when he'd answered her question.

That worry disappeared from her mind as the other guests came up to offer their condolences, and to tell her they'd be stopping by Juanita's house on their way home. Several of them promised to show up even earlier the next morning to continue the search for Linda Scarritt, even though the sheriff was taking over. One after another her neighbors thanked her, and she them, and they accepted her little offerings of leftover chili.

"Thanks, Genia," said one of the women. "Now I won't have to cook for the kids after I pick them up from the baby-sitter."

"Well, then, here," Mrs. Potter said, "please take another tub."

By the time she was finished and everybody but Che Thomas and Jed had gone, Mrs. Potter felt she had stocked the larders of virtually the entire valley with little plastic containers of 27-Ingredient Chili con Carne.

CHAPTER 19

Mrs. Potter still hoped to say good night to Jed privately.

But his other hostess, Che Thomas, walked with them to the front door. Jed and Mrs. Potter could only thank one another, politely and rather stiffly, under Che's amused eyes, and tell each other awkwardly how nice it was to have had the opportunity to see each other again. Mrs. Potter cringed inwardly at the stilted sound of her own words. It was like saying good night to him in front of her college dorm "mother."

"Good night, Genia, darling." Che leaned forward to plant a kiss on Mrs. Potter's cheek. "I'm going home to have a good cry over Ricardo, and I suggest that you go right to bed and do the same. I'll send somebody over to help you clean up the mess in the morning, so you just turn off the fire under the pots and close the door on those dirty dishes. You can always find a clean cup for coffee in the morning, and what more will you need, after all? If anything more happens tonight, you'll call me, you hear?"

"Yes, and thank you for everything, Che."

"Pshaw, girl!" Che linked an arm with Jed, and led him off the ramada steps. "You follow me, Mr. Jedders H. White, and you won't get lost on these back country roads."

"Good night, Andy," he said, turning back once.

"Good night, Jed," she called after him.

"What's this *Andy* business?" she heard Che ask him as the two walked out her front gate.

Her bedside phone rang just as she was crawling under the covers. She grabbed it quickly, in case it was Juanita.

"Hello?"

"Am I calling too late, Andy?"

"Oh, Jed, of course not."

Mrs. Potter sat up again, using her free hand to prop herself up against the pillows and to pull the covers up under her arms. It was ridiculous, she thought, how pleased she was to hear his voice, and how invigorated she felt, when only the moment before she'd been so tired she could hardly move her brush across her teeth.

"I hated saying good-bye to you like that . . ."

"I regretted it too . . ."

"But there wasn't anything we could do about it . . ."

"Not with Che standing there . . ."

"So I had to call; I hope you don't mind."

"Not at all. I'm glad . . ." Mrs. Potter found that she could only repeat those words. "I'm really so glad . . ."

"Andy, I shouldn't say this, what with all the tragedy that surrounds you tonight, but I still want you to know that I had the most wonderful time with you today. It was *grand* to see you again. I know this isn't the time . . ."

"It's all right, Jed."

"The last thing you need is some lovesick old swain showing up on your doorstep . . ."

Mrs. Potter began laughing, and oh, it felt so good, it was almost as much a release as the tears she had intended to shed privately once she was in bed. "Is that what you are, Jed? A swain? That sounds rather dashing to me."

He began laughing, too, and then said, "I wanted to stay and help you clean up the kitchen, but Mrs. Thomas . . ."

"Yes . . ."

He paused. She paused. Neither of them spoke for a long, meaningful moment. "Well, I won't keep you on the line, even though I'd like to talk to you for hours, days, months. I just want to tell you—oh, Lord, Andy, I guess I just want to tell you everything. How beautiful you still are. How grand I think your life has been, and what a success I think you've made of it. What a wonderful woman you grew up to be, and all behind my back. I'm babbling, I know, and you're thinking that this is embarrassing and not at all the proper behavior for a gently reared Bostonian, and you're wishing I'd stop and hang up . . ."

"Far from it, Jed."

"Andy, I feel like a teenager. I don't know if I can wait until tomorrow night to see you again."

Mrs. Potter was blessed with sudden inspiration. "Maybe you won't have to, if you really want to get together again sooner than that. I have to return a rental car to the Nogales airport tomorrow, Jed, would you like to go with me?"

"I'd love to," he said quickly, but then added, "How will we get back?"

"Fly," Mrs. Potter announced. "I'll tell you about it tomorrow."

"You want to hire that aerial search company to fly us over the same route that Ricardo took when he hired them, don't you?"

Mrs. Potter could only blink in admiration.

"You're wonderful, Jed."

"Hold that thought," he commanded. "Good night, dear Andy."

Mrs. Potter was left with a dial tone in her hand and a broad smile on her face . . . which suddenly grew quite pink. She'd forgotten all about the party line. Had there been any telltale clicks? How could she know, when she only had ears for his voice! Well, now the entire valley would probably know that the tall, handsome gentleman was no ordinary guest of the C Lazy U. . . .

Her embarrassed pleasure soon surrendered to the tears she had delayed crying for Ricardo. She fell asleep marveling at the exquisite capacity of the human heart to hold joy and sorrow, hope and hopelessness, in equal measure, and all at the same time.

She awoke once in the middle of the night, thinking about the list of initials on her yellow pad and about Ricardo's remark about Agatha Christie mystery novels. If she was right, and he had been murdered, then those twelve people were the suspects, because it was one of them, she felt positive, who was to meet Ricardo at five o'clock that morning.

"Who, Ricardo?" she whispered into the darkness of her bedroom. "Who killed you, and what have they done with your granddaughter?"

This time, it wasn't sadness that kept her staring wakefully into the dark room, it was anger . . . a growing fury that begged—no, demanded —resolution.

"I'll find her, Ricardo," she whispered. "I swear it to you, old friend. And then I'll find out who is trying to destroy your family and this ranch."

CHAPTER 20

Bandy's bum leg hurt him as he swung it down onto the ground and got out of his truck, in front of the garage. He grunted, a sound he didn't allow himself to make when other people were around.

At the thought of other people, Bandy glanced up at the windows of his apartment. Dark. No sign of the boys for whom he'd brought the chili. Before he lifted the plastic tubs from the seat, he checked to be sure the lids were on tight. He'd left them in the truck for a little while up at *la patrona's* while he made his usual rounds of the compound to check that the side gates were locked, and when he'd returned to the truck he'd noticed that one of the lids was loose. Good thing he'd seen it or there'd have been a mess in the front seat. Making sure that the lids were now secure, he picked up the tubs with his gnarled fingers and made his way to his own front door, hurting with every step.

He didn't hold any grudges against the pain. Didn't begrudge it the loss of most of his cowboying, didn't resent it for keeping him from riding, or doing what he'd been accustomed to do. The pain was just there, a part of his existence like daylight and starlight. Besides, it was a reminder of Ricardo. The old man felt terrible about the way that Ricardo's body had lain alone in the storm, tossed about like an elk carcass, partly devoured by predators. He wasn't responsible for that, but he felt bad about it anyway.

He wanted Ricardo to have a good burial now.

He wanted it to be the best the county had ever seen, with riders astride horses with silver trappings and women wearing lacy mantillas to cover their heads, and children crying and priests dressed in the black cassocks he remembered from the cathedrals of his childhood in Mexico.

He paused to take a breath, to ease his leg.

The pain was all right, he figured. He was lucky, he figured, to have gotten away, from as tough a life as he'd led, with only this one pain.

There could have been broken bones aplenty; he could have been gored any number of times by a bull, or tossed on his head by a horse, or even have shot himself in the foot, who knew? As it was, there was only this one bad pain and he'd earned it honestly, doing hard work. So what if he couldn't do that anymore? So what if he wasn't good for anything besides making a swimming pool safe for a woman to swim in? There were worse jobs and much less honorable ones, he figured. She was a good woman anyway and he was pleased to do that for her if that's what kept him in room and board.

He didn't know how much longer that would last, if Juanita had her way.

At least now, he thought, they'd need him awhile longer.

He was closer to the garage, only a few more steps to go. He glanced up again. Quiet, just like he'd told them to be. They were good boys, these two new ones, but too young to be making the trek. Or maybe he was just feeling too old, and so everybody else looked too young. He'd told them there was trouble on the ranch, a couple of people missing, and they'd be mighty handy scapegoats if anybody was to know they were around. Well, Mrs. Potter knew now; after giving him these tubs of her good chili, she'd have guessed it. Anybody could have seen her hand them to him and they could also have guessed what he wanted them for. Well, maybe there wasn't as much for his boys to worry about now that everybody thought Ricardo got bucked off Patches.

Not such a bad way to go, in Bandy's opinion.

He wouldn't have minded it himself, but it was too late for that, now that he couldn't ride anymore.

Bandy smiled to himself: maybe he'd fall in *la patrona's* swimming pool and drown one day. She didn't know he couldn't swim; she'd never let him do even that small job if she knew he'd never learned how to swim. They could bury him under the rose bushes and never have to fertilize them again.

Bandy was chuckling under his breath as he put his key in his door.

But there was something he was forgetting, some remaining threat to his boys. The sudden thought made him stop smiling.

Linda. At the memory of her, the old man leaned against the doorframe and broke down in tears that racked his shoulders. *Poor little girl.* Such a nice child, always so kind to him, so cheerful and hard working. *Poor child, poor little girl. Ricardo loved her so much, and now where was she . . . ?*

They could blame his boys for this. . . .

They could say his boys found them, killed Ricardo, raped her, killed her, hid her, they could say anything. . . .

He had to warn his boys, get them moving, gone from the ranch.

Bandy knew what he had to do: feed them a good dinner of *la patrona's* chili, pack them up with a few dollars and a spare shirt from the stockpile of castaways he kept for "his boys," and truck them into the next county before morning. That's the advice he'd gotten this evening from the one person he'd told about them and about what they'd heard when they had slipped over the border onto Los Palomas Saturday night. They'd been camping on the hard ground at the bottom of El Bizcocho when they were jolted out of their nervous sleep by gunshots. And a woman screaming. They'd been so scared, thinking somebody was shooting at them. Bandy had known he had to tell somebody who'd know what to do about it, because maybe it had something to do with Ricardo and Linda. Or maybe it didn't. He was torn in his heart, wanting to help his friends, and yet not wanting to do anything that might hurt his boys.

He felt a welling of paternal protectiveness surging inside him that warred with his grief over Ricardo and his fear for Linda. He wiped his eyes with his jacket sleeve and pushed the door open. He began painfully to climb the stairs to his rooms on the second floor. When he pushed open the door at the top, he walked into utter silence.

"*Hombres? Está bien. Tengo chile para ustedes.*"

Men. He always called them men even when they were young as these two, because men was what they were going to have to be from now on. *It's okay. I've brought chili for you.* They looked so relieved when they saw it was truly him. They took chairs at the kitchen table while Bandy spooned out the chili, which was still warm from *la patrona's* stove, into three bowls. He'd been too upset to eat much up at the big house, but now he knew he'd need the energy of good food to propel him through the rest of this long night when he would help his nephews escape the county. Like them, he drowned the chili in Tabasco sauce and then he ate quickly and heartily, finishing his bowl and reaching for seconds.

Before dawn, Ken Ryerson pulled his truck up to the Ortegas' garage, and gave a soft toot with his horn. When Bandy didn't appear after a few minutes, Ken tooted softly again, sensitive to Juanita and her family who might be asleep in the house. He allowed enough time for the old man to put on his hat, jacket, and gloves, to limp to the door upstairs, to close it, to limp downstairs, and to open the lower door.

When Bandy didn't come down, Ken went after him.

He opened the bottom door with his own set of ranch keys and bounded up the stairs, calling Bandy's name. He thrust open the door and stepped inside. The smell hit him first. He stayed long enough to see the damage was mortal and that there wasn't anything left for him to do for the three men in the small apartment, and then he stumbled down the stairs and was violently sick outside the garage.

When he could stand up straight and breathe again, Ken walked to Juanita's house. He couldn't run; his legs were too wobbly. It was all he could do to keep from buckling to the ground and throwing up again.

CHAPTER 21

Before the first light of morning brought out the searchers again, Mrs. Potter got into the rented Subaru and drove down to the stable to see Linda's horse, Taco.

A corral was attached to the stable, and just down the hill was the darkened garage where, she imagined, Bandy still slept. Farther on was the Ortega house, where she saw lights on and so she imagined the "children" were probably just rising now, starting to cook breakfast and get dressed to face the first official day of their lives without their father. She wondered if Juanita had slept and what Juanita would do now. Would she want to stay on at the ranch?

Well, there would be time to consider all of that later.

Mrs. Potter switched on the light in the stable, which smelled richly, comfortingly, of horses and hay.

She touched the half gate to Patches's empty stall when she passed it. Somebody—Bandy—had mucked it out since Ricardo's horse had last stood inside it. Somebody else—Ken?—had removed Ricardo's leather-tooled saddle from the body of the dead horse and returned it to its sawhorse in front of the stall. Ricardo's silver-trimmed bridle hung in its accustomed place on the post between that stall and the next, which was also empty. Mrs. Potter touched the saddle and then the reins that hung from the bridle, as if some warmth from the man or the horse might still linger there. The leather and silver were cold and inert to her touch. Her eyes filled and her throat felt swollen with unspoken grief. Mrs. Potter walked quickly on to the last stall where Taco stood alone, his head bowed low. He raised it when she spoke to him.

"Hello, boy." The dullness in his eyes matched the feeling in her heart. She kept talking, to keep from weeping. "We're so glad you're home. Where's your lady, Taco? Can't you tell us?"

Mrs. Potter peered over the half door of his stall and thought at first that the horse appeared perfectly normal. He wasn't thin or dehydrated from his ordeal; he'd been running free with plenty of grass to eat and water from the last rain. In fact, thought Mrs. Potter, as she reached out a hand to stroke his black velvet nose, it hadn't been much of an ordeal for Taco, unless he'd missed his stable and his oats, or if he now missed the familiar, soothing hands of his mistress lovingly brushing his coat and patting his prosperous flanks. He hadn't even been gone long enough for his pretty brown coat to dull, or for his black mane and tail to mat. *Your coat*, Mrs. Potter thought, as she conversed silently with him, *is exactly that Swiss chocolate shade that some of my friends favored in mink coats a few years back. You look just fine, Taco, certainly a lot better than those minks do now, except* . . . there was that inexplicable dullness to his eyes, and an odd air of stoicism about him. And then Mrs. Potter noticed that he had one leg, his left rear, lifted off the straw.

"Taco, what's the matter with your leg?"

She slipped into his stall and worked her way toward the rear, carefully stepping over a steaming pile of fresh manure, toward the left hind leg he had lifted.

"Oh, my, you poor thing!"

Dark, dried blood coated the leg.

"Didn't they see this last night?"

But perhaps the men had not noticed this blackened wound as they brought the horse in. His coat was dark, the blood would have been hard to see. Surely the horse had limped, but . . . well, they had just missed it, that was all, because it was night and because they'd brought him back in one of their horse trailers instead of trying to ride him.

Mrs. Potter went to find a bucket, which she filled with water, regretting for Taco's sake that it was so cold. She found a clean rag and carried everything back with her to his stall.

"I'll be as gentle as I can, boy, but we have to see what's wrong."

It was impossible to tell under all the blood on his leg just how bad the wound was, and exactly what might have produced it. Had he stumbled, fallen onto a sharp boulder? Mrs. Potter soothingly stroked the horse's nose and neck for a few moments before bridling him and tying him securely to a ring in the stall. She wanted his nose secured in a face-forward position so that if she inadvertently caused him pain he couldn't turn and nip at her. She then worked her way back to his hindquarters slowly, stroking his sides, taking the bucket with her. After dipping the rag in the water and squeezing some of it out, she tentatively touched the rag to his leg. Taco didn't seem to mind that small touch, so she increased the pressure a bit and stroked the wet rag down the leg.

"Easy, boy, easy now."

He began to mind the operation very much, whinnying and snorting, and moving nervously by touching the wounded leg to the stable floor, then jerking it back up into the air again. But he was an excellently trained horse, Mrs. Potter knew, and she felt fairly confident that he would stand relatively still for her ministrations. His beautiful thick tail whipped back and forth unhappily. Mrs. Potter put up her left arm to keep it out of her face.

When she finished wiping his leg clean, she was appalled at what she saw—and respectful of the horse's courage in withstanding such pain. By cleaning the leg, Mrs. Potter had revealed a long, ragged gash in it. The light in the stable wasn't good enough for her to tell how deep the cut penetrated and she was afraid to stick her face any closer. Taco, for all his stoicism, was clearly sending her the firm message: *Enough already!*

Carefully, she backed against the wooden wall of the stall, carrying the bucket with its load of filthy water with her. She edged her way back out into the corridor, then released him from the tether.

"Were you stabbed, boy? Or could you have been gored?"

That's what it looked like, as if the horse had been gored by an animal's tusk, or had actually been stabbed by a knife-wielding human. Mrs. Potter glanced around, looking at the wooden sawhorse where the other saddles usually rested, but she didn't see Linda's there; then she remembered that Charlie Watt said he didn't know what Ken had done with it.

"We have to get the vet out here for you."

Mrs. Potter stroked the horse a little longer, calming him and whispering endearments to him before she picked up her bucket and started to walk outside with it to toss its contents onto the ground.

"*Patrona?*"

She glanced up at the sound of a young woman's voice.

"Angela," she responded gently, seeing who it was. There in the doorway of the stable stood Ricardo and Juanita's youngest daughter, the one who was an accountant in Tucson. Angela Ortega's mass of black curls sprang uncombed around her pretty face, and she looked disheveled in red plaid pajamas and the incongruous addition of a pink satin bathrobe. "How are you, my dear?"

"I saw your car up here," the young woman blurted. "I came to tell you." She began to cry. "Oh, *patrona*. Bandy's dead. Ken found him."

Since Angela had run up to the stable in her bedroom slippers, Mrs. Potter gave her a ride back down the hill. They walked into the Ortega house together. *Bandy. And two young illegals. Dead. Too many tragedies, all in a row. However shall we survive it?* Mrs. Potter felt numb, as if she had lost all feeling and this were happening to someone else, not to her. She wondered, in a detached sort of way, when she would begin to feel the impact of this fresh loss. And then she saw the Ortega children, and she thought, *My loss is nothing compared to theirs.*

The first thing Mrs. Potter noticed about them was how full the house seemed with all of these "children," grown to adulthood. Where once they'd filled the house with their squealing laughter and wailing tears, now they seemed literally to fill it with all of their grown-up heights and weights and voices. The two "boys," Ricardo, Jr., and Manuel, were over six feet tall, like their late father, and almost as handsome as he had been. *But then,* Mrs. Potter thought, *I'm prejudiced, since I have always agreed with Juanita that Ricardo, Sr., was the handsomest man in the valley.* And the "girls," why, they were still stair steps, starting with the smallest and youngest, Angela, and going on up to Estella, who was the oldest child, and the tallest of the women. Francesca, the middle girl, who was Linda's mother, was still in Brazil.

By one of those unplanned coincidences that works as well as a potluck dinner, none of the married ones had brought their spouses or children. Each, she learned later, had felt the house was too small to hold them all, each had thought the events too upsetting for their children to attend, and each couple had determined that one spouse needed to stay home, take care of the children, and keep working. So the Ortega children were —probably for the first time in many years—all together, solely as brothers and sisters, under their parents' roof.

It had been Ricardo's secret sorrow—told, at least, to Mrs. Potter—that not one of them had chosen to make a life out of ranching in the valley. But then he had Linda. . . .

"Have you reached Linda's parents?" Mrs. Potter had asked Angela on the ride down, and had been told no, they were still trying, always trying, they'd sent word, but now they had to wait until one of their messages got through. In the meantime it was agonizing to them that Linda's mother didn't know, that Francesca wasn't here with them. . . .

"*Patrona,*" Mrs. Potter was greeted, and she went to each of them for a handshake or an embrace. "*Lo siento,*" she murmured over and over. "*Lo siento mucho, lo siento a cerca de sus padre.*"

I am so very sorry about your father.

Mrs. Potter was struck by the contrast Ken Ryerson made to the family of his fiancée. Do they know? she wondered. Something about the emotional space between them made her think: no, he hasn't told them yet. Seated on a couch in the living room, his head bent over into his hands, the young cowboy looked unattractively pale next to the vividness of the Ortega family. But that was unfair, Mrs. Potter chided herself. Obviously he was still sickened by what he had seen in Bandy's apartment. Her own stomach felt queasy at the thought of it, and she hoped she would never have to hear the details. Mrs. Potter crossed the room to sit beside him.

"Are you all right, Ken, dear?"

He took a deep, shaky breath, but offered a wry grin as he said, "I don't think so."

You'll be all right, Mrs. Potter thought, seeing his bravado attempt at a grin. Still, it was awful for him, to walk into that room of terrible death. Food poisoning, Angela had suggested, based on what Ken had told them, or maybe even a virulent influenza. Surely not, Mrs. Potter thought. Whoever heard of the flu catching its victims and killing them in their tracks, like that?

"Where's your mom?" she asked the others.

"Mom!" one of the "boys" called, as boys always will, Mrs. Potter thought.

Angela walked into the kitchen to get Juanita, but she came back in a minute, saying, "She's not in there. Check her room, Rico." Ricardo, Jr., left the living room to do as his little sister suggested. But he, too, came back without their mother.

"I'll look upstairs," Estella offered.

But in a few moments she was back, too, spreading her hands wide in bafflement. "She's not in any of the rooms upstairs. I guess she's in the bathroom down here—"

"No, she's not," Rico said. "I checked."

"Well, where is she?" Manuel asked.

"Everybody go look," Angela directed, and the Ortega children dispersed to look for their mother. One by one, they straggled back to the living room, each of them looking as if they expected one of their siblings to produce their mother.

None of them did.

"This is ridiculous," Angela pronounced. Although the youngest, she also seemed to be the spunkiest, the most outspoken. The most, Mrs. Potter thought again, like her mother. "Where is she?"

None of them could answer that. Juanita Ortega wasn't in the house—not the basement, not the attic—and she wasn't anywhere they looked in the yard.

"But she was here just a minute ago, right before Angela came back with Mrs. Potter!" Estella exclaimed. "She can't have gone anyplace! The cars are all here. And anyway, she was still in her nightgown, for heaven's sake!"

Mrs. Potter, like the Ortega children, began to wander about the house, doing everything but opening drawers and cabinets to look for their mother. In the kitchen, she saw that somebody else had been opening drawers and doors—the door to the broom closet was open and a pile of brown paper grocery bags had spilled to the floor. The door to the supply shelf under the kitchen sink was wide open too.

"Maybe she's gone off by herself to cry," Rico said.

"*Mother?*" Estella retorted.

They all seemed to agree that scenario was an unlikely one.

Begging the question: where was Juanita, and why had she picked this moment to disappear? None of them, Mrs. Potter noticed, including herself, appeared willing even to broach the idea that not being able to find a grown woman—one who was last seen in her nightgown in her own house—had anything to do with the deaths of their father, the old man, and the two young Mexican illegals, or the disappearance of their niece, Linda.

"I have to git."

Ken stood up abruptly, drawing their attention back to him. His complexion was still as pale as the lighter blond hairs in his mustache, and his mouth was still set in a tight line that suggested he was holding back nausea. "I've got to get out to the windmill."

"We ought to concentrate on the area where you found Taco," said Manuel, and other heads nodded in agreement. When Estella objected, "But what about Mama?" Manuel said, "I'm not worried about Mama. She'll turn up."

"But what if she *doesn't*?" Estella insisted.

"Taco!" Mrs. Potter exclaimed. "I almost forgot. Ken, do you realize he's badly wounded? His left rear leg. Looks like he got gored, or—" She halted, not wanting to say "stabbed" in front of these uncles and aunts of Linda, who might hear the word and leap to a logical and terrible conclusion about their niece. "I cleaned the wound as well as I could, but we'll have to get the vet out here. I couldn't tell if it went to the bone. I'm just hoping we can relieve the poor thing's suffering without losing him altogether."

Ken headed for the door with the Ortega men, saying, "You'll take care of that, *patrona?*"

"Yes, but wait . . ." She looked around the room, at the unhappy, worried faces of the young people. "Did anybody call the sheriff about Bandy and those two poor lads?"

"Mama did," Angela told her. "He's on his way here anyway to take over the search for Linda, now that Papa . . ."

"He'll need to talk to you, Ken," Mrs. Potter said.

"He can find me," Ken replied, as he, Ricardo, and Manuel left the house.

"I can't believe you two!" screamed Estella through the screen door.

"You call yourselves sons? How can you leave without knowing what's happened to Mama?"

Rico turned back. "We'll *look* for her, Stella! On our way to the windmill. What do you think we're going to do, close our eyes? Calm down! Nothing's happened to Mama. She can probably hear you screaming right now. If *that* doesn't bring her running back, there's nothing we can do that will!"

Soon the women heard the sound of Ken's truck starting up and leaving the yard. Mrs. Potter used a telephone extension in the living room to call the nearest large-animal veterinarian, who promised to come out as soon as she could get away from her clinic.

Estella, who was tall and handsome like her father, sank down on an easy chair and began to cry into her palms. When Mrs. Potter went to comfort her, the young woman whispered, "They don't know anything, my dumb brothers. Where is she? How could she do this, just walk away like that? Has she gone loco? I wanted to go look for Linda, too, but how can we go, when now we have to stay here and look for *her*? We don't need this! Doesn't she realize that? Why can't she think of *us*? Papa's dead. Linda's gone. Now Bandy and those *pobrecitos*." *(Poor little boys.)* "How could she be so selfish, to worry us like this? Why doesn't she just come back from wherever she's hiding? I could kill Mama for doing this to us."

The small, furious figure of Angela Ortega appeared briefly in the doorway between the kitchen and the living room.

"You'd think people could clean up their own messes," she said, her pretty face tight with resentment. "You'd think people could close the broom closet door after they open it. And shut drawers. And close the door under the sink. And pick up paper bags if they spill them. You'd think if we all have to live here together again for a couple of days, people could pick up after themselves. You'd *think* so."

She stomped back into the kitchen, and soon Mrs. Potter heard the sounds of doors and drawers being jerked open and slammed shut, and then Angela yelled, "Who hid the Lysol? Where'd somebody put the Comet? Where the *hell* is the darn mop? How can I clean up after you all if I can't *find* anything?"

Mrs. Potter thought, *It's too much for this family to bear.*

She left Estella on the couch and walked into the kitchen, where she found Angela down on her hands and knees scrubbing the linoleum floor so hard it looked as if she were trying to rub the pattern off.

"You remind me so much of your mom," Mrs. Potter told her gently. "When she's the most upset, that's when she works the hardest too."

For a moment, Angela's hands kept pushing the sponge, but then they stopped. She looked up at Mrs. Potter and Mrs. Potter stared down at her as they both had the same appalling thought at the same time.

"Oh, my God!" Angela said. "You don't think so?"

Mrs. Potter nodded grimly. "Did you look there, any of you?"

"I didn't. I'm sure nobody else did, either."

Angela started to get up off her knees.

Mrs. Potter stopped her with a gesture. "No, dear, let me do this, please. I'll find her. I'll talk to her."

CHAPTER 22

From the bottom of the stairs leading to Bandy's apartment, Mrs. Potter heard the sound of water running upstairs. There were twelve steps going up and Mrs. Potter's imagination worked overtime on every one of them. But when she drew near to the last step, she smelled only the fresh scent of cleaning solvents. A cold breeze reached her, telling her that Juanita had opened the windows to the cleansing air of the morning. Still, Mrs. Potter braced herself before stepping into the room.

"Juanita, dear."

The other woman was startled by Mrs. Potter's sudden appearance, and she jumped up guiltily. Juanita had pulled on a pair of Bandy's old jeans, and wore one of his sweatshirts on top of that. On her feet she still wore her bedroom slippers—just like her daughter Angela, who looked so much like her and who was also down on her hands and knees in a kitchen, trying to scour her own grief away. Juanita's silver hair was tied up into a ponytail with a piece of string whose ends dangled down the back of her neck.

"I couldn't bear it," she said.

"I know, dear." Mrs. Potter looked around, and her heart filled with sorrow for Bandy and compassion for the bereaved woman who stood like a sentry with a mop in one hand. On the counter by the sink sat the missing bottle of Lysol, along with the missing can of Comet; there was a brown paper bag on the floor, which Juanita had used as a container for the cleaning supplies she had brought over from her own house. Bandy's body lay faceup on his narrow bed, and the bodies of two other men—*Oh, they were no more than boys!* Mrs. Potter thought—lay on cots near him, the cots he kept folded up for just such visitors. Their eyes were closed, their brown hands folded over their chests. They were dressed in clean, neat shirts and trousers, and there were socks on their feet, though no shoes. "You changed their clothing and washed their bodies, didn't you?"

"I couldn't leave them like that."

"And you've washed the floor, haven't you? And the dishes."

"I washed everything," Juanita stated flatly. "Dishes, floor, table, chairs, bathroom, walls. Took their clothes outside to the incinerator and burned them."

"I guess you know the sheriff will be furious."

"Let him be." Juanita set to work with her mop again, but then looked up at Mrs. Potter. "There's something I have to tell you."

"Can you sit down to do it?"

Juanita propped the mop against a wall and sat down with Mrs. Potter at the kitchen table. She seemed eerily calm, as if her frantic labor had drained emotion from her, as if there weren't three dead men in the room with them. Mrs. Potter had a much harder time displaying a tranquil face to match Juanita's.

"I have to tell somebody, señora. It's my fault, whatever has happened to my granddaughter. I set her to checking up on Ricardo. I made her follow him around for the last couple of weeks, because I thought he was behaving strangely. Maybe it was the thought of retiring, I don't know. But he was upset about something and he wouldn't talk to me about it, he seemed angry sometimes and depressed some other times. I screamed at him, I said, 'What's wrong with you, tell me what's wrong with you!' But he wouldn't. He said something that didn't make sense, he said that he didn't want to hear what I'd have to say. He said that if he told me, then I'd tell him what he didn't want to hear, and then he might have to do what he didn't want to do. What kind of answer is that?"

Her brown eyes pleaded with Mrs. Potter, who had no answer to give.

"It was getting so he was gone at odd times, when he should have been here. So I wanted to know what was going on with him. If he wouldn't tell me, I had to find out what he was doing and where he was going. So I told Linda to follow her grandfather." Juanita's face was suddenly expressive of pain. "She's a good girl, she did as her grandmother wanted. Her *stupid* grandmother," she said bitterly. "Linda said that man was spending his time driving around the valley! That's all! Up one country road and down another, staring at cows, if you can believe it, and following tractors and looking at hay piles." The stern brown face grimaced with distress. "So that's why he was talking about retirement, because that man knew he was getting senile. I didn't want to tell you, señora. He knew he was losing it. But so fast, so soon! And to lose him, to lose him like this, so fast, so soon . . ."

Juanita bowed her head, but didn't weep.

In a moment, she looked up again.

"So on Saturday he called you, because he was crazy, and he called all those other people for a nonsensical meeting, because he was going nuts. I don't know why he did it, he didn't know why he did it. And the next morning, he got up for no reason to climb to the top of a mountain he would never have climbed if he was in his right mind. And because I told her to do it, our granddaughter followed him, and now she's been washed away by the storms. . . ."

"They didn't find her—"

Juanita waved that comfort away. "They will, I'm sure. I accept responsibility. I killed my own granddaughter, just as much as if I'd held a gun to her head and fired it. I may as well have put the gun to my daughter's head as well, and I wish I could put it to my own. Perhaps Francesca and Les will kill me; I deserve to die. I hope they want to kill me."

"Oh, Juanita, my dear . . ."

Mrs. Potter looked over at the three bodies on the cots, and then gazed around the now-immaculate apartment. Cleaning it, she thought, must have felt to Juanita like crawling on bare, bloody knees up to the cathedral door to beg for forgiveness, for expiation of what felt to her like the most awful, most terrible sin.

Juanita saw her looking around, and said, "I didn't clean up just for Bandy. I did it for you, too, Genia."

Mrs. Potter looked up at her, surprised.

"It was your chili they were eating that made them sick."

Mrs. Potter reached out her hand for the support of the tabletop. There was a roaring in her ears and she suddenly felt so ill herself that she thought she might faint. She barely heard Juanita's next words.

"But there's no reason for anybody but you and me to know now that I've got it all cleaned up."

"What? What did you say? My *chili*?" With horror, Mrs. Potter thought of all her neighbors who had been to supper at her house last night and of all the little plastic tubs of leftover chili they had taken home with them to eat for lunch today. Juanita didn't know about that. Juanita was wrong; this could not be a secret to be forever kept between them.

Mrs. Potter practically ran back down the stairs, clinging to the banister.

"Angela! Stella!" she called out as she burst into the house.

The daughters rushed in at her summons.

"You found Mama?"

"Yes, she'll be here in a little while. But listen to me, please, you have to help me. I'm going to give you a list of names and you have to call every single one of them and keep on trying until you get all of them. Tell them not to eat the leftover chili I gave them last night! Tell them it may have killed Bandy and two other men, tell them it may be spoiled, they might get ptomaine poisoning!"

Quickly, Mrs. Potter grabbed one of the yellow pads that Juanita kept for her even at the Ortegas' house and she scribbled on it every name she could recall, terrified that she might forget somebody. She thrust the list at Stella. "Call every one of them. I'm going to drive to their houses myself to collect that chili to make absolutely sure that nobody else gets sick from it!"

But even as she started her car, Mrs. Potter was having doubts about the real urgency of her mission. She'd used only fresh ingredients. She hadn't left anything out to cool so long that it might get spoiled. Her utensils, her pots and dishes, even the plastic tubs, were sparkling clean. It wasn't possible that her chili had developed a bacterium that was virulent enough to kill people.

But just in case it *was* possible . . .

Mrs. Potter stepped harder on the Subaru's gas pedal.

CHAPTER 23

As she sped from neighbor to neighbor, collecting little yellow tubs, Mrs. Potter thought about Juanita's words. Could Ricardo's wife be right? Was it all a mirage created by a man whose faculties were failing him? Were there no suspects, no suspicions; was there no murder; was Linda's body really going to show up washed farther downstream? Maybe it was true that a hunter's shot had caused Patches to do a houlihan, and that Ricardo had been bucked off down the mountain. And maybe Linda, in attempting to go to her grandfather's rescue, had been caught by a rushing torrent of water. . . .

But then Mrs. Potter remembered Ricardo's strong, sure voice on the telephone. That was no feeble old man who'd called her. She recalled the undertone of satisfied amusement in his voice, as if he'd figured out something important and he was feeling just a tad smug about the whole thing. Ricardo, senile? Not the Ricardo she'd talked to on Saturday!

That man knew exactly what he was doing.

She thought of what had happened to him not twenty-four hours later, however, and wondered, *"My friend, were you finally too smart for your own good?"*

The headquarters of Highlands Ranch sat on a ridge above the valley. From the valley floor, one could see the outcropping of rock well enough, but not any of the buildings that perched there. For a visitor, the only visible structure was the guardhouse at the front gate. It was impressive enough, containing a fortress' worth of communications and television-monitoring equipment, which was visible from the road in front of the electrically locked gate. The gate itself rose ten feet high, and on the rare occasions when it was opened, swung wide by electric command when one of the men in the guardhouse pushed a button.

No one gained entrance to Highlands except by that gate, not even Mrs. Potter with her message of emergency.

"I'm sorry, ma'am, but Mr. and Mrs. McHenry are not available to visitors today," said the burly young man who walked out from the guard-house to greet her. He was uniformed, though subtley so, in navy-blue trousers and short-sleeved matching shirt and cap that might have passed for normal street clothes were it not for the discreet embroidered ranch logo on the flap of his breast pocket and above the bill of his cap. The holstered gun at his waist would have aroused comment on the street, too, even an Arizona street. Mrs. Potter guessed it was a .45 caliber, for no other reason than that it looked awfully big, and she had a vague notion that .45's were huge compared to, say, .38's. But then she'd never had any interest in guns or their nomenclature. It was enough for her to notice that he had one and that it was a "great big one" and that his right hand rested oh-so-casually on the butt of it all the while he chatted so courte-ously with her as she peered up at him from the driver's seat of her car.

"Are they out on the search party at my place, do you know?"

"I couldn't say, Mrs. Potter, ma'am."

That was undoubtedly true, she thought: he *couldn't* say, or he might be dismissed from his job.

"You will get the message to them, though, won't you?" she insisted. "It's so important, lives could depend on it. Do they have a cook who ought to be told, perhaps?"

"I'll let them know at the house," was as much as she could get out of him. She had to be satisfied with that and his polite smile as she backed out of the drive again. She was annoyed at the whole encounter, which hadn't been the first of such run-ins she'd had over the past few years since the McHenrys had moved into the valley. They were her neighbors, for heaven's sake! Who did they think she was, a Russian spy? Even *that* wasn't the threat it used to be. What was the matter with those people, she wondered, and what were they hiding in their fort on the hill?

"I will," Mrs. Potter declared to the world, "find out at dinner to-night."

Compared to Highlands, it was easy to get onto the C Lazy U dude ranch owned by Che Thomas. It had a "guardhouse," too, but that was only a cute little cabin built to mimic an early Arizona sod house, and it was staffed by a pert young woman in a Western skirt, blouse, fringed vest, cowboy boots, and a smile bigger than her skirt.

"Howdy! My name's Megan!" she shouted out with cheerleader vigor. If this child were paid by the decible, Mrs. Potter thought, she'd be rich by the end of the tourist season. Or perhaps she'd been instructed to shout at all of the many older guests who might be hard of hearing. Mrs. Potter was not flattered by the notion that she might appear to this child to be of an age that required younger persons to raise their voices. "Y'all can just go on up the road, if you like, although I'll have to sign you in, if y'all don't mind telling me your-all's name. Do y'all need a map of the ranch?"

"No, thank you, Megan. Where are you from, dear?"

"Atlantic City! I don't know how everybody can tell so easily."

Mrs. Potter thought about explaining that it wasn't only Megan's accent, but also her incorrect use of the colloquialism "y'all," that gave her away. (It was always plural, never singular.) She decided that it wasn't worth the effort and that the girl was perfectly charming just as she was. Loud, but charming.

"Is Mrs. Thomas up there?"

By "up there," Mrs. Potter meant the complex of guest houses, stables, recreation/dining hall and main lodge where Che entertained hundreds of paying guests every year.

"Oh, y'all here to see Ms. Thomas personally? Well, I can save you the trip! She's gone out with a bunch of folks to look for that poor girl got lost over at that other ranch, y'all know about that?"

"Yes, I do." As she carefully formulated her next question, Mrs. Potter felt her face grow warm. "Megan, would you happen to know if a guest by the name of Mr. Jedders H. White is in? Or has he gone out too?"

The young woman brightened even more. "The handsome one, looks like a movie star?"

Mrs. Potters was quite taken aback by that. "Well, I don't know. He's tall and slender, with dark hair that's turning silver, and—"

"Sure, he looks like that actor, you know, that old guy . . ."

Mrs. Potter knew she didn't dare speak, for fear she'd sputter. *Old guy?*

"Oh, *you* know, *what's* his name, I see him all the time on the old-time movie station, Gary or Cary or Dick or something. Anyway, Mr. White looks just like him and I even told him so. Yeah, he's gone. Took one of the ranch Jeeps and left, I don't know, maybe an hour ago. He's all the time going off by himself, doesn't hardly ever do any of the regular guest stuff. First night he gets here, he drops off his bags, borrows a Jeep, and he's gone. Then he's out early the next morning, even before the sun's up, I couldn't believe it. Said he was bird watching. Heck, I figure there's no bird worth getting up to see at four o'clock in the morning, except maybe if it was a flock of eagles on a *really* big stack of silver dollars." Megan smiled, and then hooted with laughter at her own joke. This was clearly a child of the Atlantic City casinos, Mrs. Potter thought. "Then he's out with the Jeep most of the next day. And every time he says he's bird watching. How many birds can you see at night, huh? I figure he's got himself a bird of a different sort, don't you?"

"I beg your pardon?"

"You know, how they used to talk back in the sixties? How they called women birds? Dumb clucks, I guess they meant!" Megan laughed, or rather, hooted. "Boy, people used to be so *back*ward, you know?"

"Megan, how in the world do you know when Jed—Mr. White—took all those Jeep trips? Do you sleep here? Do you staff this guardhouse twenty-four hours a day?"

"Oh, that's funny! No, see, we keep a log of who goes in and out, specially if it's a guest with one of the ranch vehicles. And I get pretty bored sitting here sometimes; I mean, you can only read so many romance novels, you know? So I always look over the log when I come in. That way I can see who's out and who I should be expecting back during my shift. I like to know they're coming, so I can call them by name. I think that's kind of a nice thing to do, makes people feel welcome, you know?"

A nice child, Mrs. Potter thought, and she said, "Yes, I do. May I take a look at your log, Megan?"

She was amazed at her own temerity. Why in the world should the girl let her see it? On the other hand, as she had tried to drill into her children as they were growing up, a person had nothing to lose by asking, as long as the request was politely put. Perhaps Megan was still young enough to be intimidated by any grown-up asking for something.

"Sure," Megan said, shrugging, not seeming the least curious at the odd request. Mrs. Potter realized then that the young woman had such a trusting nature that it simply hadn't occurred to her to say no. Mrs. Potter felt a bit guilty about that, but it didn't keep her from taking the logbook from Megan's hands and putting it down on her own lap. She flipped back to the early morning of the day that Ricardo died, to see if any hunting trips had departed from this gate. Evidently one had, just as Che had told her, judging by the fact that three vehicles, carrying what looked like six guests and two employees, had passed through. The initials beside the entries looked like Che's, so Mrs. Potter thought she could safely assume that the C Lazy U hostess had accompanied her guests that morning. That was a detail Che *hadn't* mentioned.

She passed the book back through the window to Megan.

"Thank you, dear."

"You're welcome. Y'all come back!"

"I'm going to go on up to the main lodge anyway, Megan, because I need to have a word with Mrs. Thomas's kitchen staff. When Mr. White returns, will you please tell him that I'll come back for him about noon, and that we'll go to lunch?"

Megan's eyes grew wide, and she grinned. "You bet!"

Mrs. Potter felt as if she should fess up by saying, "Yes, dear, I'm the 'bird.' " Instead, she merely waved, and smiled back. She followed the neatly paved road, which was lined with artfully planted cacti and yucca. Perhaps Jed could take comfort from the fact that his young admirer might have meant either Cary Grant, Gary Cooper, or Dick Powell, she thought with some amusement. A resemblance to any one of them was enough to flatter any man's ego. Megan had only omitted Alan Ladd and Ronald Coleman to complete the list of the most handsome stars of Mrs. Potter's youth.

Old guys, indeed!

Mrs. Potter drove into Charlie Watt's front yard just as Charlie was getting out of his pickup truck. He saw her, stopped in his tracks, and came over to her driver's window. She peered up into his tanned face and thought she could see the lines of sorrow that his wife's death had etched in this past year.

"Good morning, Genia. Any news?"

"Not about Linda. Did you get a call from my ranch, Charlie? From one of the Ortega girls?"

"No, I just this minute got back to the house, Genia, as you can see. I've been out checking on a fence line where one of your bulls got through last night, I hate to tell you."

"Oh, Charlie, I'm sorry." She was distracted from her immediate errand by this fresh piece of bad news. "It wasn't our Charolais, was it? He's such a big, fiesty old thing. He didn't get in with your heifers, did he? What kind of damage am I going to owe you for this?"

"Don't worry about it, Genia, it wasn't that big white monster. It was one of your littler fellows, and it was a bunch of my older cows who are already pregnant anyway, so I don't think he could do any damage. You can pay for my new stretch of barb wire, and a couple of posts if you want to—"

"I do, you just let me know how much."

"But, hell, even if he did sire himself a couple of young'uns, I ought to pay you for his services. He's a lot better bull than any that I got. I was tempted to keep him on my side of the fence!"

"You're kind to say so, Charlie. Lord, what am I going to do, with Ricardo gone? If he were here, you'd have called him, wouldn't you? And he'd have come right over to help you, and instead, you had to manage all the work by yourself—"

"Oh, hell, Genia, it can't be helped."

"I'll have to hire somebody quickly, I guess."

"That ain't no decision to make lightly. I'll help where I can, you know

I will, and there's a bunch here in the valley who'll pitch in every chance they get. Meantime, you get that Ken to cut down on his work for all them other folks, and help you out more. You thinkin' of giving him Ricardo's job?"

Mrs. Potter had been more than thinking about that probability; in fact, she'd been actively worrying about it, for reasons she didn't feel she could discuss with him. "It's a consideration," she replied in her best Western-vague manner. "You think I ought to?"

"Man knows ranching, all right. I'd think he'd be glad to settle in to one good job instead of holding down a dozen dinky ones like he does. And he's got that little spread of his own that he's building up, over to the western slope. Got too many irons in the fire, you ask me, but then some people like the smell of smoke better'n I do."

"Charlie, did you have words with him yesterday, over at the windmill? I thought I saw you and Ken arguing."

"Nah, only one of us was arguing, Genia." Charlie's smile creased his faced even deeper than usual. "Me and my big mouth, I made the mistake of saying something about how he was sure quick to take over for Ricardo, and it seemed to tick him off something terrible. Told me he wasn't doin' no such thing, and I could mind my own business, if it pleased me to do so. Well, I told him it did, but that didn't soothe him down none and he run off like a bull with a burr up its tail. But you didn't come over here for this," Charlie said suddenly. "Unless you got ESP or somethin', and you knew that bull was out. What's this about a call I'm supposed to have got from one of Ricardo's girls?"

"Oh, Charlie, I hate to tell you, but I have more bad news. Bandy's dead. Ken found his body this morning in his apartment, along with two young Mexican illegals who were staying with him. It looked like food poisoning to Ken and to Juanita, and that's why Angela and Estella are calling around, to warn you not to eat any of my leftover chili. That may have been what killed them."

"Damn it!" He jerked off his cowboy hat and threw it violently to the dirt at his feet. "Now it's happened, Genia, just like I *told* Rico it would, over and over. How many times did I tell him? Now you got two dead wets on your hands, and how are you going to explain that? What are you going to do with their bodies? They won't have any identification, you can bet on that, no way for you to send them on home, 'cause you won't know where their home was. Hell!" He bent down to pick up his hat and when he straightened up again, his face was red. "I told Ricardo, I said you're going to get Genia in trouble, if you don't care about yourself and Bandy, think about your employer. Think about what the immigration people are going to say to her when they find out you're harboring wets on her place. Dammit, Genia!"

"Oh, Charlie, nothing's going to happen to me. It was Bandy's doing, and that's what I'm going to say, and that's what they're going to believe, wouldn't you?"

But he fisted his hands and placed them on his hips, and stared beyond her toward the mountains behind her ranch. "Yeah, they'll buy that. And just as well it ended this way, I guess. . . ."

"Charlie!"

"Not that I'd have Bandy die such a mean, hard death—I don't mean to say that—but I'm saying it's better that he won't be taking in no more wetbacks. Governor's been asking me to sit on a special board, Genia, one that's going to look into this state's immigration problems and solve them once and for all, if I have any say about it. Hell, if I have my way, we'll take that electrified fence of Reynolds McHenry and we'll string it all along our border, keep them damn freeloaders out of our country. The way I figure, if they could keep all them East Germans out of Berlin for all those years in an entire country, we can manage to do it for an entire state."

"Our own Berlin Wall, Charlie?"

"Oh, I know you don't like this kind of talk, Genia, but I'm a realist, not like you and Ricardo."

A "realist," Mrs. Potter often thought, was what unimaginative people called themselves when they couldn't come up with any better solutions than ones that involved pain to other people.

"I don't have to tell you how I feel about your opinions on this subject, Charlie."

He almost smiled. "No, you don't, Genia. You and me, we tell each other what we think, always have, and so did Ricardo and me. I hate to say it, but with Rico and Bandy dead, that ends the wetback problem for this valley, and I can't say as I'm unhappy about *that*, bad as I feel about them. Wish it could have been accomplished in some other way than killing them and a couple of innocent young wets, but there you have it, that's as it is."

"You really do think Ricardo may have been killed by illegals?"

"I do, and they got Linda, you mark my words. I feel bad not being out on the search for her this morning, Genia, but you understand I've got to take care of things around here, too, before I can leave." This time his smile was wider, and gentle, a reminder of her problem with the stray bull. "But I'll head on over to your place this afternoon, if they haven't found her yet."

"Of course, Charlie, I do understand that everybody's got their own chores to do. Cattle won't wait for our emergencies. Why don't you give me that container of chili, Charlie? I want it in my hands, so it won't find its way into anybody else's mouth, and so I can personally destroy it."

Charlie's face suddenly flushed a deep red.

"Well, I can't, Genia. I don't know how to say this, but I don't have that tub of chili anymore. It's already been eaten."

"Oh, no, Charlie! By whom?"

His flush deepened to purple, and he wouldn't meet her eyes. "Well, hell, Genia, by Shep, that's who."

"Shep?"

A mixed breed collie came trotting around the corner of Charlie's truck and came up to stick his wet nose into his master's hand.

"Heard your name, did you, boy?" said Charlie.

Mrs. Potter burst out laughing. "You fed my best chili to your *dog*, Charlie?"

"Eats everything I do," he said, defensively. "It's no offense meant to your chili now, Genia, so don't you go to taking any."

"Well," Mrs. Potter said, still laughing as she reached down out of her window and stroked the dog's head, "at least I can see that he's still alive to tell the tale. What'd you think of it, boy? Did you like that chopped sirloin I put in it? I'll bet you did, and the ground pork too."

"Aw, hell, Genia!"

CHAPTER 24

A FOR SALE sign hung on the fence that abutted the gate to Saguaro Ranch. Mrs. Potter knew from Ricardo that Walt and Kathy Amory had got in over their heads when they purchased the five-thousand-acre spread, but she hadn't known things had reached this state and so soon. Driving up the gravel road to their house, Mrs. Potter thought, Somebody's going to "steal" this ranch; it's so run-down, it's bound to be a bargain for some lucky buyer.

Not just anyone could have detected that it was run-down.

But after twenty years of ranching, Mrs. Potter could spot leaning fence posts that should have been replaced and sagging barbed wire that needed tightening. She saw pastures that looked overgrazed, and a few cattle that appeared underfed. Ricardo would have had a fit if he'd seen them, she thought. There was nothing he had detested more than ranchers who spent their money on themselves while they let their livestock suffer. But as Mrs. Potter approached the Amorys' home, with its big barn off to one side and various items of farm equipment scattered about the yard, she wondered if Walt and Kathy *had* spent it all on their own comforts. If they had, the results were not visible. The buildings needed painting, and judging from the way the weeds had grown up beneath the rusty equipment, it didn't appear to have been used for some time. Overall, there was a desolate, dreary look to Saguaro Ranch, Mrs. Potter thought, the look that children get when they aren't sufficiently loved and tended to.

Walt Amory stood on the front porch, looking her way, so Mrs. Potter stuck her arm out her car window and waved. He waved back, a diffident-looking gesture, and remained standing there until she walked up onto the porch. "We threw the chili away," he said immediately, in a quiet voice that she rather had to strain to hear. "As soon as Mrs. Ortega's daughter called. I was sorry to hear about your hired man, Mrs. Potter."

"Thank you, Walt. I'm beginning to think it wasn't my chili, but I don't want anybody taking any unnecessary chances. Did you throw it where the dogs can't get it?"

"Yes, I think so. Kathy took care of it."

Mrs. Potter smiled. "Charlie Watt's dog seemed to like it fine."

Walt smiled a little, too, and she thought: what a nice man he seems when he does that. "Charlie fed it to his dog? Not much of a compliment to you, was it?"

"He says the dog's his best friend."

"Well, then, I guess it is a compliment, after all."

Mrs. Potter waited for him to invite her into the house.

After an awkward moment he did, even throwing an offer of coffee into the deal. Mrs. Potter walked through the doorway, past the screen door he held open for her, and into a home that was shocking in its bareness. There was a kitchen table with a vinyl top, and four matching chrome chairs with vinyl seats and backs, and that was all, not even a television, or a couch to view it from. Mrs. Potter saw newspapers scattered on the tabletop, and when she took a seat at Walt's gestured invitation, she saw those papers included the *Wall Street Journal* and the *New York Times*. They were opened to the employment sections.

Walt Amory caught her staring at the ads and he smiled that sweet, rather sad smile of his again. "Well, there's my secret, out in the open for everyone to see."

"I'm sorry, Walt—"

"Please don't be, Mrs. Potter. It's plain enough, or should be, from the 'for sale' sign by the gate. I don't suppose it was hard for you to tell that we've sold off most of our cattle, and we're having a hard time keeping up with the few we've got left." He stuck his hands in his pockets again. His expression was almost peaceful behind his horn-rimmed glasses. "We had great plans for decorating this house." He laughed a little, and Mrs. Potter was surprised that it didn't sound at all bitter. "Didn't get very far with that plan, as you can see." He nodded toward the papers. "Not getting very far with *that* plan, either. Nobody's much interested in a forty-year-old with a computer software company in bankruptcy and a cattle ranch on the skids. Your man Ricardo—I'm awfully sorry about him, too, by the way—told me it was going to be tough, and he was right. I don't blame him for saying he wouldn't give us a loan from that bank of his down in Nogales. Heck, I wouldn't loan me any money, either."

For Walt, he was almost chattering, she thought.

But then he seemed to get snagged on another thorn of shyness, not seeming to know what to say next. To cover it he turned toward the single item on the kitchen counter, a full coffeepot, pulled a single mug out of a nearly empty cabinet, and poured it full to the brim. He handed Mrs.

Potter her coffee, then stepped away from the table and stuck his hands in his pockets.

"I hate to say this," he blurted, "but as sad a thing as Ricardo's death was, it may turn out to be helpful to Kathy and me." His glance was apologetic. "I don't think the rest of his bank board is as savvy as he was, and without him to dissuade them, we might even get that loan after all. I don't know, though, if it'll help. May be too late for anything, except if we won the lottery." He smiled slightly. "Any lottery."

"Walt . . . what happened?"

He sighed. "Amateurs. We're amateurs, Mrs. Potter, who fell for the romance of ranching without understanding any of the realities of it. I knew it was an expensive hobby, really, I'm not such a fool as I must look by now. But I thought we could pull it off. At first, we only took a reasonable amount of money out of our software business, but then as the bills kept coming in, we kept taking out more and more, until our business began to suffer as much as our hobby. . . . It's seductive, in a way, ranching is—you keep draining your one real source of income in order to prop up your unreal source of income."

He laughed a little, as if he amused himself.

"And you keep thinking, if I can just cover this one invoice, and then this next one, and then we'll sell some cattle and we'll put the money back in the other business. . . . But, heck, the feed bills have been enormous, so much bigger than I ever anticipated, and I think our tractors and our other rolling stock must have worn out faster than a car on a one-year warranty. It seems that we're always taking them in for repairs." He paused, and Mrs. Potter felt for the first time that he was struggling to contain some bitter emotions. "Well, we've even stopped that now. All that expensive machinery that's in our yard? You saw it? I call them Agricultural Artifacts. They're no use to us anymore, we can't afford to fix them or run them. Sometimes I think the cost of fencing alone put us under. Seemed like I'd buy a roll of fencing long enough to encircle Eastern Europe and it'd be gone before our hired hands had it half up. And then I'd buy more, and none of it went as far as I thought it would. Oh, heck, you've got your own troubles, Mrs. Potter, and a lot more tragic than ours. . . . Aren't you sorry you drove up here to hear all about mine?"

"No, Walt, not at all, I'm just sorry that—"

He nodded, cutting her off, though nicely. "Thank you."

"Where's Kathy today?"

"She went to visit the Steinbachs this morning. Gallway says he's got a real estate agent that's better than the one we found, so he's taking Kathy in to Tucson to meet the woman."

Mrs. Potter couldn't help but react to that startling piece of news, delivered without so much as a blink of Walt's brown eyes. "They drove out of town? Together?"

"Yeah, but I don't think it'll help much. What we need is a miracle or, barring that, a friendly neighborhood millionaire. You don't think the McHenrys would like a few more thousand acres to play with, do you?"

Mrs. Potter tried to match his apparent serenity in regard to Kathy's little trip with Gallway. "Have you asked the McHenrys?"

"Seriously?"

"Sure, why not?"

"Well, no, it was just a joke."

"I'm having dinner with them tonight, Walt. Would it be all right if I sounded them out on the subject? I mean, you're probably right, and it's unlikely, but how will you know unless you ask?"

His sweet smile appeared again. "That's what Kathy's always telling me, that I need to ask for what I want, that the worst anybody can say is no."

"She's right."

"She's a saint, is what she is."

Mrs. Potter looked at him, startled at the wetness in his eyes as he said that, and the vehemence in his young voice. Kathy Amory, a saint? Now, there was an interesting perception, one that would certainly boggle the minds of Lorraine and Che. Mrs. Potter wondered at the apparent naïveté of this young husband who waved his wife off on a trip out of town with the very man who was known all around town as her lover. Didn't Walt know what everybody was saying? It couldn't be that he didn't care; his last words and the look on his face showed that he cared about his Kathy very much.

The coffee was some cheap brand, watered down.

Mrs. Potter drank enough to be tactful, then set it aside.

"If there's anything I can do to help, Walt. . . ."

He laughed a little, but it had a strange, giddy sound to it. "Write a check for about a quarter of a million? No, no, that isn't funny. Thank you, Mrs. Potter, that's very kind of you, but I think we got ourselves into this fix, and I think there's nothing much that anybody else can do to get us out of it. Unless Ricardo's bank in Nogales comes through."

"I'll keep my fingers crossed for you."

He escorted her back to her car.

"I haven't seen your saguaro cactus patch for a long time, Walt. Would you mind if I drove into your pasture to take a sentimental look at them? I dearly love those crested saguaros, and they're just so rare to see anymore. And you never know how ranch owners will be, you could sell this place tomorrow and the new owners could be like the McHenrys, and never let anybody on the place again. It's just through a couple of gates, isn't it? I'll certainly close them behind me."

He gently shut her door for her, and pushed down her lock.

"I wish you could, Mrs. Potter, maybe next time. We've got a couple of bulls in there that can't be trusted. I've tried to sell them—heck, I'm trying to sell everything, but who wants a couple of mean-tempered scrawny bulls who'll sire mean-tempered scrawny calves?"

"It's too bad people can't be so sensible," Mrs. Potter joked, trying to raise another smile from him. "We'd have fewer skinny curmudgeons in the world."

It worked. When he waved her off, the gesture was almost jaunty.

On the way back to the main road, Mrs. Potter determined to call Walt Amory back in a day or two and offer to buy his remaining cattle, including those bad-tempered bulls. Maybe they were ill-nourished, which was enough to make any creature mean. Maybe they'd been ill-treated by owners who meant well but who didn't know the front of a cow from the back of a computer terminal. Or maybe they *were* mean, and in that case she'd try to sell them herself, and probably have better luck at it. As Mrs. Potter gazed out at the Amorys' sparse pastureland, it hurt her to see their cattle looking so runty, at this time of year especially, when they should have been fat with pregnancy and with rich feasts of thick grass. *Ken!* she thought, suddenly. Ken Ryerson was trying to build up a small herd of his own; this might be a good, and sadly cheap, way for him to increase his numbers. She'd have to remember to suggest it when she saw him next, which would be soon, she hoped, as she had some potentially disturbing questions to ask her ambitious young part-time hired hand. Like, just how ambitious was he? Did Ken Ryerson want his late boss's job, did he want his late boss's granddaughter . . . and did he want them badly enough to kill the one man who might stand in the way of both of those desires?

As Mrs. Potter exited the gate of Saguaro Ranch, where the FOR SALE sign hung, she wished she'd gotten one last look at those magnificent fan-shaped cacti. What an irony it was that the Amorys had right on their property a small fortune in endangered flora, but as it appreciated in blackmarket value, all they could honorably do was . . . appreciate it.

Mrs. Potter knocked on many doors, rang many doorbells, left many messages, collected many margarine tubs. By the time she finished, she felt sure that between her and the Ortega girls, they'd managed to reach everybody who might have been a potential victim of her cooking—if that was the culprit.

One of her last stops was at Lorraine and Gallway Steinbach's home. She had to double back to reach it, because she wanted to save it until last in the hope that she'd catch Gallway there, back from his trip to Tucson with Kathy Amory.

"Tucson?" said Lorraine Steinbach. "Gall's not in Tucson, Genia."

Mrs. Potter stood on Lorraine's front porch. "Well," she said, feeling acutely awkward, "I wonder where I got that idea."

"I can't imagine. No, Gall's over at your place, has been all day, Genia, helping out in the search for poor little Linda. Won't you come in, dear? You look plumb frazzled, if you don't mind my saying so."

"I don't mind at all, Lorraine. That's exactly how I feel."

"Iced tea?"

Over cool, minted glasses of sun tea, served at Lorraine's kitchen table, Mrs. Potter relayed the news of Bandy's death, and of her sojourn through the valley that day in search of "deadly tubs of ptomaine." Mrs. Potter's smile was embarrassed. "I'm not making light of this, Lorraine, please believe me. I think I'm half goofy from the heat and from riding around in the car for so long."

"Have they figured out what killed Ricardo, Genia?"

"I haven't been home to find out." Mrs. Potter saw a flash of something that looked very much like malice cross the sweet, plump face of her neighbor. "Lorraine? What are you thinking?"

"I'm thinking that I ought to be ashamed of myself." And the other woman's expression did, indeed, quickly alter to one of contrition. "I'm having a hard time grieving over Ricardo, Genia, because the truth is I've just been so mad at the man. Now I should feel guilty about that, but I don't. I guess I'm still mad, can you believe it? I haven't a shred of decency, I guess."

"Don't be silly, Lorraine, of course you do." Mrs. Potter saw Lorraine's lower lip tremble and couldn't help but think, *Oh, dear, here we go again. . . .*

"You wouldn't know about this, Genia, because Lew was such a good, faithful husband, I'm sure, but . . . oh, I've never said this to anyone before . . . the truth is that the worst part is other people knowing." She looked up and Mrs. Potter saw the angry defensiveness in her eyes. "I think I could live with his philandering. Well, I have lived with it, haven't I? And for a lot longer than any of you know, that's for sure. And do you know what? When he . . . does that . . . and nobody knows but me, then I'm kind of okay about it. Then I can pretend I don't know, or I can pretend it isn't happening, and he can pretend that I don't know. . . ."

Mrs. Potter didn't move a muscle or make a sound, but she thought, *When we wish we could be flies on the wall, in order to overhear somebody's secrets, we don't know what we're asking.*

"But the minute somebody else knows and they *say* so, then everything changes. Before that I was just a wife with a private problem, but after that, I'm a fool. That's the hardest part, being a public fool. That's what Ricardo made me when he went up to Gallway that day in the grocery store and told him that everybody knew what was going on and that if Gallway had any respect for me he'd stop seeing Kathy Amory. And I heard that, Genia. Ricardo didn't know it, but I was just around the corner, where I could hear it. And even that would have been okay, but Gallway knew I was there. And so then we couldn't pretend to each other anymore. And then we both knew—that the other knew—that everybody *else* knew." She glanced up at her guest again. "Like you. And Che. And everybody else I see all the time. And then I had to think about how you'd all been thinking about us and talking about us, and how foolish, foolish, foolish you must all think I am."

"Oh, Lorraine . . ."

Mrs. Potter reached out to cover one of the pudgy little hands with her own, but Lorraine withdrew from her touch.

"I hated Ricardo for doing that to us."

"He wanted to help you, Lorraine."

"I know that, Genia. But I don't *care* what *he* wanted. *I* want people to leave us alone. We're just *fine* when people leave us alone and don't stick their noses into our business. I've put up with it all these years, I could keep putting up with it. But now, now . . ."

She looked utterly despairing.

"He won't quit seeing her. And now that I know the whole town is aware of it, I can't lift up my head. I hate Ricardo for making it like this. I hate him, and I can't stop hating him, and I ought to feel guilty about it, and I don't. Oh, Genia, go home, please. . . . I've made a bigger fool of myself than ever before."

Mrs. Potter knew she couldn't offer comfort where it wasn't wanted, and so she did the most respectful thing she knew to do: she got up to leave.

At the door, Lorraine saw her off with the words, "So he went to Tucson today, did he, instead of to your ranch? And I guess we both know who went with him. Thanks for the information, Genia."

The bitter, hateful tone sent chills down Mrs. Potter's spine as she looked back once, then turned around and kept walking to her car.

With all she'd done that day, it was still only noon.

Mrs. Potter had risen from bed very early, planning on seeing Linda's horse, planning on stopping by Juanita's house, planning on going out to the windmill to greet the searchers on this second morning. But Bandy's death had changed all those plans. There remained only one left to fulfill, and she spared a thought for the impossible wish of going home to freshen up first.

Mrs. Potter glanced in the rearview mirror of the Subaru.

She patted a few loose strands of hair into place, pressed her lips together to smooth out what little remained of her lipstick, ran a finger over the crease in each eyelid where gray shadow had glommed up in an unattractive clump. (It was one of the mysteries of life, Mrs. Potter thought, that eye shadow never stayed where you put it. It "traveled," and no matter where you applied it to begin with, it always ended up in the same place: in the valley where the eyelid met the skin that came down from the eyebrow. It contradicted the laws of physics, eye shadow did, because it regularly defied gravity by moving *up* the eyelid before sliding down into that valley. She felt she would understand that phenomenon when she learned where socks disappeared and why the telephone always rang when you stepped into the shower.)

Ready or not, eye shadow or no, it was almost time for her to pick up Jed.

CHAPTER 25

They opted for Sally's Café at the crossroads for lunch.

"Based on your sworn testimony that she serves the best pork tenderloin sandwich in the whole Southwest," Jed teased.

Mrs. Potter very much appreciated his effort to make her smile; there'd been so little reason to do so for the last forty-eight hours. And after hearing her tale of woe of the last six or seven hours, Jed was doing well, she thought, to still be able to make a small joke. Another thought flitted through her mind as well: *this is what companionship is all about, offering solace and comfort to one another, finding a spark of happiness and hope even in the darkest times. This is why people fall in love, why they live together, why they get married, and why in spite of divorces and deaths, they never give up. And these are dangerous thoughts, these are presumptuous thoughts, and I will put a stop to them at once.*

It was hard, though, considering the company she was keeping. Jed seemed to be so relaxed, and so happy just to be in her company, that Mrs. Potter was nearly able to forget how dusty and grubby she felt in comparison to how nice and clean he looked in his brown cotton shirt, open at the neck, over attractive tan gabardine slacks, topped by a light wool jacket in a brown heather tweed. His feet were shod in sturdy brown leather walking shoes of which she completely approved because they looked as if they had traversed some mud and rocks in their time, which indicated that maybe he spent enjoyable times outdoors and that he was smart enough to wear appropriate footwear in rocky Arizona. Surprisingly, very few of her out-of-state guests were so prescient—otherwise intelligent women showed up at Las Palomas in spike heels, and brilliant CEOs of major international companies came calling in Italian loafers. That was why Mrs. Potter had long kept on hand not only a variety of serapes, but also a small shoe store of men's and women's boots and hiking gear in several sizes. Pride of fashion went out the window, she knew, where blisters were concerned. On top of everything else, Jed smelled "simply divine," as one or two of her friends back East might have said.

"You can only eat pork tenderloin sandwiches in a restaurant, did you know that, Jed?"

"Why, no, Andy," he said, playing along with her, "I never heard that before. Why is that, do tell?"

"Well, because there's home food and there's restaurant food, that's why. I'm surprised you don't know that. I offer the pork tenderloin sandwich as proof. Have you ever eaten one in anybody's home?"

He began chuckling. "No, now that you mention it."

"Of course you haven't. It can't be done. I suspect there must be some sort of unwritten law against it. But if you ever *did* have one in a private home, it wouldn't be any good at all."

"Is that right?"

"That's right. I don't know why. No one does. I've asked the greatest chefs from Paris to Harrington, Iowa, and they all claim they don't know. I don't believe them, of course. They're hiding a trade secret, something that gets passed down from one short-order cook to another. It's probably posted in a hidden spot in diners and greasy spoons where the customers would never think to look. Otherwise, we have to assume that something magical happens on the grill in a restaurant, some alchemy that transforms a frozen slab of breaded pork—"

"You make it sound so appetizing, I can hardly wait."

"—into a succulent morsel of tenderness."

"There's a parking space, right in front."

She laughed, feeling for the moment much happier than she had in such a very long time. "Hungry, are we?"

On the way into the café, they bantered back and forth about what comprised "restaurant food" as opposed to "home food." Mrs. Potter held that meatloaf could only be prepared at home, "preferably by the mothers of sons," but Jed maintained that he knew men who swore by certain truck stops' meatloaf. "Orphans," Mrs. Potter scoffed. "Obviously. Poor motherless things. Now, sausage and gravy, that's definitely restaurant cooking." Jed agreed, and he guessed that crepes also were strictly to be eaten "out," but Mrs. Potter claimed not only to have had them in people's homes, but actually to have prepared them herself. "No!" he exclaimed, as he held open the door of Sally's for her. "Then I suppose you 'do' corn dogs, as well?"

Mrs. Potter smiled into his blue eyes.

"Not *nearly* as well," she said.

* * *

Just as she'd promised, the pork tenderloins overflowed the buns and filled the plates. The breading was light, the meat was tender and juicy, the buns had been slapped on the grill just long enough to get the edges brown and crisp and the centers buttery brown. Fresh, fluted leaves of lettuce hung out the sides of the buns; the sandwiches were thick with sliced tomatoes and onions, creamy with mayonnaise that had been slathered by a generous hand. Potato chips decorated the edges of the plates, and tall glasses of iced tea rose beside them. Jed took a first bite of the sandwich and closed his eyes, a beatific expression spreading across his face.

"Another convert," observed Mrs. Potter.

He didn't open his eyes until he had finished chewing and swallowing that bite. Finally, he said, with a look of awe, "Is this what they call an epiphany?"

"I think it's a little lower on the scale than that." Mrs. Potter smiled before she raised her own sandwich to her mouth. "More along the lines of a 'meaningful experience,' I believe."

He chewed, looking, as her grandchildren might have said, "blissed out." After he swallowed again, he said, "Haven't you people ever heard of low-fat, cholesterol-free diets?"

"Oh, of course," Mrs. Potter assured him, "and we practice them every second Thursday in March. You're in cattle country, Jed. Our theory is that the fresh air evaporates the calories."

"I do believe I like that theory."

Mrs. Potter assured him that Sally's pork tenderloin sandwiches were a carefully allotted treat, in which she probably indulged no more than a few times a year. "And which I make up for with carrots and celery lunches for the rest of the week."

"No sacrifice," Jed said, holding the sandwich high, "is too great."

"Precisely." Mrs. Potter smiled at him. "It's nice to see that we still agree on the important things."

"White Tower hamburgers . . ."

"Steamed clams . . ."

"And Sally's pork tenderloin sandwiches."

He held her glance for a long moment, during which she felt as if a movie of their earlier time together played before her eyes. The years fell away, and the man seated opposite her was still young Jed, so full of exuberant intelligence and curiosity and fun. As that young face faded out, and she saw again the lines and wrinkles of the older one, she felt a stirring of something like tenderness. She, too, had lines and wrinkles, and she knew the pains and joys that had put them there. Mrs. Potter had to restrain an impulse to reach out to smooth the creases between Jed's eyebrows, and to touch his cheek, as if to say *"yes, I know, it's been hard sometimes, but here we are again. . . ."*

"Andy, I . . ."

"Yes, Jed?"

The waitress who had taken their orders and delivered their food had trotted off to serve other customers, but now Sally herself appeared and leaned an arm on the top of Mrs. Potter's side of the booth. She stared frankly at Jed. She'd already quickly greeted Mrs. Potter at the door and offered sympathy for the consecutive tragedies at Las Palomas Ranch. But Mrs. Potter knew—and wasn't offended by the fact—that it wasn't possible for Sally to remain morose for any longer a time than it took her to boil a pot of water. The restaurant owner was a stout woman in her mid-fifties, with a broad face that always looked reddened from cooking, and a tightly frizzed blond mass of what she herself called her "beauty shop hair." Neither she nor any of her waitresses or cooks wore uniforms. Blue jeans and T-shirts were the order of the day, every day, at Sally's, with only plastic name tags to identify the servers from the served. Sally's tag displayed her first name in red block letters.

"You must be Genia's old friend from college," she said.

Jed looked startled, and Mrs. Potter jumped in quickly to rescue him. "You're right, Sally, as always. Jed, this is Sally Thompson, who owns this fine establishment. Sally, may I present to you yet another satisfied customer? This, as you no doubt already know perfectly well, is Jed White."

"Jedders H.," said Sally with a grin. "Don't know what the *H* is for. This is Gossip Central, Mr. White, everybody stops here, and they talk about everything that's going on, and can I help it if I just happen to be walking through when they say whatever it is they're saying? It's not like I *try* to listen." She turned to Mrs. Potter in a confiding way, and leaned down until her name tag was even with Mrs. Potter's right shoulder. "Listen, Genia, you won't believe who was in here yesterday. Together. At the same table. That old stinker, Gall—"

"—way Steinbach," Mrs. Potter said, "and Walt Amory."

Sally pretended to pout. "Well, you're the stinker! Take the wind out of my sails! How'd you know that, anyway?"

"Just happened to be driving past, Sally."

"Well, then you don't know what they were saying!" Sally retorted triumphantly. She glanced at Jed. "Your Mrs. Potter here doesn't approve of gossip, I want you to know, but she knows that she can't stop me from telling it, so I think she's come to think of me as more like the valley newspaper, sort of a communication link with the world, you might say." Sally pretended to preen a bit, and Mrs. Potter and Jed both smiled. She bent still closer to Mrs. Potter. "Besides, Genia, this is really interesting.

So they were in here together, and you wouldn't believe what I was hearing. I had to keep walking by, so I couldn't hear the whole thing, but I was just so shocked I nearly dropped a whole entire bowl of homemade chicken noodle soup on old Mr. Ford in the next booth."

She hunkered down still further, until she was nearly whispering.

"That awful old Gallway had the nerve to lecture that young Walt Amory on how he ought to keep better tabs on his wife."

Mrs. Potter couldn't help it. "What?" she exclaimed.

"That's what I said! I heard him with my own ears. I heard him say, 'Walt, you've let 'er get completely out of control.' And he said, 'You've got to keep a tight grip on them.' Women, he meant! Can you believe it? I almost ran to the kitchen and got a spatula to come back and hit the old goat with it. And then he says, he said, 'Some men have got what it takes to take care of business, and some men don't! You can't handle 'er, Walt,' he says, 'that's obvious, and you're absolutely right if you think I can.' Are you just shocked, Genia? Did you ever think Gallway was *that* arrogant? And then he says, 'But I don't know if I want to take 'er on! Got enough on my plate as it is,' he says, talking about that sweet wife of his! Lorraine would die if she heard him! Why, I was walkin' by with hot coffee at the time when I heard him say that, and I wanted so bad just to dump it in his lap. See what he could handle after that! What do you think of all that, Genia?"

"What did Walt think of it, Sally?"

"Walt!" Sally made a dismissive, contemptuous gesture. "He *took* it, is what he did, just sat there nodding his head and looking humiliated and taking it, and letting that awful Gallway shake a finger in his face and lecture him about his own wife. I'll tell you, I was shocked." Sally straightened up and shook her head, smiling and looking as if she was having a great time. "Just shocked, that's what I was. Aren't you?"

"Sally," Mrs. Potter said with mock repressiveness, "do you have any rhubarb pie left for us?"

"Oh, you." The restaurant owner touched Mrs. Potter's shoulder affectionately, and grinned at Jed. "Too nice, that's what she is. But I love her anyway." The smile grew a bit mischievous. "Don't you?"

"Pie and coffee, Sally?" said Mrs. Potter, emphatically.

"Coffee too? Well, you *are* demanding! I might just have to give you some of the mud left over from Ken's pot. Her hired man," Sally said in an explanatory sort of way to Jed. "Ken Ryerson. Lives upstairs here. Bless his heart, he makes a pot of coffee every morning when he goes out, fills up his Thermos, but he always leaves me some. 'Course, as early as he goes, it's usually sludge by the time I come rolling in."

"How early does he go out, Sally?" Mrs. Potter asked.

"Crack o' dawn, or even way before the dawn cracks."

Jed laughed, and Sally nudged Mrs. Potter as if to say, "See there? Got a sense of humor, he does." Mrs. Potter fixed her with a penetrating stare and said slowly and with even greater emphasis than before so that maybe this time Sally wouldn't miss the point: "I've told Jed all about your rhubarb pie, Sally, dear. He can't wait to taste it. Neither can I. Sally. Dear. And coffee surely would taste fine too."

Sally nudged her again, and broadly winked.

"Comin' right up, madam!"

It was a moment before Mrs. Potter could meet Jed's eyes, and when she did, she was comforted to see that he looked quite as pink in the face as she was.

On their way out of the café, Mrs. Potter recognized two of the McHenrys' burly employees coming in. One was the guard who'd stopped her at the gate, the other was the muscular young man who'd accompanied Marj and Rey to the windmill the previous morning. She nodded to them in greeting, but they appeared not to recognize her, or even to be in the habit of being polite to strangers who were polite to them. She noticed that they both stared hard at Jed, however, and then exchanged quick glances. They were watching when Jed stopped Sally long enough to say to her, "It's Harold."

"What?" Sally looked baffled, but then she burst out laughing.

It was a marvelously invigorating sound that carried all the way out the door with them. In the car, however, Jed said quietly to Mrs. Potter, "That was our son's name, too, only we called him Haj. He would have been thirty-seven in a couple of months."

This time, it was Mrs. Potter who reached over to grasp one of his hands, and to press it in silent comfort.

CHAPTER 26

Mrs. Potter drove the little brown Subaru onto the two-lane highway leading south to Nogales.

"I hate this stretch of road."

"Do you want me to drive it?"

Mrs. Potter laughed a little. "I don't want anybody to drive it. Except me. I want it all to myself all the way to Nogales. No, thank you, Jed, that would hardly be fair. At least I know the road, and a little about how to play their game."

"Their game?"

She narrowed her eyes. "Those big trucks that you see barreling down on us? Tomato trucks. They come all the way up from Mexico with the sole intent of terrorizing innocent drivers on this highway. It's even worse going this way, because they're hauling empty, as they say. I call this the Nogales 500."

"Wait a minute then."

Mrs. Potter slowed a bit, and looked over at him.

Jed had brought with him a tweed hat with a little red feather in it, and now he plunked it on his head. He smiled at her, looking quite debonaire, she thought. "Just wanted to put on my crash helmet," he said. "And make sure I had myself strapped in."

"Check," Mrs. Potter said, and pushed her speed up to seventy miles per hour merely to keep from getting squashed by the monster on wheels that was right behind them. "Pardon me if I don't talk much, Jed, but I can't talk and drive this suicide trap at the same time. Don't ask me about the scenery—I've never seen it. Don't expect me to point out spots of interest along the way, because I don't even know if they're there. All I have ever seen on this road are taillights and yellow lines."

"That bad?" He sounded skeptical.

A monster truck seeming to come out of nowhere suddenly passed them, blasting its horn as it drew even with them and leaving their little car rocking in the wind in its wake. It appeared to miss hitting another oncoming truck by all of ten yards.

"I see what you mean," Jed said, sounding a bit shaken.

Mrs. Potter couldn't resist asking, "Still want to drive, Jed?"

"No, no." He laughed as he tightened his seat belt. "You're doing fine, Andy, you're doing just fine."

"I'll try not to kill us," she said.

It was a promise that would prove hard to keep.

The day was developing in a typical Arizona spring way, with the nippy dawn passing into a pleasantly cool morning, which melted into a warm afternoon, which was already working its way up to "mighty hot." Mrs. Potter knew that by the time they returned to the valley, she'd be ready for a long, cool swim in her pool, and she wondered whether or not to invite Jed to join her. It seemed to her that presenting herself in a bathing suit after forty years was displaying a great deal more courage than she probably possessed. . . .

They were thirty miles down the road, and she was passing one of the trucks, when her steering wheel suddenly grew stiff and hard to manage in her hands, and the car began to ride roughly beneath them. She couldn't hear anything amiss because of the roar of the truck beside them, but Mrs. Potter knew something was dreadfully wrong. Her palms were suddenly slick with sweat on the steering wheel and her heart was pounding. She suspected that Jed had no idea anything was amiss, but she wasn't sure she could control the car long enough to push it past the truck and around the front far enough to pull safely off the road. She looked ahead and saw to her horror that a second huge truck had just crested the far hill and was speeding toward them.

There was a third truck coming up fast from behind.

Nevertheless, Mrs. Potter saw no alternative but to ease off on her gas pedal and to try to fit herself back in between the two trucks that were going south with her.

The third truck driver blasted his horn and speeded up, narrowing the gap so that now she couldn't manage to squeeze in. She would have sworn that he did it on purpose.

Jed had straightened up in his seat.

Out of the corner of her eye, and because everything was beginning to move in a strange sort of slow motion, she saw him look up at the truck beside them, then look up the road at the truck that was coming, and then glance in the passenger-side mirror on his door to check out the truck behind.

Mrs. Potter made a split-second decision and drove the car off the side of the road on the left, moments before the truck heading north sped over the very spot in the pavement where she had crossed it. It seemed as if all the horns of hell were blasting, as all three truck drivers registered their indignation at the same time. At that moment, if she'd had a rifle hanging in her back window as practically everybody else in the valley did, Mrs. Potter would have happily taken potshots at all three trucks.

"Whew," Jed said.

"You can say that again."

"We could have been killed."

"Are you sure we aren't dead?"

"You handled that marvelously well, Andy."

She held up her shaking hands for him to see.

He grabbed them and held on tight.

"Jed?" Mrs. Potter said hesitantly, softly.

He looked deep into her blue eyes. "Yes?"

"I have to tell you something."

"Yes, Andy?"

She squeezed his fingers.

"I'm afraid we have a flat tire, Jed."

By the time they'd changed it, Mrs. Potter was a good deal more than merely dusty and Jed's neat clothing was dirtied at the knees and elbows and his hands were reddened and greasy from manipulating the jack.

As they got back into the car, and limped on into Nogales on the little emergency tire they'd found in the trunk, Mrs. Potter felt utterly depressed.

Typhoid Genia, she thought, *that's what Jed must think I am.*

He was so nice about it, so sweet and patient and understanding, but good heavens! First, coming upon the body of her ranch manager slung over a horse. And then the search party for Linda. And then her chili—which he ate, too—which might have killed three men.

And now this, near-death on the highway.

If I were he, Mrs. Potter thought sadly, *I wouldn't have anything more to do with me.*

The people at the rental car agency felt so sorry for Mrs. Potter and Jed that they gave them a ride to the general aviation side of the airport and let them off right at the front door of the office of Arizona Aerials. But not before Jed had insisted that the mechanics at the agency check the flat tire to determine what happened to it.

"Nail," the mechanic finally said, and held it up for them to view. "Big sucker."

Mrs. Potter thoroughly agreed; she thought it looked long enough to fasten five thick boards together. Seeing it, and hearing the explanation, seemed to satisfy Jed's need to know. He took the nail out of the mechanic's hand and slipped it into his own wallet, as if it were a souvenir. Mrs. Potter thought of telling him that he could get ceramic salt and pepper shakers in the shape of cacti, if he really wanted mementos of his stay in Arizona. She wasn't delighted at the idea of Jed walking around with a long, sharp, pointed reminder of just how hazardous she could be to his health.

With the wallet tucked away in his pocket, Jed finally agreed to let a young woman from the agency chauffeur him and Mrs. Potter across the airport grounds to the little aviation company that had located Linda's horse from the air the day before. Only a few minutes later they walked back onto the airfield behind their pilot, a woman named Lucy who was one of the two owners of the business. Lucy was a garrulous, thin brunette whose dyed hair and deeply tanned face hid her true age, which could have been anywhere from thirty-five to fifty. Considering that both she and her husband had flown planes in the Vietnam War, though, Mrs. Potter guessed they were both pushing the upper end of that age scale. Notwithstanding that she was middle-aged, Lucy seemed fairly to bounce on the soles of her feet with all evident eagerness to get up in the air. Mrs. Potter had taken off her sweater and Jed had shed his jacket long before, and now it was so hot that she felt as if her own soles might bake into the tarmac if she didn't pick them up and walk fast enough.

"Maybe you'd better stay safely on the ground, Jed," Mrs. Potter suggested, "instead of taking another chance with me."

She secretly hoped he would laugh that off and squeeze her hand again to reassure her that he didn't blame any of these misfortunes on her, but Jed didn't reply. He seemed lost in thoughts that he apparently wasn't going to share with her. Climbing in after him and the bouncy pilot, neither of whom appeared to show the slightest hesitation or awkwardness about putting a foot on the struts and pulling themselves up into the cockpit, Mrs. Potter felt hot and old and unattractive and clumsy. Sweat ran down her face, and she took a tissue out of her purse to dab it away.

Lucy leaned over to inquire, "Need a hand up?"

"No!" Mrs. Potter snapped. "Thank you."

"Can you make it all right, Andy?"

"Yes!" Mrs. Potter said as she hoisted herself up into the cockpit. She tried not to glare at the two faces gazing at her so solicitiously. "That was easy. I'm set. What are we waiting for? Let's go!"

Lucy opened the little window on her side and yelled, "Prop!" to warn any pedestrians to move out of the way. She started the single engine. The propeller blades came to life, with a jerk and a wheeze and finally, a roar.

CHAPTER 27

The little airplane lifted off just in time to clear the palo verde trees at the end of the runway. Mrs. Potter breathed again, and then watched as the pointer on the altimeter climbed to five hundred feet and then rose slowly to one thousand feet above the ground. The little plane bumped about in the air as if they were still racing down the dirt runway.

"Thermals," the pilot, Lucy Dermitt, yelled during one particularly rocky stretch when the altimeter jumped from one thousand feet down to nearly nine hundred and then up fifty feet again in the space of a few seconds. It was noisy inside the four-seat, high-wing airplane. "It's the heat rising from the ground, makes the air a roller coaster sometimes. You folks okay? You're not going to get sick on me, are you?" She twisted her head around a bit in order to holler into the back. "There are bags behind the seats, there, Mr. White, if you or Mrs. Potter need them. Me, I never get sick, but then pilots usually don't. It's you passengers who suffer, because you're not in control, you don't have anything to do but sit there and worry that I'm going to kill you. I promise I won't. I think it helps, too, that I've got this wheel to hang on to, it kind of centers me, gives my equilibrium something to hang on to, so to speak."

"Will it stay like this?" Mrs. Potter asked, raising her own voice.

Lucy shook her head. Mrs. Potter could see now why she wore a sleeveless T-shirt and shorts with sandals; it was beastly hot inside the little plane. "Nope. Might get worse, once we get close to the mountains, 'cause then we'll have updrafts and downdrafts to worry about in addition to these thermals. But listen, you'll be so busy looking out the window that you'll forget you have a stomach."

Mrs. Potter doubted that very much, but she swallowed hard and vowed not to disgrace herself during the flight. She glanced back at Jed, who sat behind Lucy. He was staring out the small triangular-shaped window beside him. As if reading Mrs. Potter's mind, the pilot said, "It's worse for Mr. White back there, 'cause in the back you get more slipping and sliding, more drift in the air. Us, we're flying pretty straight, but he's going side to side as well as up and down. Be glad you're sitting up here with me, Mrs. Potter."

Actually, Mrs. Potter was glad. Despite the heat, despite everything, she was beginning to feel the adventure of their little flight; the sheer joy of seat-of-the-pants flying began to infect her and to help her to ignore her feelings of physical and emotional discomfort. She turned her face toward the rear seats.

"Are you all right, Jed?"

He glanced up and smiled at her. "I'm fine."

"So," said Lucy, with the air of an exuberant child, "where we goin'?"

They wanted to fly wherever Ricardo had flown, that was the plan.

And so Lucy swooped them down over the southern range of mountains into Wind Valley, where Mrs. Potter and Jed learned exactly why it had been so named. The little plane was buffeted in every direction, as if there were gods stationed in the North, South, East and West, blowing their powerful breaths into the valley where they collided in a maelstrom above the ground.

"You got wind comin' off those mountains," Lucy explained, pointing at the Rimstones, "and those," pointing toward Mexico, "and those goin' up toward Tucson, and those over there," pointing west. "And we still got those thermals comin' up off the desert floor. It was like this in Vietnam, which is why it doesn't bother me, I guess. You know how mountainous that country is. You ever been there? No, well, I guess you've seen pictures, all those mountains, and it's a hot sucker, like here, although the air's a lot dryer here, of course, and the nice thing about flying here as opposed to flying there is that nobody's going to shoot us from the ground. And if the engine gives out or we lose oil pressure I got a million places to glide us down to a safe landing. And there aren't any snakes in the trees, hell, there aren't any trees to speak of, and once we get down, there also aren't any little men in cone hats, carrying rifles, come to take us prisoner." A particularly strong thermal lifted them and then violently dropped them again. The top of Mrs. Potter's head brushed the ceiling of the plane. She tightened her seat belt. "This is a picnic, really," Lucy assured her with a big grin. "This is a ride in an amusement park. This is Disney World, compared to 'Nam. Okay, Mrs. Potter, if I remember correctly, this is about where we started, Mr. Ortega and me, here on the edge of the valley, and he directed me to fly toward that little crossroads settlement. . . ."

Lucy Dermitt took her plane down to five hundred feet, which increased the turbulence even more, but which also made it possible for her passengers to see the lines of wire strung between fence posts, the faces of people in pickup trucks, many of whom waved out their windows as the plane flew over, and to see dogs and cattle, children in the schoolyards, and clothes hung out to dry in backyards.

"He had me just basically fly back and forth over mostly this part of the valley while he took pictures."

"He had a camera with him?"

"Oh, yeah, I'm surprised you didn't bring one, most people do when they come up for one of these rides. It's a wonder to me they can shoot anything, what with their camera riding up and down in front of their faces. But, yeah, he took lots of pictures, mostly of scenery, it seemed to me, pastures and cows and stuff."

Mrs. Potter remembered that Juanita had mentioned a new camera, a fancy one that printed the date and time on each photograph.

"What else did he take pictures of, Lucy?"

"Come on!" the pilot said, banking the plane so sharply that Mrs. Potter's left shoulder brushed her right one. "I'll show you." Mrs. Potter looked toward the back seat and saw that Jed was pressed up against the window.

For the next half hour they swooped over one ranch and then another. She flew them over the C Lazy U, where they spied on two of Che's hired cowboys conducting a calf roping demonstration for the dudes. Several children spotted the plane and jumped up and down excitedly as they waved at it. Mrs. Potter thought it wonderful that a small plane could still evoke such a thrill in the young, whom one might expect to be jaded by air travel. But, no, even the grown-ups in the valley seemed to take pleasure out of the buzzing airplane.

Charlie Watt was out in one of his pastures with his pickup truck, and he got out and waved up at the plane. Lucy waggled her wings in reply, which caused Mrs. Potter to grit her teeth and swallow hard again. She drew back from the window so that the man below couldn't see her, figuring that if she could so easily identify him from this height, it wasn't beyond possibility that he might recognize her when the little plane dipped toward him.

"We're coming up over the McHenrys' ranch," Mrs. Potter yelled back to Jed.

"Oh, no, we're not," Lucy yelled back.

"What? Why not?"

"Because they've asked me never to fly over their property with tourists, that's why. And they pay me a nice sum of money to keep my promise. My husband and I, we don't ever fly over the Highlands. That's the bargain, and I keep it. I'm sorry, but, hey, don't worry. I didn't fly your ranch manager over it, either, so it wouldn't help you any to see it."

So instead of zooming over the huge McHenry spread, the little plane flew its boundaries for a short time and from a discreet distance.

"Did you take some aerial photos for them, Lucy?"

She grinned. "*I* didn't."

Mrs. Potter got the message.

"Did they tell your husband why they wanted them?"

Lucy shook her head, giving the impression that she really didn't know. She banked to the north and flew on toward Walt and Kathy Amory's place, Saguaro Ranch.

Mrs. Potter thought she could have counted with two hands the number of cattle she spied there.

"Jed," Mrs. Potter called back to him, and pointed out the window. "Look down here to the right. See that clump of tall cacti? Those are crested saguaros, and they're a very rare sight to see. They're the prize of this ranch, and they wouldn't be there except by some fluke of luck or nature. Nobody knows if some early settler actually planted them, or if they just happened to grow up like that. But there are so few of them left, what with illegal harvesting, that those down there are literally worth tens of thousands of dollars on the retail market."

From the air, Mrs. Potter counted four of the impressive cacti.

It saddened her that they should be a tourist attraction like this, when they ought to be common sights along the roadways of Arizona. Every time she drove anywhere in the state, whether up to the red-rock country around Sedona or over toward New Mexico, or west to Baja, she kept her eyes peeled for that distinctive fan-shape, but in all the years of living in the state, she had yet to come across one by happenstance. The only way she knew to see them was to go where the tourist brochures directed her to go to view them. Or to catch sight of one in somebody's private garden and, ever after, to wonder and worry about how it got there.

"You ought to get a picture of it!" Lucy shouted.

"I wish we could," Mrs. Potter said.

"Well, maybe you can get a copy of the one your Mr. Ortega took. He must have had me circle them a dozen times until he got what he wanted. Ready to see your ranch, Mrs. Potter?"

Mrs. Potter was.

Oddly enough, for all the years she had resided off and on at Las Palomas, she'd never before viewed it from the air. And she was taken by surprise that the sight of it shining beautifully golden in the sunshine would move her nearly to tears.

They spent some time swooping through the canyons, with Jed and Mrs. Potter keeping their eyes peeled for signs of Linda's presence. They followed several different sets of searchers, viewing from above what those people could only see from below. The fact that the searchers were still there at all told Mrs. Potter all she needed to know about the search for Linda Scarritt.

Once, Lucy started to buzz a small herd of cattle, which would have made them stampede in fright, but Mrs. Potter quickly stopped her by grasping her arm. "No, please." Stress was no better for livestock than it was for human beings; Mrs. Potter remembered how Ricardo's goal had always been to keep her cattle "fat and happy."

She did encourage Lucy to circle the top of El Bizcocho several times, however. Mrs. Potter noted how one could, indeed, see all of the valley from way up there, and everybody's fence lines. You'd feel like king of the mountain, she mused, or queen, as the case might be. If you took a stranger up there, you could point out every landmark for miles around, show him or her where everybody in the valley lived or worked, and all the roads and pastures, barns and houses, even the shops in the cross-roads. If you turned around, to the west, your view would be blocked by the mountains leading into government land. You'd have absolute privacy up there, too, more privacy than perhaps anywhere else in the valley. You could see everything, but nobody could see you, especially if you parked your horses behind a couple of cacti or boulders.

"Okay," Mrs. Potter said, after Lucy had flown around El Bizcocho four or five times, "if we've seen everything that Ricardo saw, we can go down now."

The arrangement was that Lucy would land them on the dirt strip at the C Lazy U, where Mrs. Potter would hitch a ride home with one of Che Thomas's young employees.

As Lucy bounced in for a crosswind landing, she shouted over the noise of the engine, "Oh, how I wish I were a crook!"

Startled, Mrs. Potter looked over at her. "Why?"

Lucy throttled down and lowered the flaps and put the gear down and talked through her headset radio microphone to any other airplanes that might happen to be flying in the vicinity and kept the plane level and descending, all in seemingly simultaneous maneuvers that Mrs. Potter thought should surely require at least three hands. Plus, she managed to reply to Mrs. Potter's question at the same time. "Because the country's full of great smuggler's airports, that's why. Like this one. Dirt runways. Middle of somebody's pasture. No cops for hundreds of miles around. Nobody lookin'. Nobody carin'. No lights at night. Just drop your load of cocaine or whatever, or pick one up, and off you fly, with nobody the wiser. A halfway decent pilot could make enough dough to open his own FBO in a couple of years."

Mrs. Potter clutched her armrest as the little plane bounced onto the dirt, then bounced into the air again, before settling to earth. "FBO?"

"Fixed-base operation." Lucy turned off the fuel and opened her side window and guided the little airplane to a coasting stop at the end of the runway. "What my husband and I want someday, our own little airport at the crossroads of Podunk and Plumbdamn. Hope y'all enjoyed your flight."

Jed stood with the door to the C Lazy U car open as he gazed down at Mrs. Potter in the front passenger's seat.

"Never a dull moment," she said, and smiled up at him. "What time should I be ready tonight, Jed?"

"I feel awful about this, Andy, but I'm going to have to cancel tonight."

"You're not going to dinner at Highlands after all?"

He shifted his gaze from her own for a moment before looking at her again. "I'm just not going to be able to take a guest, Andy. I'm awfully sorry. This is awkward, and I feel like an utter fool to be doing it. Please, I hope you'll forgive me, and let me make it up to you. May I call you later today?"

"Of course, Jed."

He closed the door gently, and she heard it click.

Mrs. Potter waved back at him, where he stood waving at her as one of Che's young cowboys drove her away from the C Lazy U. But she was thinking of Jed's last words: *"I'll call you."* They were, she knew, three of the most dreaded words in the lexicon of dating, no matter what the age of the man or woman. Mrs. Potter had many times dried her daughters' tears over disappointments when that particular promise wasn't kept by young men who had probably never intended to be cruel. She knew that much from her own son. "Hey!" he had protested when his sisters once accused him of leading a girl on in that way, "I didn't know what else to say! What was I supposed to tell her, 'Sorry, I'll never call you, because you're boring and I had a horrible time and I don't care if I never see your ugly face as long as I live'?" "Just say thank you," his sisters had lectured him. "Just say good night. Don't make promises. She'll get the picture."

Mrs. Potter suspected she had the picture.

She felt as tired and sad and discouraged as she had ever been, and she couldn't wait to get home. *After everything that has happened in the last two days,* she thought, as she rode silently beside the young driver, *who could blame Jed if he never called me again?* Mrs. Potter tried to convince herself that the absence of Jedders H. White from her life would be just one inconsequential little loss added to the larger, much more important ones. *After all, I got along perfectly well without him for forty years!*

The young man let her off at her own front gate.

Normally, the sight of it would have lifted her heart, but on this late afternoon in May, Mrs. Potter's heart felt terribly heavy as she lifted the latch.

CHAPTER 28

Mrs. Potter didn't even walk all the way through her front gate before she changed her mind and her course. She looked in at her swimming pool and saw that it was still covered. The meaning of that hit her hard: there was no Bandy to pull the cover off and neatly fold and store it. Mrs. Potter glanced at the nearest rose garden and spied a dead head, which had been a yellow flower. Bandy was no longer there to snip it off. She'd used firewood last night, and today there wasn't any Bandy to replenish the baskets in the house.

Because she suddenly couldn't bear to face her empty home, not just yet, she turned around and headed up to her carport instead. There was something she had to do, and she might as well use this time to get it over with. Something unpleasant. Something she dreaded. Something she'd been thinking about off and on all day. And she decided that she might as well do it while she was already feeling miserable, since not even a shower or a change of clothing, not even a swim, was likely to put her in a better frame of mind.

But once in the carport, she found she had to change course again.

There, dumped near her car, was Linda Scarritt's saddle.

"So this is where Ken put you last night."

Mrs. Potter walked over and crouched down beside the saddle. The fabric of the seat felt wooly and perfectly dry in spite of its drenching, but then nothing but a cactus could hold moisture for this long in Arizona. She ran her hands along the saddle, feeling the fine tooling of its leather, thinking of the horse that had worn it and of the woman who owned it. This saddle had been a high school graduation gift to Linda from Ricardo and Juanita, if she remembered correctly. Mrs. Potter wished she had psychic abilities, that she might touch the saddle horn and receive vibrations or somesuch, telling her what had befallen its owner.

"Charlie's right, this saddle has nothing to tell us."

She started to grab it at both ends to move it farther back into the carport and in so doing she lifted one stirrup, meaning to throw it over the saddle seat. When she did, she glimpsed something lodged under the strip of leather that connected the seat to the stirrup. Mrs. Potter didn't attempt to touch the object until she had pulled a tissue out of her purse and wrapped it around the fingers of her right hand so that her fingerprints wouldn't contaminate the surface of the object.

Only then did she tug at it, and out came a wallet. It was thin, made of some sort of synthetic fabric, folded over into thirds, and closed by means of a Velcro strip. The wallet was a greenish brown with darker stains; the black trim around the edges looked frayed, as if this wallet had resided in somebody's back pocket for many months. Careful to employ the tissue as a shield, Mrs. Potter pried open the Velcro and saw that the wallet had narrow compartments for cards, photos, or cash, but there was no coin purse. In the cash compartment, she found a five-dollar bill and three ones. The card compartment held only two items: a tiny photograph of two adults and a girl, and an Arizona driver's license. Mrs. Potter recognized the adults as Francesca and Les Scarritt and the girl as Linda Scarritt only a few years ago, when she was maybe about fourteen years old. The driver's license carried a more recent photograph of her, perhaps only a couple of years old.

Although she carefully looked through the rest of the wallet, Mrs. Potter found nothing else in it. So she was left with the question of how the wallet got stuck up in a crevice of the saddle, who put it there, and why.

"It had to be Linda who slipped it in there," she whispered in the still, shadowy heat of the carport. "There's no reason anybody else would do it. She could have stuck it up there to keep somebody from stealing it, but I doubt that, because there's not enough in it to worry about. Eight dollars and a driver's license, I don't think she'd go to this trouble over that. . . ."

Then why would she go to the trouble?

"To let us know . . ."

Mrs. Potter's eyes filled with tears.

"That she's alive!"

Then. She was alive then. If I'm right, Linda hid this wallet in her saddle. But is she still alive? Mrs. Potter suspected the dark stains that had soaked into the fabric of the wallet were blood. She raised it to her nose to sniff, but couldn't smell anything except the scent of horse and leather. If it was blood, only a lab would be able to detect if it was animal, perhaps from Taco's wounds, or human.

"I have to get this to the sheriff . . ."

And she had to get down the hill to the Ortega house to show Juanita this one and only piece of evidence, and do it without raising a desperate grandmother's hopes too high.

"Mrs. Potter?"

She jerked around, her heart pounding.

"Oh, Ken, hello, you startled me."

If she felt dirty and worn, the tall cowboy standing in the shadows looked even more so. He ducked his head apologetically. "I'm sorry, ma'am, I didn't mean to. I came to get Linda's saddle, and then I saw you was up here. I thought I ought to tell you what's been going on and how the search went today. We haven't found her yet, Mrs. Potter."

"I was so afraid of that, but look, Ken, at what I found!"

She held out the wallet, in the tissue, for him to see.

"That's hers," he confirmed, his tanned face growing pale. "Where'd you find it?"

"Tucked in under the saddle seat."

"My God. I don't get it . . ."

"Well," Mrs. Potter said gently, "she was alive to put it there."

"If it was her who did it."

Mrs. Potter felt almost guilty for having shown it to him, because he seemed to take it so hard, as if he just couldn't believe it meant anything in the way of good news. And she had to tell him that there wasn't anything in the wallet, either, to point them in the right direction.

"Was that you," he asked, "flying overhead a while back?"

"Yes, I knew the bad news when I saw all of you down there."

"I don't know what to do next, Mrs. Potter. We got the vet in to look at Taco. She says he got gored, maybe by javelinas. That could mean Linda got hurt, but where is she?" His face twisted with emotion, as he glanced down at the wallet in her hands. Mrs. Potter wished she could put it away, out of his sight. "Why can't we find her?"

"What about Bandy, Ken? Do we know what killed him?"

The cowboy shook his head. "No word yet. I don't think it was your chili though, I mean, all those poisons he had around the place, fertilizers and bug sprays and all, hell, he coulda got confused and thought he was pouring vinegar into the chili, when he was really pouring poison. Coulda used those bowls for mixing chemicals, then served the chili out of them. You know?"

"That thought has occurred to me, too, Ken."

She walked toward him, and gestured toward a bale of hay outside the carport. "Come on, let's sit down." As long as he was already here, she thought unhappily, she might as well get the next job over with. Mrs. Potter had thought she was going to have to go looking for Ken Ryerson —that was why she had gone to the carport in the first place—but here he was, ready or not. While his back was turned, she took the opportunity to place Linda's wallet on the driver's seat of her car.

When they were both seated on the hay, Ken with his back slumped up against the side of the carport and one long leg bent so that his right cowboy boot rested on top of the bale, she began the speech she had rehearsed in her mind throughout the day.

"Now that Ricardo is gone," she said, "I have to look for someone to take his place. Ideally, that would be a person who is already familiar with our operation, and one who has many years of experience with cattle and who is ready to move up to a responsible, permanent position as ranch manager." She paused, and only the sound of the hot wind moving through the grass reached her ears. "You're the obvious candidate for the job, Ken. Do you want it?"

His answer came quick and ready.

"Nope."

"What?"

"Thank you, Mrs. Potter, really, I do thank you a lot, but it ain't the job for me."

"But you and Linda—"

"Oh, I know it would give us a mighty lot of security, and maybe that's what I ought to be thinkin' of, but it ain't what I want, exactly. What I want—and Linda's with me on this—is a spread of my own. I guess you know I've been building my own little herd over west of here, a cow at a time, you might say, and one of these days, I'm going to have a decent herd can support me and a family. That's what I'm aimin' at, Mrs. Potter, that's why I work all these different jobs, to make enough money to keep buying land, a little piece at a time if I have to, and everything else that goes with ranchin'. Like a hay baler." He laughed shortly, ruefully. "Right now I'd sell my soul for a good used baler—hell, I'd take one ten years old and near total rusted out. I got a beautiful couple ten acres of sweet grass just beggin' to be cut and baled. But everything costs money, which I got to earn before I can spend it. Can't even expect to borrow stuff like that, 'cause I don't have anything to trade for it except my time, and I need to get paid for that. A full-time manager's job, hell, I'd make a better living in the short term, but I wouldn't have any time for my own little place in the long run."

Mrs. Potter felt a swelling sense of relief upon hearing his words.

"Well," she said, "it was yours if you wanted it."

He rose to his feet and looked down at her. "Like I said, I do thank you, and I'll be glad to help out same way as always, long as you need me."

"Until you get your own ranch."

"Exactly," he said, with an air of such fierce determination that Mrs. Potter had no trouble believing him. "Excuse me, now, but I got to get on to my other chores."

She watched him stride off to where his own pickup truck was parked down by her front gate. An ambitious young man, that one. But not so ambitious that he would kill his boss in order to take over his job. All day long, Mrs. Potter had known that she had to offer Ken the job so that she might see for herself the awful eagerness with which he took it. And now he'd turned it down.

Mrs. Potter sat a moment longer, savoring the relief she felt, before she got up again. She had to take the wallet to show Juanita and Linda's aunts and uncles.

But Juanita's home was dark, everyone was gone.

Mrs. Potter suspected that if she had taken time to stop at her own house, she might have found a message on her answering machine, telling her that the Ortega family had gone into Tucson, where Ricardo's funeral would be held, because that was where his parents were buried. Mrs. Potter would have liked to see him buried in the valley, but she felt it wasn't her business to say so. On that day, she knew there would be a long line of cars and trucks traveling to the city so that the residents of Wind Valley might pay their last respects.

After only a moment's hesitation, Mrs. Potter let herself into Juanita's house with her own key. *While I'm here*, she thought, *there's something else I may as well get done.* . . .

She knew right where to go to dig out Juanita's photo albums, and she hoped that would also be the place to find the pictures that Ricardo had taken while he was up in Lucy's airplane.

"Eureka," Mrs. Potter said, upon spying a new-looking yellow envelope that was thick with developed photographs. After a glance to confirm that it did, indeed, contain aerial pictures that were labeled with times and dates, she took the package with her and traveled back up the hill to her own home.

CHAPTER 29

Mrs. Potter was quick to switch on the lights—a lot of them—in her house, because as she walked up her front walk she became acutely aware of how completely alone she was now on her own property. Ricardo was gone, Bandy was gone, and Juanita and her family were gone. There was no one in the house down the hill, nobody in the barns or corrals, in the pastures or the garages, no one; except her, all by herself in the big house. Mrs. Potter had grown accustomed to relative solitude since Lew's death, and even before that when he traveled on business, but this was different. *That* had felt like privacy—sometimes it had felt good, even luxurious, to be alone with her own thoughts and needs and wants and with nobody else's to consider—but this did not feel like privacy.

It felt lonely, and not quite safe.

In her front hall, Mrs. Potter slipped off her dusty walking shoes and shoved them into the closet, where she picked up her favorite sewn-leather moccasins. She was just starting to slip into them when the phone rang, and so she hooked a finger over the heels of each of them and carried them in with her as she trotted to her office to answer the phone.

"Hello?" she said rather breathlessly, as she dropped her moccasins on the floor beside her, grabbed the telephone receiver, and tossed the envelope of photographs onto her desk. She sank down into her desk chair. "Hello?"

"Andy, is that you? You sound out of breath."

Hearing his voice, her shortness of breath seemed to worsen. Mrs. Potter inhaled deeply to calm herself. *I always seem to have to do this when he calls,* she thought wryly, and put a hand on her chest where her heart was playing at being a teenager again. But, oh, she was so glad he'd already kept his promise to call her. "I was just coming in, Jed, and I ran to the phone."

"Mrs. Thomas tells me there's no word about Linda."

"That's right."

"I'm so sorry. And Andy, I also called to say that I'm sorry about this evening . . ."

"It's all right, Jed . . ."

"No, it isn't, it was unforgivable . . ."

"Well, maybe not that bad."

He laughed a little. "Thank goodness you feel that way. Andy . . ." She noticed that suddenly he seemed to be picking his words with great care, and the unexpected thought came to her that Jed was feeling inhibited by the party line. What was it, she wondered, that he would have said if he'd felt free to say it? She was greatly surprised by what he did say next. "Have you had dinner yet?"

"Supper, Jed," she said, stalling while she tried to adjust to this new, odd tack of his. "When you're west of the Mississippi, it's dinner at noon and supper at night."

"What ever happened to lunch?"

She smiled as she said, "I think they still serve it in schools."

"And to ladies?"

"No, those are luncheons."

"Of course, I should know that."

There was a pause, a most comfortable pause, and Mrs. Potter could almost literally feel the two of them falling back again into the happy companionship they seemed to share so naturally. But then she realized they had digressed considerably. "No, to answer your original question, I haven't eaten yet."

"May I take you to dinner, Andy?"

"But I thought—"

"I can't offer a fancy French dinner, I mean, supper . . ." He interrupted her so quickly, almost rudely, that she had the definite feeling that he was trying to keep her from saying what she had been about to say, which was that she thought he was going to dinner at Highlands Ranch as the guest of Marj and Rey McHenry. Was that what he didn't want the party line to hear? "But if you don't mind eating at Sally's Café again, I thought I could drive by and pick you up and we could—"

She wondered why, if he wanted to take her someplace nice for dinner, he didn't take her to the best restaurant in the valley, the one right there in the big lodge at the C Lazy U.

"Jed, I'm sorry, I'd love to, but—"

"I understand," he said, so quickly that she knew he didn't.

"It's just that I'm so tired, Jed," she said with utter truthfulness. "And I have to get some things accomplished around here," she added, with equal truthfulness, if not quite candor. She also didn't want to divulge to the party line exactly what it was she needed to get done at home, such as go through Ricardo's photographs of the aerial views of the properties of the very persons who might just happen to be causing the many clicks on the line this evening.

"Yes, of course, I understand."

But she thought he sounded disappointed, and a little hurt.

Well, there wasn't any way for her to cure that, Mrs. Potter thought with a touch of inner asperity. He was the one who'd originally broken their plans, after all, not she. And now she *was* too tired and dirty to even think of getting ready to go out, and she really did have things to do. She wasn't about to allow herself to be whipped about, first one way and then the next, by his whims. Still, she felt in herself the same dissatisfaction she thought she heard in his voice when they said good night to each other after only a little more conversation. "May I call you tomorrow?" he said.

"I hope you will," she said.

But will you? she wondered as she hung up.

Her glance fell on the yellow envelope, and she opened it.

At first, she couldn't make any sense of the contents.

It seemed that Lucy the pilot was right: Ricardo had snapped pictures of cows and pastures, flora and fauna, fences and farm equipment. She recognized certain properties by the buildings or landmarks: there was Charlie Watt's pickup truck apparently parked in one of his pastures on Section Ranch, and there were some of the far cabins at the C Lazy U, just beyond the dirt runway where she and Jed had disembarked that afternoon, and there was the guardhouse at the front of Highlands Ranch, and the saguaro cactus patch at the Amorys' place, and even the roof of Sally's Café, and she recognized the brand of the Lost Dutchman on a few of Gallway and Lorraine Steinbach's cattle. He'd gotten a great picture of the crossroads, good enough for framing, she thought, and lovely vistas of the valley as seen from some vantage point toward the eastern end of the valley. "El Bizcocho?" she wondered, and peered more closely at those particular photographs.

There were multiple pictures of things, single pictures of others, and pictures of things she couldn't imagine why he wanted to photograph . . . trucks going down country roads, and tractors entering gates and just plain clumps of cattle in fields. They were things that Ricardo Ortega had seen every day of his life, nothing to get excited about, surely nothing to want to catch on film when he could see it all "up close and personal," as they said on the sportscasts on television.

It was all color film, and each individual picture had printed on it the date and time that Ricardo took the photo. There appeared to be five rolls all together. After thumbing quickly through them once, and then again, Mrs. Potter felt nearly despondent. But then, as her eye began to skip over the obvious landmarks in the photos, certain other, smaller, less noticeable things began to catch her attention.

She didn't, at first, understand what she saw.

It was so unexpected, so out of place, that her mind couldn't at first compute it. It was like seeing an apple falling up. "No," one's mind declared, "this is impossible, therefore I'm not really seeing it." But there it was, the apple falling up. Again and again, in photo after photo. She even counted the objects in one picture, touching each one with the tip of her finger, until she comprehended the meaning of them. Then it became easier for her eyes to see and her mind to accept. It was not nearly as easy for her to reach the only obvious conclusion and to accept it emotionally.

"Oh, dear," Mrs. Potter heard herself say, exactly as her own grandmother might have murmured when she was the most distressed by some heinous moral failing on the part of someone she knew, and of whom she had expected something better, although that counted nearly the entire population of Harrington, Iowa. "Oh dear, oh dear."

Mrs. Potter slid the photos back into the yellow envelope.

"I've got to stop saying 'oh dear,' and start notifying the sheriff," she chided herself. But how to do that, with the party line? She couldn't risk calling Sheriff Ben Lightfeather, that was clear, so she'd have to get into her car and drive the many miles to see him. "Oh dear," Mrs. Potter said again, as she realized that meant another run on the Nogales 500, and this one at night when she was frightened and exhausted. But what else could she do? And then it came to her: she didn't have to drive all the way to him, all she had to do was get out of the valley, to a phone that was off the party line. "Thank goodness!"

She pushed her chair away from the desk, and felt stiff in body and sore at heart as she did so. And cold, oh, she suddenly felt so cold. Her face, her hands, her feet, her whole body was so cold that she was shivering.

Mrs. Potter swiveled her chair toward her fleece-lined moccasins and started to bend over to put them on to walk back into the foyer to get her walking shoes again.

They lay in a shadow cast by the desk, out of the illumination of the room lighting, so she almost didn't see the small movement in the heel of one of them.

She almost stuck her fingers inside both moccasins.

Almost slid her feet into them.

Instead, the small movement registered, and she drew her hands back and both her feet up into her chair, gasping as she did so.

A scorpion arched its tail in the soft fleece of the heel of her right moccasin.

Without even stopping to think, Mrs. Potter grabbed the closest heavy object she could find and dropped it square on the shoe. When she could bear to open her eyes again and look down, she saw that she'd squashed a scorpion with *Webster's New Twentieth Century Dictionary*. After a few more moments, during which she worked up her courage, Mrs. Potter reached down and lifted the huge book off the floor.

The scorpion was still moving a little.

She dropped the book a second time.

This time, when she picked it up, bits of the scorpion clung to its cover. *I cannot deal with this*, she thought with a shudder. *If my kids were here, I would pretend it was nothing, I would be brave and I would scrape that scorpion off this book as if it were cake crumbs, but with nobody here to test my courage, I haven't any!* She simply dropped the dictionary down on the floor, in a different spot, and vowed to clean it up later. Next week. Next year.

But the moccasin was another matter.

She had to make sure the scorpion really was dead and not just maimed.

Mrs. Potter took from her desk drawer the longest thing she could find, which was an old wooden ruler. She hooked the end of it into the shoe, and shook. The squashed scorpion's body started to fall out, she thought, but then it just dangled there from the shoe. Mrs. Potter shook harder. Yes, it was definitely dead. But still the scorpion dangled, and so she was forced to bring it closer to her face and look again.

What she saw was a thread, tied around the scorpion's tail and pushed inside the shoe and then wound around and knotted to one of the leather bindings that sewed the sole of the moccasin to its top. Mrs. Potter dropped the whole thing, scorpion, shoe, and ruler, into her wastebasket under her desk, and leaned back in her chair, feeling very, very shaken.

Who?

After studying the photographs, Mrs. Potter knew who.

Why?

She had to think for a while on that one, because there didn't at first seem to be any logical reason, only malicious, vicious, and irrational ones. But then she remembered something that had very recently been said to her, and she suddenly realized that she probably had the awful answer to "why," as well. She didn't have to give the question of "how" any time at all; her "secret" housekey was the obvious answer to that . . . everybody who knew her, and probably a good many who didn't, had easy access to her hall closet or anything else they wanted. The only question remaining was what to do about this new event, and the answer to that seemed easier than anything else she'd had to think about all day: Sheriff Ben Lightfeather.

Mrs. Potter walked very carefully, in her stocking feet, to that same hall closet, where she peered into her walking shoes first, and shook them out well, before starting to put them on, just as parents in the Southwest— land of scorpions and brown spiders and other stinging, crawling things— always instructed their children to do.

The children, Mrs. Potter thought with a sudden flash of insight. She jolted up straight, her shoes still in her hands. *The children!*

CHAPTER 30

Mrs. Potter had phoned each of her own three children right after the discovery of Ricardo's body and before the discovery of the other three men. They didn't know that Linda was still missing.

She had to call them.

Not because they knew Linda Scarritt at all—she being considerably younger than they, and they having spent their teenage summers on the ranch before Linda was even born, and then, while she was still just a baby living with her parents, in university towns . . . and not merely to keep them informed, either, as Mrs. Potter knew they were concerned about her, their mother, and about the situation . . . but to ask them something very specific that she hadn't thought to ask before. A simple question and an obvious one, and they were the perfect, perhaps the only people she could ask.

Why hadn't she thought of it before? Her very own children!

She dialed her eldest, Louisa, first, and pulled her yellow notepad toward her to make notes.

"Darling," she said, "where are the best places to hide on this ranch?"

"Mother." Louisa laughed. "The questions you ask! Well, now that I'm all grown-up, I'll confess, there's a little hidden arroyo a couple of miles south of Bandy's apartment. If you ask Emily, I'm sure she'll tell you it was her favorite place to hide from Benji and me. Do you think Linda might be there?"

"I don't know, darling, but it occurred to me that you children would know this ranch better than any of us grown-ups. And Linda spent a good part of her own childhood here, so if she had to hide out, maybe she'd go where none of *us* could find her . . . but maybe you three would know where to look."

"Oh, Mom, what can have happened to her? And poor Bandy. I'm just shocked, but you can't think it was your chili that killed him! I don't believe it for an instant. I mean, we are talking about the same mother who wouldn't put mayonnaise on my salami sandwiches for school for fear it would spoil and kill me before recess!"

"Everybody makes mistakes."

"Not my mother, not in the kitchen."

That left, Mrs. Potter thought, a rather wide world in which to make other errors. "I appreciate your loyalty, dearest."

"Will you call me as soon as you find her?"

"Yes, Louisa, of course."

"Love you."

But Emily, her middle child, sighed upon hearing of Louisa's prediction. "Oh, Mom." She sounded frantically exasperated. "Louisa has it all wrong, as usual. It wasn't that arroyo at all, and anyway, if it was my secret place to hide, how would she know about it? I'll tell you what it was, it was a cave—"

"A *cave*?"

"Don't sound so horrified, Mom."

"But you were absolutely forbidden—"

"Sure." Emily laughed a little. "It was a little cave back in the hills, not exactly on the ranch—"

"What do you mean," Mrs. Potter said ominously, "not exactly on the ranch?"

"Oh, dear, can I still get grounded after all these years?"

"I'm not so sure you're too old to be spanked!"

"That's what I was afraid you'd say. Okay, true confession time. It was a cave off the ranch, on that property that's owned by the Bureau of Land Management, you know? I can't describe it exactly, but there was a high ridge to the left, and a trail to the right—"

"To the left, Emily? Would that be east, west . . ."

"I have no idea. It's been a long time ago. Benji would know."

"I thought it was your secret hideout."

"He tracked me down. All I remember is, I'd run down that trail through some trees and up a hill and there it was, almost hidden by some other small trees. Which may be big trees by now. And the neat thing was, you couldn't see it unless you knew where to look."

There was a sudden, appalled silence as both women comprehended what that might mean in regard to Linda Scarritt.

"Ask Benji," Emily advised.

"And I thought you were such *good* children," her mother said.

"Love you," her daughter replied. "Call me!"

And so it was Benji who gave her exact directions, which she mapped out on the yellow pad in front of her.

"You've got to find her, Mom," he said. "I don't mean you, personally, but Ken or somebody, somebody's got to find her, and she's got to be okay."

He was her youngest, and he took things hard.

In her heart, as she hung up from talking to her son, Mrs. Potter knew that subconsciously Benji meant his words quite literally: she, Mom, had to find Linda Scarritt. As she'd found the children's socks and their toys, their teddy bears and, later, their car keys. Mothers found things. Mothers were *supposed* to find things for their children, for anybody's children, for everybody's children. After a moment's hesitation, Mrs. Potter flipped over a page in her yellow pad and began writing quite a few other things down on the paper. She did it as fast as she could, because now there was no time to waste.

Afterward, she ran into her bathroom to put together a first-aid kit, even ripping up a clean sheet in case she needed bindings for wounds, putting in plenty of antiseptic spray and what pain medication she could find, which was a few old pills of codeine 3, probably leftover from the misery of old dental work. Then she raced to the kitchen to fill a Thermos with water and to stick some bland food—bananas, crackers, bread—into a plastic bag. It was while she was filling the Thermos that she realized that nobody had found *Linda's* Thermos, the one her grandmother said she always made the child carry. It should have been attached to the saddle, but it was not. That seemed to Mrs. Potter to be the best news, perhaps even the only possibly good news, she had heard yet. Maybe there really was hope.

If, that is, she hurried.

By this time three days had passed, and a Thermosful of water wouldn't last long in the desert, especially if somebody had been injured. Food she could live without for a long time, but not water, not for very long in this country.

"Now . . ."

Mrs. Potter stopped dead in her tracks in her kitchen.

How was she going to get to that cave without anybody else being the wiser?

Mrs. Potter set her supplies down on the kitchen table, and walked to the telephone in the kitchen. She thought for a moment and took a deep breath before she picked up the phone. *Please!* she thought, and then, *Oh, yes!* when she immediately heard voices talking.

Mrs. Potter began to moan piteously.

"Got to call the hospital," she said, breaking in to the conversation between a woman and a man. "Ohhh . . ."

"Who's that? What's the emergency?" a woman's voice demanded.

"Genia Potter," she said. "Bit by scorpion, oh, it hurts so much . . ."

"Mrs. Potter?" the man said quickly. "You stay right there, I'll be right over to get you—"

"No, no," she said quickly. "Bit more than once, afraid I'm allergic, can't wait, going to drive myself to the county clinic. . . . Call them, will you? Ohhh!"

She hung up.

Immediately, the phone rang again and kept ringing.

"Get off my phone," she said to it, "and start calling everybody else around here!"

Mrs. Potter wanted everybody to know she was leaving her home and was on her way to the county health clinic many miles away from Wind Valley, and she couldn't think of a more efficient way to do it than through the "dadblamed, goldarned, infernal" party line, as the locals were wont to call it. Before the man on the line had a chance to make good on his threat to drive to Las Palomas and pick her up, Mrs. Potter grabbed her supplies again and stuffed them into a backpack that she found in the hall closet. She was just about to race out the door when she thought of one more thing . . .

What if she needed a weapon?

There was no rifle in *her* back window.

But sometimes, just when you needed the miracle of a brilliant idea, there one was. Mrs. Potter hurried back to her kitchen and created a most ingenious weapon, if she did say so herself, on the spot. She slipped it carefully into the backpack, put on a jacket and a pair of cowboy boots, stuffed gloves and a hat into the pockets of her coat, and *then* she ran to the carport to get her four-wheel-drive vehicle.

She was going to need the power of all four wheels, and more, where she was going.

CHAPTER 31

The desert had never seemed emptier, the night had never seemed blacker to Mrs. Potter as she turned north out of her own front gate and drove off as if she were, indeed, going to the county clinic. She didn't even have to hide her hurry, but could drive like the proverbial bat out of hell. She tried to remember that she was supposedly in agony, and swerved the car a bit now and then, as if she were having trouble controlling her pain, just in case anybody was watching. In truth, she only had less than a mile to go, and she wanted that short distance to be utterly convincing.

For that brief, frightening ride, she saw no headlights, no taillights, no sign of any other vehicle on the road.

Too bad horses don't have headlights, she thought as she slowed the car ahead of the unobtrusive gate that was her immediate goal. *Too bad they don't wear reflective saddles at night.* Because if anybody was observing her from the vantage point of a horse, she'd never know it. Mrs. Potter's left hand moved automatically to her signal indicator, but she stopped it just in time. *That's all I need to do*, she told herself, *announce to the world which way I'm turning and where I'm going.*

She was going to have to get out of her car to open the gate.

Feeling exposed and vulnerable, she scurried to accomplish that. She drove on through, and then had to get out and close the gate again. There were cattle in these pastures, and just because it was a matter of life or death didn't mean she could leave the gates open. *That* would have been a good way to have cattle wandering across the road where somebody might hit them, and even die doing it. She didn't want to be responsible for the death of any living creature on this strange night.

Mrs. Potter had never driven through her own pastures alone, at night. She could only see as far ahead of her as her headlights shone.

The car bumped up and down, so she was forced to go much slower than she wished, and there were still other gates to open and close. At every moment, she was afraid of coming upon a big cow in the road too suddenly, of hitting it, of plowing off into a ditch. She was afraid of boulders she might strike. But more than anything, Mrs. Potter was afraid of getting there too late. . . .

She glanced quickly up at the sky. *Oh, if only I could turn up the wattage on the stars. If only there were a celestial rheostat so that I might shine their lights brighter on my path!* But any light that illuminated her road would show her, as well, to anyone who happened to be looking for her. . . .

Mrs. Potter drove on, having once or twice the strangest feeling that she was not alone, that there was somebody else along for the ride. Shivers ran along her spine, and her hands grew ice cold. *"Ricardo, is that you?"* she whispered. *Or was it Lew?*

Or was it simply a haunting feeling of being watched by a thousand eyes, of being quietly observed by the creatures of the night and the desert and the mountains, of attracting the silent, watching attention of the wolves and coyotes, the desert rats and mountain lions, the rattlesnakes and owls, the scorpions on the ground and the hawks in the air?

She only knew that the closer she got to the mountains, the stronger the feeling grew that she was not alone.

At the base of the Rimstone Mountains there was a rocky path winding up, over rocks so large they looked as if no car could pass them, and between cacti whose thorny arms grasped anything within their reach. Mrs. Potter kept her windows rolled up, and her car in first gear all the way. The route wound up and up, just as Benji had directed her, until it simply ran out at a point where a massive oak tree, the last and farthest up the mountain, stopped the trail.

At that point, again as directed by her son, Mrs. Potter got out.

She slipped on the backpack and her canvas hat with the brim that hung down. She zipped her jacket to the neck, pulled up its collar, and put on a pair of leather gloves. She shoved her pants legs down into her boots.

Benji had no idea I'd be doing this alone, she thought, and if he had, he wouldn't have wanted to tell her, but at the time, she didn't know she'd be doing it alone either. Mrs. Potter would have given nearly anything *not* to be doing this alone.

The going from there was rough and taxing, and sometimes so vertical that she pushed herself up—by shoving against huge boulders—as much as climbed up. She had to stop many times to catch her breath. Her clothes got snagged on cactus thorns, her feet slipped painfully, even in their thick shoes, on the jagged rocks that lined the way. But she kept going, breathing ever more raggedly as she climbed. *"I'm too old for this!"* her mind protested more than once. *"That's all in your mind!"* her heart retorted. Nearly laughing at that, feeling a bit hysterical for a moment, she nevertheless kept climbing.

Benji's directions were good, clear ones.

But it was night, and she'd never done this before.

Stop the car by the oak tree, he'd said. *You can't drive any farther than that. Climb straight up. You'll get to a fence.* GOVERNMENT PROPERTY *on the other sign. Posted on the other side. Their side.* NO TRESPASSING—*on our side. Climb the fence.* Easy for you to say, my dear son! *It'll get a little easier for a while. Go north from the other side of the fence, maybe you'll get lucky and you'll come across a little path. Should still be there, because it was an animal path, probably deer and elk.* And where there are deer and elk, she thought, there are wolves and coyotes. Where there is prey, there are predators. Finding the trail, she plunged into an even darker thicket of tall ocotillo shrubs. New and tiny cacti sprouted from the ground, as hard to walk on as rocks. "Thank goodness I thought to wear boots!" she murmured.

And suddenly she was face-to-face with a rock wall.

Mrs. Potter was also suddenly so afraid, she thought her knees might collapse on her, sending her tumbling to the ground upon the rocks and baby cacti, causing her to lose her balance, and go rolling violently down as Ricardo must have done. Then she realized it was just the sheer dreadful darkness of the rock wall that so unnerved her, and the fear of what might be lurking in its holes and crannies.

But its holes and crannies were what she had come to explore.

Mrs. Potter prayed to find the right one the first time.

Turn south at the rock wall, her son had said. South? *she'd asked.* Does that mean right or left? Right, *he'd said, laughing at her a little.* Turn right and walk along the face of the rock cliff. Go about fifty paces. Children's paces? *she'd asked,* or grown-up paces? Good question, Mom, *he'd agreed.* Well, just consider that we were teenagers when all this chasing and hiding was going on, and I was taller than you by then, so grown-up paces, I guess. *Mrs. Potter murmured "Mother, may I?" under her breath, and walked off fifty paces along the face of the cliff. It was difficult, for* things *had naturally sprouted during the intervening years. More cacti. Scrub brush. Rocks had fallen, blocking her path. Mrs. Potter climbed over and around, blessing her boots and gloves and long pants and sleeves with every rugged step. The route took her into the shadows, to what surely, she thought, must be the darkest side of the mountain.

Fifty paces in, there was no mouth of a cave.

Her heart, which had beat so strongly throughout the climb, caught for a moment on a snag of hopelessness, and took its time kicking back in again. Feeling utterly desperate, Mrs. Potter called out softly, "Linda? Linda?"

She heard nothing but a rustling in the brush that made her mouth go dry, so dry that she had to moisten it before she could repeat her call, and make it even louder this time.

"Linda! Linda Scarritt! It's Genia Potter! Can you hear me!"

The rustling in the brush stopped.

All time seemed to stop as well.

And then Mrs. Potter heard another sound, a low moaning, as though from a terribly wounded animal. She plunged on through the scrub and over the rocks, following the sound, calling out its name . . .

"Linda, Linda, *Linda!*"

The sound was coming from inside a dark hole in the cliff. Mrs. Potter swallowed hard, pulled her flashlight out of her packback, and pointed it into the mouth of the cave.

Linda Scarritt lay curled in a fetal position on the rocky ground, uncovered except for her own clothing, with her saddle blanket rolled under her head. The beam of Mrs. Potter's flashlight caught a flicker from the young woman's eyes as they opened the merest slit, and then quickly closed again. The moaning began again. Mrs. Potter had to bend over to run to the girl's side, where she knelt and nearly wept, both in relief and in pity for what she saw. Linda had been wounded, like her horse, gored by the same animal that injured Taco, and her jeans were ripped where the tusk had gone through. Mrs. Potter lay her own hand on Linda's face and found the skin to be terrifyingly dry and hot. The wound was infected, Mrs. Potter was sure, and the child would have died soon from thirst, hunger, and infection.

She quickly took off the backpack and lay its contents on the ground to her left, moving the flashlight over them as she worked. First, she twisted off the Thermos lid and held it gently to Linda's lips, managing only to wet them at first. But then she maneuvered well enough to lift Linda's head and lay it on her own lap so that she could slip a little water between the parched lips. Mrs. Potter stroked the girl's head, murmuring the comforting endearments of a mother to a precious child. She would make Linda as comfortable as possible, she decided, try to get her to swallow some pain medicine, and more water, and then she would go as quickly as she could for assistance. . . .

Now that she'd finally found her. . . .

"Good work, *patrona.*"

Mrs. Potter jumped at the sound of the voice at the mouth of the cave. She couldn't see the face in the darkness, so she swung her flashlight around until she could.

"Put that damn thing down," Ken Ryerson said, and when she saw the gun in his hand, she did as he told her to do. Mrs. Potter lay the flashlight on the floor of the cave, so now all three of them were together in the darkness.

"I led you right to her," Mrs. Potter said sadly.

"Yes. Too bad in a way. She's hurt, isn't she? Probably gored by the same javelina pigs that got Taco. If you hadn't found her she'd have just died here without anybody ever knowing, and I wouldn't have to do this."

Kill us, Mrs. Potter thought. *That's what he "has to do."*

"Why did you have to do any of it, Ken?"

"Ricardo found out I've been borrowin' pastureland and equipment, even a few head of cattle to build up my own place. When the owners are away, the help will play." Mrs. Potter heard, though she couldn't see, the cynical smile on his face. She already knew all that he was saying, because the proof was in Ricardo's pictures, but she didn't say so. She didn't say that she'd seen photos of cattle with Ken's brand on them in the Amorys' pastures, where he was using their grass to fatten his own livestock. She didn't say that she'd seen a photo of a fancy air-conditioned tractor that she knew for a fact belonged to the Steinbachs being driven onto Ken's property. She didn't say that she'd seen hay being transported that she suspected Ricardo could have shown belonged to somebody else besides the man who was driving it down the roadway. Not all of the pictures had been taken from the air; some of them had been taken during those "random" drives around the valley that Ricardo had taken, with his granddaughter tailing him on Juanita's instructions. Mrs. Potter didn't say that what she'd seen had led her to come to the same conclusion that she suspected Ricardo had come to: Ken Ryerson was using his position of trust—of helping out around the valley, of overseeing ranches in their owners' absences—to "borrow" his employers blind. Hay, equipment, pastureland, it all added up to great expenses for the owners and great savings for Ken Ryerson himself. No wonder the Amorys were going broke; they were probably the biggest victims of all, because they were the newest, the least knowledgeable, the most likely to take the advice of a trusted and experienced hired hand like Ken Ryerson. *Anybody could be a rancher*, Mrs. Potter thought, *if he used other people's land and equipment to do it!*

Ken took a step into the cave.

"Are you really engaged to her, Ken?"

He laughed. "Of course. A little respectability don't hurt none. And what's more respectable than marrying the granddaughter of the king of the valley?" The last was said in tones of great, triumphant bitterness. "Said he knew what I was up to, said he wanted me to meet him, so we could look out over this great valley of his, so he could show me what a great wrong I was doing to good people, so he could set me straight in my ways. And then, we were going to come down off the top of El Bizcocho and he was going to hold a meeting of the ranchers and I was going to tell them I wanted to make amends and they were going to decide what to do about me. I could work real hard, Ricardo said, work real hard and over a period of years I could pay it back to everybody. Earn back my reputation and my self-respect. Be a man." Ken's laughter burst out and bounced off the walls of the cave until Mrs. Potter thought she could no longer bear the sound of it. "King of the valley. Pompous fool is what he was."

Ken stepped closer to her and even in the darkness, she sensed that he had brought the gun up a few inches in the air. He'd probably aim for her first, she thought, because Linda posed no threat to him, and there was no telling what she herself might do if the gun went off and he shot Linda first.

Mrs. Potter slowly reached behind her with her left hand.

Her fingers landed first on the Thermos, then slid over to what felt like the package of crackers and bananas. Finally, they landed on something smooth and long and rounded. Mrs. Potter's hand closed around that, and inched it silently toward her.

Ken walked closer, obviously intending to place the gun right against her head before he shot her.

Mrs. Potter waited, trembling.

She waited as he bent over in the cave and crouched toward her.

She waited as he stooped near and the gun came close to her head.

She waited until the gun was almost touching her hair.

And then she whipped out the plastic spray bottle she held in her hand and squirted its contents into his face. Ken screamed in pain and dropped the gun, whirling in the cave with his hands covering his face, knocking his head into the walls and the rocks, screaming in agony as the liquid burned his eyes. He tried to plunge out of the cave, but banged his forehead against the edge of it and knocked himself out cold.

Mrs. Potter, with shaking hands, put the spray bottle down.

Before she left home, she had poured into it the juice from a bottle of jalapeño peppers.

When she stepped outside the cave to take a few deep breaths before trying to drag him out of it—without the slightest idea of what she would do with him next—she saw many headlights converging below, at the foot of the mountain. Mrs. Potter ran back into the cave for her flashlight, and used it to signal whoever was down there.

In a fairly short time, but what felt like an eternity to her, it seemed that half the residents of Wind Valley were there at the mouth of the cave with her, and Jed was leading them all. While the others took Ken away, and tenderly began the task of carrying Linda back down the mountainside, Jed took her into his embrace and held her as if he would not let her go for another forty years.

"I was afraid you were mad at me," he said, half laughing, while she tried, unsuccessfully, to keep herself from crying, "when you wouldn't come out to dinner. I mean, supper. I was afraid I'd offended you, and that you didn't want to see me again. And the only reason I canceled dinner . . . damn, supper . . . was because I'd decided I didn't want anything to do with people like the McHenrys who were so secretive and who were so ill thought of by their own neighbors, and I had already hinted as much to them over the phone today. Then, when we had our flat tire, I got this idea that those two men of theirs—the ones we'd seen at Sally's Café—had done it. And I didn't want to pull you into any sort of bad situation. Eventually, I just phoned them and scotched the whole deal, and then I was free to see you. But you didn't want to see me! So I drove to your ranch, and when I saw you weren't there, I let myself in with your key so that I could leave you a poem on your yellow pad. And that's where I saw the notes you had written, explaining the situation, and I saw the photographs, and I finally I saw the map you had drawn. So all I had to do was go for help . . . which was already right outside your door."

"It was?" she murmured happily into the snuggly warmth of his nice wool vest. "Why's that?"

"Because people had come from miles around." Jed was laughing again. "To take you to the hospital. For your scorpion bite. Is that all better now?"

She looked up at him, and he wiped tears from her cheeks.

"Yes," she said, smiling up at him. "It's a miracle."

"Yes," Jed said, wrapping his arms even tighter around her. "It is."

And Mrs. Potter didn't even care what the neighbors thought.

CHAPTER 32

When Mrs. Potter drove up the winding drive through the detached guest cottages of the C Lazy U, past the tennis courts, the swimming pavilion, and up to the entrance of the large main lodge, she thought again what an appealing place it was. All the buildings were of simple, Spanish-style adobe construction, all of varying warm shades of tan and buff, all built in the simple pueblo architecture known in Arizona as "New Mexico style." The buildings were flat-roofed, and dark, heavy, peeled timbers (which appeared to support the roof construction) protruded from the exterior adobe walls at ceiling height.

She parked in the guest lot and stepped out into the twilight. A delicious fragrance hung in the air, of juniper and mesquite and desert plants and nearby horse corrals at the end of the day. The big double doors of the main lodge were opened and there were warm lights, the glow of a huge fireplace, the laughter and hum of people indoors at cocktail time.

She had agreed to meet Jed at the C Lazy U for Che's Wednesday night tostada fiesta, and she was early, several minutes earlier than the time upon which they'd agreed. Mrs. Potter had planned it that way to give herself enough time to visit the ladies' room to check her dress, her makeup, her hair before she saw him again.

The first thing she saw when she stepped inside the lodge was Che's enormous buffet table, set up in the grand two-story lobby, and loaded to the edges with delicacies, both familiar and exotic. One of Che's standard ploys for entertaining her guests was to give them a Mexican meal that appeared sufficiently foreign, yet was reassuringly and immediately familiar in its ingredients. Even those visitors who were sure that any hint of Mexican food was going to disturb their digestions could thus be lulled into confidence and enjoyment. Che's favorite dish for this purpose was what the valley had come to call her "Make-Your-Own-Tostadas."

Each ingredient was presented in its pristine, virgin state, in a panoply of foods covering the sideboard. On the electric heating trays were the warmed crisp round corn tostadas, which Che bought commercially made. To spread lightly upon each of these was provided a *cazuela* of hot *refritos*—the mashed pink Mexican beans, so inaccurately named because as far as Mrs. Potter could determine, they had never been *fritoed* even once, let alone refritoed. These, too, Che purchased commercially canned, although occasionally she had her cooks make them from scratch (Mrs. Potter thought them better that way). To strew upon the thin layer of hot mashed beans, there was hot cooked shredded chicken, or freshly cooked, still-a-bit-pink lean ground beef, or any number of other chipped or shredded leftovers from the kitchen.

None of these would be seasoned beyond a small touch of salt, and Che always pointed out to each of her guests that he or she alone was in charge of what dangerous additive would be included: diced fresh tomatoes; sliced ripe olives; chopped green onions; grated Monterey Jack or white country Mexican cheeses; cooked sliced zucchini, hot or cold; sliced crisp radishes; sweet dark raisins, earlier plumped in hot water; thinly shredded iceberg lettuce. Che might also bring out from the larder such items as cooked carrot rounds, warm or cold, or sliced papayas, garnished with their own black spicy seeds. There might be chopped cucumbers or cottage cheese with a sprinkling of chives, or drained, canned pineapple chunks. She had been known to add dishes of crumbled crisp bacon, or diced cold baked ham. There could be whole salted peanuts or chopped blanched almonds. There was sure to be any other leftover vegetable on hand—cauliflower, broccoli, beets, or turnips, sliced or chopped, or cooked fresh corn cut from the cob. Sweet green peppers, called "bell peppers" in Arizona, might appear crisp and raw or might be chopped and briefly sautéed in hot oil, then served cool. Sometimes there were all of those, sometimes only some; and tonight, Che appeared to have outdone herself with most of those and even a few others.

Mrs. Potter saw that on this night her hostess was standing, as usual, right by the buffet, coaxing her out-of-state-guests to be . . . daring! Che was attired, as usual, in daring and inventive ways too—adorned in lots of turquoise and bright Mexican colors and fabrics to bring just the right appearance to her fiesta. "Do try things in *combination*," Che was assuring her more timid eaters in her bold, vigorous voice. "That's the only way to make it *authentic*! You're building a pyramid, do you see?"

Copper trays held the final toppings—a big emerald bowl filled with finely sliced crisp lettuce with silver tongs alongside, to strew over the entire structure; a second large bowl filled with pale, cool crescents of ripe avocado; and for a graceful touch . . . to top each layered serving, each as high as the appetite and inventiveness of the concocter would take it . . . there was sour cream for a snowy flourish. The final cascade (or dribble, if the guest preferred) was pale green tomatillo salsa with only a touch of Mexican fire. It was ground cherry, really, the same paper-skinned pale-green fruit, rather like a paper lantern flower, that her Grandma Andrews used to grow around the entrance to the storm cellar in Iowa, and from which she made an innocuous fig-like jam that nobody much liked. Whatever they did to ground cherries in Mexico by blending them, obviously, with mild green chiles, the thick green tomatillo salsa was the crowning glory of the make-your-own-tostada, and very pretty over the sour cream and avocado slices.

Depending on her guests, Che served milk for the eight-year-olds, iced tea, fruit juice and decaffeinated soft drinks for the nondrinkers, and for everyone else, Mexican beer—Carta Blanca or Dos Equis. Great-aunts from Appleton might sip it dubiously, but unless she saw them actively shuddering she did not fetch the pitcher of ice water at the end of the buffet table. A little beer was the proper *digestivo*, Che would advise them, and often the conversation brightened as they sipped, telling each other they'd *never* thought they could tolerate Mexican food, but wasn't this delicious, and it just went to show.

Mrs. Potter walked over to say a quick hello.

"Che," she said quietly in her hostess's ear, as she watched all the young employees scurrying about to do her bidding. Mrs. Potter had decided that she was, by gosh, going to find out once and for all what everybody in the valley wanted to know, even if meant asking a question so rude her own grandmother would have gasped to hear it. "How do you *do* it? Maintain this place so beautifully, travel, keep up your other place in Europe, employ all these people . . . ?"

Che turned astonished turquoise-blue eyes on her.

"You don't think I *pay* them, do you?" she whispered back. "Genia, I thought everybody knew . . . these are rich kids from back East whose parents are paying *me* to keep their offspring for a season. All except my head chef, that is. Why, they call it an 'adventure,' my darling. Or even an 'apprenticeship,' some of them. Poor dears. I call it free help."

The enterprising hostess turned away to encourage a quiet little mouse of a guest to "try the anchovies, they'll add such a delightful *piquancy*!"

Mrs. Potter saw Charlie Watt bearing down on her and, fond as she was of him, she tried to escape because getting to the ladies' room was a far more urgent matter for her at the moment. But he had longer legs and a longer stride.

"Genia, I'll be driving to Ricardo's funeral tomorrow and taking Che with me. You need a ride?"

"Thank you, Charlie, that would be a great help."

Bandy was to be buried a day later, right there in the valley, and the two poor young Mexican men were being returned to their country, where it was hoped their homes and families could be located. Ken Ryerson had doctored their chili, it seemed, while it sat unattended in Bandy's truck, after the old man had confided to Ken that his two "nephews" had heard shots and screaming early that fatal morning near El Bizcocho.

"I'm sorry I said that about those two young fellers," Charlie said. "But it's just as well you're out of the wetback business, if I'm going to get that governor's appointment."

"If you do, you're going to have to stop saying wetback, Charlie."

He grinned. "You'd like that."

She patted his arm, and made her escape.

At least she didn't have to worry about running into the McHenrys, who never showed up at these fetes. Jed had told her again the night before how uneasy he felt about doing business with people who were so ill-regarded by their neighbors, and how he even feared they might be wanting to use White Research for right-wing political purposes—like international arms and munitions operations—that he didn't want any part of. He'd been taking early-morning rides, he'd told Mrs. Potter, thinking things through—and bird watching! He'd seen Mexican white-wing doves, he reported to her, and Gambel quail, and a wonderful, scalloping flight of blue-breasted western bluebirds, plus a million (he claimed) rosy-headed house finches.

Mrs. Potter finally reached the ladies' room, but didn't even find herself alone there.

Primping at the mirror was Kathy Amory, looking all duded up, as Che might have said, in cowgirl fringe and denim. *Well*, Mrs. Potter thought with a resigned sigh at her own failings, among which she counted a small streak of busybody, *I may as well say it to her and get it over with.* "Kathy, dear?"

The young woman turned around with a bright smile.

"Kathy, Lorraine Steinbach doesn't understand that you're only interested in her husband because you and Walt hope that Gallway will buy your ranch. She thinks you're in love with him."

It was almost comical to watch the young woman's bright smile turn a little sickish, and to see her tanned complexion grow pale. "Oh, my God," exclaimed Kathy. "Me? With that yucky old . . . oh, my God! Mrs. Potter, we don't even care if he *buys* our ranch, we'd be happy if Gallway would just *lease* it from us. His place adjoins ours, after all, and he's got plenty of money." Kathy still looked appalled at the very idea, which Mrs. Potter had to admit she also found appalling. "What should I do, Mrs. Potter? Should I tell her?"

"No," Mrs. Potter said quickly, imagining the tactless ways that Kathy might find to do that, "probably not."

Kathy screwed up her face as if struggling with a difficult question. "You think I flirt with him too much? You think anybody notices?"

Mrs. Potter restrained her own smile. "Lorraine notices."

"I'd better quit then." Kathy suddenly brightened to her own sweet, if rather vapid self again. "Anyway, he's about to say yes. He's out there right now telling Walt how we don't know a thing about running a ranch. 'You just can't handle her,' he keeps saying. 'She's a handful and you aren't up to looking after her.' Why are cars and ranches always 'hers,' Mrs. Potter?"

Mrs. Potter allowed as how she didn't know, but that perhaps a little less flirting with Gallway Steinbach was the right thing to do.

And finally, she was alone.

With the mirror, however.

For this evening, she had put on her favorite long dress, an off-white wool, as plain as a T-shirt and as comfortable, long-sleeved and high-necked. No more makeup than her usual bare minimum. The less the better as she grew older, she thought—a quick bit of gray color above the lashes, a touch of pink lip gloss. She had added gold hoops at her ears, and a few rounds of pearls and bright Mexican beads at her neck in the hope of deflecting attention from what she saw was a tired face—moreover, a face clearly forty years older than it used to be. "At least I smell good," she told herself. "Well, I am the age I am and except for once in a while in a good light, I look it. But I can be scrub-brush clean, I can afford good perfume, and—no matter what happens—I can try to be pleasant."

All of this was not enough reassurance.

She still felt that she looked a million years old and in about one second she was going to see Jed again and he was going—finally—to get a really good look at her and one of life's small, secret dreams was going to die forever.

Mrs. Potter looked at herself in the mirror one more time.

Then she gathered her courage and walked out to meet Jed.

He was waiting for her at the front door, staring outside, as if he thought she would be driving up at any moment.

Mrs. Potter walked to his side and put a hand on his arm.

"Jed? I'm here."

He turned, and when he looked at her she saw in the very first moment that she had nothing to fear. "You look lovely," he told her. And then he took her right hand and gently placed it on his own chest, above his heart. "You've always been here, Andy."

Jed bent down to greet her with a kiss, which she returned, and then she said, "Let's go in to dinner, Jed."

"I think you mean supper," he said.

"Let's eat," she said.

AFTERWORD

Several years ago, I picked up a mystery called *The Cooking School Murders* by an author named Virginia Rich. I loved it. I wrote to her to say so and to mention some coincidental similarities in our lives and our books. She wrote me back a lovely note in which she mentioned that she was working on a novel called *The 27-Ingredient Chili con Carne Murders*. I waited what I hoped was a tactful period of time and then I wrote to her again, only to receive a reply from a nurse telling me that Mrs. Rich was too ill to correspond. Soon after that, I learned that Virginia Rich had died. I was shocked and saddened, as were the thousands of mystery readers who had loved that first book as well as the next two Eugenia Potter mysteries, *The Baked Bean Supper Murders* and *The Nantucket Diet Murders*.

After her death, the three books in her series not only remained in print, but grew in popularity. During that time her husband, Ray Rich, came across boxes full of notes that Mrs. Rich had made for future books she had in mind, and even first drafts of some chapters. He approached her editor, inquiring whether the series might be continued by other writers along the lines that his wife had set forth in her notes. That editor approached my agent who then asked me, "How would you like to write a book by the name of *The 27-Ingredient Chili con Carne Murders*?"

It felt like fate to me.

The book in your hands is the result of that rather amazing sequence of events coming full circle. I thank everyone concerned with this labor of love: my gratitude goes out to Jane Rosenman; to my agent, Meredith Bernstein; and to Mrs. Rich's agents, Susan and Robert Lescher. Heartfelt thanks to my editor on this project, Emily Reichert, whose tact and patience is equalled only by that most gracious of gentlemen, Raymond Rich.

Virginia Rich, this novel is my letter to you.

Yours truly,
NANCY PICKARD